REBEL
SOUL
a romantic comedy

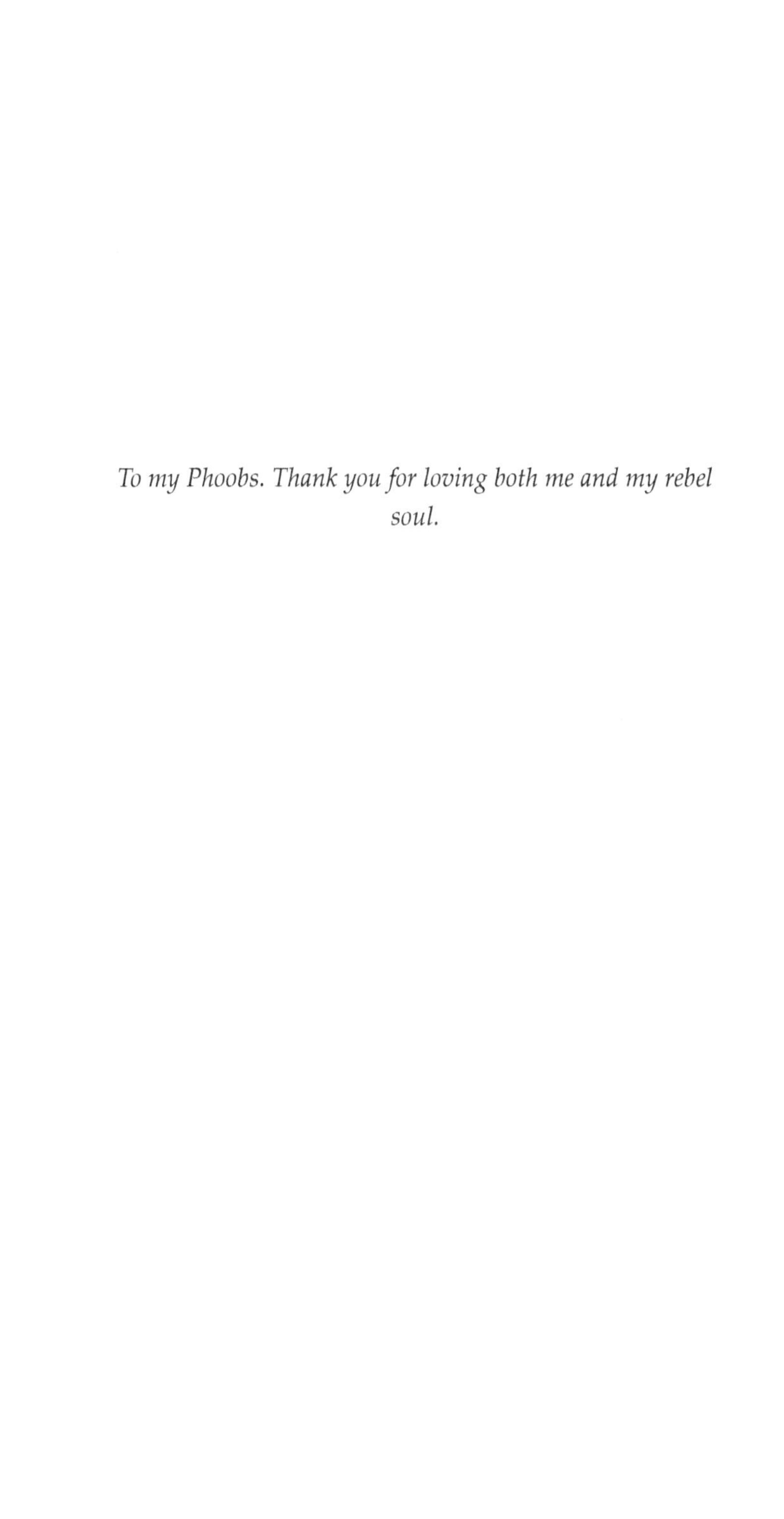

To my Phoobs. Thank you for loving both me and my rebel soul.

CHAPTER 1
WEST

"This… there's no way…" I pause my pacing to look over the page before me. I must've read it wrong, because Jesus-fucking-Christ, this is some bullshit, and I'm well-versed in bullshit. Anyone in my position—broker by day, virtual porn app developer by night—has to be. From the boardroom to the bedroom, it's practically my second language.

…provided he produces an heir by the age of twenty-five. Failure to do so will result in forfeiture of the trust, henceforth relinquishing any right to the estate…

My eyes snag on that particular line again and again. Hell, the words may as well be circled, highlighted, and in bold, with little arrows pointing at them. My grandpa was a hateful old jackass who loved fucking with anyone and everyone. He was the puppet master and everyone in his life nothing more than marionettes. And now, here he is, tugging on my strings from six feet under. *I wonder if my cousin Brock is in a similar boat*—and by boat, I mean up shit creek without a fucking paddle.

"This is for real?" I arch a brow at Colton—my

lawyer—waiting for him to tell me I'm being punked. He's only a few years older than me, but he's smart as a fucking whip and in a sea of sharks, he's a moray eel: lean, unassuming, but fucking vicious when provoked.

"Unfortunately, yes. Ironclad, too." Colton delivers the news, his voice even and bland, as if we're two strangers discussing the weather and not longtime friends.

My hands tremble as I read over my grandfather's will for the fourth time in as many minutes. My family has been known to do some fucked-up shit over the years, but this... yeah, it takes the cake. "How ironclad?"

"Battleship," is his only reply. The fact that he's being so frank tells me just how serious this is. Usually Colton goes all lawyer-y on me, refusing to make hard statements. But he's talking to me as more than my lawyer right now—he's speaking as one of my most trusted friends.

The walls of my corner office feel like they're closing in on me as I resume my pacing, wearing a trail in the plush sheepskin rug that takes up most of the floor space in front of my desk. Unwilling to accept defeat, I stalk over to the bookcase on the far wall. My eyes flit over the spines, searching for the title I have in mind. "This can't be legal." *Right?* I mean, in my line of work, legalities are huge, and this just seems fucking fishy.

Colton crosses the room and stops me with a heavy hand on my shoulder. "Yes and no."

I spin on him. "Explain."

He rubs a hand over his five o'clock shadow. "Things that in the real world would be considered batshit crazy are easily upheld in wills and trusts—they're interesting like that."

"Interesting isn't the word that comes to mind," I mutter, tugging at my collar before heading over to the bar cart in the corner. I pour myself a healthy measure of scotch, swallowing it in one gulp, relishing the burn as it goes down.

"You realize you just downed that single-malt Glenlivet like a frat boy on a mission to get blackout drunk?"

I lift a brow. "Your point?"

Colton scoffs. "My point is that bottle costs more than said frat boy's entire college education. Respect it."

My eyes roll of their own accord. "You're insufferable." Even still, I pour myself two fingers, not wanting to rile him up—asshole's passionate about his scotch, and one of us needs to remain level-headed.

"You fucking love me," he challenges, collapsing onto the navy blue plush velvet couch situated in the center of the room. "Pour one for me and take a seat."

I do as he says before recapping the bottle and joining him. We sit in silence, my mind racing like a Formula 1 car. A whole gamut of emotions rocks my system—shock, anger, frustration, despair, anger, incredulity, sadness, fear, anger... *did I mention the fucking anger?*

"You're acting like you've been sentenced to death."

A groan slips past my lips as my eyes close and my head drops to the back of the couch. A vision of a nagging wife with a crying baby on her hip flashes through my mind, the very picture of domesticated misery. "I may as well have been. I'm twenty-four. I'm in my fucking prime. I don't want a wife or—"

Colton makes a dismissive noise, stopping me. "Who said anything about a wife?"

My head snaps up, and my eyes fly open. "What?"

He shrugs, a calculating glint in his blue eyes. "An heir is required, not a wife."

I lean forward. "Wait, wait, wait. You mean to tell me they're all but legally requiring me to have an illegitimate child?"

Colton arches a brow. "Didn't think a contractually binding sex clause would ruffle your feathers so much."

"Normally I'm not the one signing on the dotted line to fuck," I grumble under my breath before polishing off my drink.

Swear to God, if this was happening to any-fucking-one-else, I'd find it hilarious. But it's not. It's me. My eyes flit to my desk where the damning paper sits, the words already burned into my brain. A baby with no marriage? Talk about shortsighted. However, if I want the Cottonwood Estate—the place where every good childhood memory I have lives—an heir is the price I'm required to pay.

"So, okay, one more time. The papers over there on my desk state that I have to knock someone—anyone— up before my next birthday but in no way require me to marry her?"

Colton's lips tip up into a calculating grin. "Precisely."

I hear what he's saying, but my brain... my brain simply can*not* process it. One of my dad's brothers— whom I've never met, if that tells you anything—had a baby out of wedlock and refused to marry the girl, and he was disowned, disinherited, and said to have disgraced the Larson name. Which is a load of shit, given that my dad's *other* brother used to beat his own son and verbally abuse his wife. Even so, my grandpa all but sawed his branch off of the family tree in an effort to erase the so-called dark mark he left on our legacy. And yet, here we are… with legal papers drawn all but telling me to have a bastard. *The fuck…*

"I need a drink."

Colton's gaze drops to the tumbler in my hand, eyeing it skeptically. "You had a drink. Two, in fact."

The urge to roll my eyes at his blasé attitude is overwhelming, but I manage to stifle the urge. "Let me rephrase. I want to go out and drink. At a bar. Surrounded by scantily clad coeds with tight pussies and loose morals. You never know…" I grin sardonically. "I might even find my baby mama."

Unlike me, Colton doesn't fight it, and his eyes damn near roll back into his skull. "As your lawyer, I've gotta say, this is a horrible idea."

I stand up and head toward the door. "And as my friend?"

He stands and follows, retrieving his keys from his pocket. "As your friend… let's go get you wasted, motherfucker. I'll even be your DD."

We bump fists as he walks past me and out the door. "Hell yeah! My lawyer can go fuck himself."

***

Two hours later, I'm three sheets to the wind and surrounded by an eclectic mix of women with sober-as-a-judge Colton at my side. There's a Botoxed blonde grinding on my lap to the low bass-y beat thrumming through the speakers, a knockout redhead plastered to my side whispering dirty promises in my ear, and a tantalizing ebony-skinned temptress dancing in front of me, her luscious curves on full display for my hungry gaze. I could easily take one of these women home with me—hell, I could probably take all three.

But I won't.

Maybe it's the knowledge that I actually have to impregnate someone—something I've been actively avoiding since the onset of puberty—but even in this den of iniquity, with a cement mixer load of lust and alcohol swirling through the room, my libido seems to have taken the night off. Not to mention, Colton would shut that shit down faster than I could blink.

Or maybe it's the fact that whoever I end up knocking up is someone I'll have to deal with for the next… *forever*. That, in and of itself, is a stellar reason for a little discretion. Which means my dick won't be getting wet for the foreseeable future—at least, not until I find a suitable baby mama.

Fuck. That thought's depressing as hell. Not to mention, sobering. So much so that I dislodge the pretty blonde grinding on my lap. "Let's roll," I bark, and she smiles eagerly, licking her blood-red lips as she takes me in. "No, not you. Colton."

Her face crumples, and a thread of guilt stitches its way into my heart. That is, until I see her set her sights on the next schmuck in an expensive suit, her two friends in tow.

"On it." He pays our—my—tab and guides me out to his car. "I was starting to worry you were considering taking Barbie and her playmates back there home with you."

I shrug; the movement disrupts my equilibrium, causing me to stumble. "Fuck. Nah. She was hot, but not have-my-baby-hot." Colton guides me into the passenger seat of his BMW M8 Coupe. Drunk as a skunk, reality sets in. "Colt, man, what am I gonna do?"

He closes the door without a reply and rounds to the driver's side, where he slides behind the wheel. "Tonight? There's nothing you can do. Get some sleep. Tomorrow, we'll hit the ground running."

I nod, agreeing without really hearing him. My ears are ringing, and my vision swims as the events of today rain down on me—and I don't mean a little sun shower. This is a fucking Category Five hurricane.

CHAPTER 2
WEST

he sound of my father's ringtone—because, yes, a call from him requires extra warning—wakes me from my slumber. The blaring trill combined with the harsh rays of sunlight filtering in through my open curtains has me groaning.

Slowly, I attempt to sit up; the small movement sends a riot of pain through my skull. *Fuck.* Accepting defeat, I collapse back into my pillow and fumble around my nightstand for my phone, wondering when in the hell I even put the phone on the charging dock. Finally, after a few misses, I palm the sleek device and lay it on my face. "Yes, Father," I croak, my voice hoarse and groggy from my night of heavy drinking.

"Weston," my dad barks into the phone, his voice as pleasant as stepping on a Lego. From what I'm told, that shit doesn't feel very nice. But if I want to gain access to my grandfather's estate—and I really fucking do—I guess it's something I'll know for myself soon enough. *Shit… at what age do kids even play with Legos?*

"Yes, Father?" I reply, barely suppressing my sigh.

"Your mother asked me to invite you to join us at the house this evening." He pauses before adding, "Dinner will be served promptly at five—dress appropriately, and for God's sake, be on time." *And by on time, he means early.*

"Yes, Father." The silence on the other end lets me know he disconnected. Crazy how an entire conversation can pass with me only saying the same two words the entire time.

The rest of the day passes much too quickly, in a blur of electrolyte-enhanced beverages, carbs, and headache meds. Then again, I slept until noon, so that may have something to do with it, too. Regardless, it all boils down to the same thing: not enough time between my unwanted wake-up call and my summoning—I mean, family dinner.

At half-past three, I snag my phone and keys off of the bar, thumbing through my notifications as I walk out to my car. Just as I'm about to pocket my phone, it buzzes with an incoming text.

COLTON

You survive?

ME

Ha, funny.

COLTON

Hey, can't fault me for checking.

ME

I'm good. Thanks for last night.

Colton

Always, man. Let's set up a meet time
for Monday to discuss yesterday's bomb
and the impending fallout a little more?

ME

Just tell me when and where.

COLTON

AKA tell Veronica.

ME

Yup, you know it.

I know he'll text me at least a few more times, but I need to hit the road if I want to avoid getting my ass chewed out for being late.

The drive from my place to my parents' is an easy one, but the minute their ostentatious brick wall and iron gates come into view, my heart starts racing in my chest and sweat beads my hairline. At twenty-four, I fucking hate the fact that the mere sight of this house can elicit such a visceral response from me—probably because I'm acutely aware of the terrors housed within its walls. Sure, my parents never raised a hand to me, but they didn't *raise* me either. I was more like a prop to them, no more important than a piece of art or a vase. If it weren't for the house staff taking care of me, I'd have probably starved to death before I turned two.

I steel my nerves as I turn onto the curving paver-stone drive, pausing long enough for the gate to swing inward to allow me entry. On the outside looking in, nothing seems amiss. Tasteful landscaping, pristine brick, spotless windows, and a welcoming front entry— but it's all a lie. The inside of this house is as cold as a goddamn crypt.

After a small pep talk, I leave the safety of my Mercedes and head to the door. I knock twice and wait, my spine straight, shoulders back, and head high, projecting an air of confidence I don't actually feel.

A few seconds pass before the crypt-keeper herself answers the door. Reining in my shock at seeing Prissy Larson doing something she deems beneath her station, I lean in and hover my cheek next to hers. "Mother." I draw back and step inside. This house was custom designed, foundation to roof, no expense spared, but the one they really nailed was the wall color—a deep charcoal, fitting to match the hearts and souls of its owners. "Did you give Eliza the day off?" I ask, wondering where the house manager is.

Mother clucks her tongue. "Her granddaughter is sick. Though, I hardly see how that's an excuse not to be here."

My fists clench at my sides. "Her granddaughter lives with her," I remind her. How she doesn't know this is beyond me—Eliza has been raising the kid since her first birthday, when her mother passed away, and that was ten years ago.

"Oh, yes, right." She brushes her hands down her skirt. "We're dining on the patio today since the weather's so nice."

"Sounds great," I reply, even though she's already walking away.

I follow behind her through the immaculate house and out to the backyard. Everything out here, from the travertine tile patio to the oversized pool complete with a waterfall, is a show of status. Hell, I can't even remember the last time someone dared dip a toe in the crystal blue, perfectly heated water.

Noticing my presence, my father makes a big show, eyeing me and then his watch. "West, how good of you to join us."

He and my mother both are dressed to the nines, looking more fit to attend a derby than a backyard dinner, and like a good puppet, I'm decked out in my Sunday best as well, bowtie and all. Then again, even a backyard meal is a five-star affair for Roland and Prissy Larson.

"Happy to be here," I lie dutifully, playing the part of the good son, even though there's no one here to see the show.

A smug, victorious grin graces my father's aristocratic features. "Come, sit. We have much to discuss." He claims his place at the head of the table, not bothering to pull out my mother's chair. *Jackass.* I pointedly make up for his lack of chivalry before taking my seat across from her.

Always one for dramatics, he takes his time getting to the point. However, Mother and I know better than to speak before him. Instead, I let my mind wander—to the will, to work, to the women from last night, random thoughts racing by at lightning speed.

Finally, after what feels like a lifetime of silence, he speaks, his tone every bit as smug as the smile on his face. "I assume you've read the will?"

He's after a reaction; he so desperately wants to see me mad and miserable so he can feed on my defeat. Fucker is like a demon who subsists on the misery of others.

I'm determined not to give him what he wants—ever. So, with a carefully blank face, I nod. "I have."

His outward expression remains calm and stony, but

the pulsing vein in his forehead is a dead giveaway to his mounting irritation. "And?"

I shrug. "And what? Are you worried about what your grand-name will be? I was thinking Pappy, but I'm sure that's far too informal for you." I do a mental fist pump when I see his jaw clench. This entire conversation is like a game of Battleship, and I'm determined to sink him. "You're probably more of a grandfather though…" I allow my words to casually trail off, as if I'm simply thinking aloud and not pouring gasoline over an already raging inferno.

"Surely you don't intend—" my father starts, but I quickly cut him off.

"Oh, I absolutely do. In fact, I've already begun looking for viable… candidates."

It's a rarity, but such a sight to see, when Roland Larson loses his composure, and right now, he's damn near nuclear. "You mean to tell me you're going to marry and produce an heir by your next birthday?" he asks, his voice strained as he raises a rocks glass of whiskey to his lips.

I grin, knowing good and well I'm about to tip him over the edge. "Oh, no, Father. I have no intentions of getting married. I guess *you* should have read the will better. I only need to knock someone up."

He pitches the crystal tumbler at my head, but I duck, letting it shatter against the brick facade of the house. *Crazy motherfucker.* "You've shamed this family enough! I will not stand for you furthering it with a bastard child!" my father seethes before storming back into the house, undoubtedly heading to his study to re-read the document in question. *Too bad he's not going to like what he finds.* My mother scurries after him, ready and willing to bear the brunt of his displeasure.

I remain seated, knowing the first course should be out momentarily. As awful as being here in this house is, the food Mrs. Zelda cooks up makes it almost worth it.

I check my watch, and, sure enough, the minute the second hand hits the top of the hour, the french doors open and a lone server steps out. He places my plate before me, and my mouth waters. "Butternut squash ravioli with rosemary browned butter. Enjoy."

I turn in my seat to thank the server, but he's already scurried back into the house, no doubt scared of my father's wrath. Roland Larson makes it a point to never be friendly with his staff—be it here or at the office, he firmly believes that thanking someone for their services is beneath him if he's paying them. Like I said… *jackass.*

With nothing else to do, I dig into the food before me. The aromatic flavors burst across my tongue, and my eyes damn near roll back in my head. How in the hell Mrs. Zelda packs so much flavor into two small pockets of dough is beyond me, but I'm thankful all the same. Idly, I wonder if I could convince her to come work for me instead.

Shortly after the second course—a dope-ass salad with these little candied walnuts—my parents return to the table, acting as if everything is peachy keen. If I didn't know better, I'd swear they were both fucking robots—alas, they're simply heartless and not mechanical. Hell, I'm fairly certain robots have more authentic feelings than my parents.

I focus on my food, trying my hardest not to listen to any of the mindless garbage my parents are gossiping about. That is, until I hear a very familiar name.

"It's really a shame about Ken Kellan." My mother tries her best to sound sympathetic, but if anything, she's more like a dog with a bone.

I glance up from my food and ask, "What about him?"

She brings her cloth napkin up from her lap to blot her lips. "Oh, that's right, you know his daughter. What's her name again... Stacy?"

I barely refrain from rolling my eyes. "Stacia. Now, back to her dad."

"Oh, yes, that's it." She takes a dainty sip of her water. "He was arrested."

I reel back. *Arrested...* "For what?"

Ever dramatic, Mother leans forward and stage whispers, "Embezzlement."

"To the tune of over a million, I've heard," my father adds, sounding utterly bored.

Mother brings a hand to her chest as she shakes her head solemnly. "Thank God you didn't invest with him..."

I tune their chatter back out, my mind racing. I've met Mr. Kellan a few times in passing, and he's always seemed like an honest man. His wife is sweet as hell, and don't get me started on his daughter—that girl is finer than fine. *Shit.* I guess I should check on her—indirectly, of course.

While my parents are busy yammering away about the latest trophy wife's nose job, I discreetly slip my phone out of my pocket and text Brock, my cousin, under the table.

ME

How's Stacia? Shit... how are you?

BROCK

I'm good. She's… in rough shape.

ME

Meet up tonight?

BROCK

Come over tonight. Ab's is doing taco
fries.

ME

Fuck. Yes. I'll be by around 6.

CHAPTER 3
STACIA

ack and forth. Back and forth. My silver-glitter Doc Martens wear a trail in the hideous puke green rug as I continue to pace back and forth. The cramped motel room limits my range of motion, which only serves to make me feel even more confined.

I check the clock, trying to ignore the way it hangs crookedly on the wall; it's a quarter past three. *Why haven't you called yet, Dad?* I look over to where my mother sits on the bed, worrying the scratchy polyester coverlet between her slender fingers. Her usually wrinkle-free face is etched with concern as we both wait on his call.

"He's okay," I say, though I don't know which of us I'm trying to reassure. Ever since life as we knew it came crashing down two days ago—*God, has it really only been two days?*—my mother has become almost a shell of herself. It breaks my cold little heart in a way I never knew possible to see my once-vibrant mother so desolate.

I'll never forget the way she broke down when the uniformed officers hauled him away...

"You have the right to remain silent." The officer's words are muted by my mother's wailing cries as she collapses to the ground, landing hard on her tailbone.

"Ken." She howls Dad's name with a desperation I've never heard before—like her entire universe is being ripped away. I crouch beside her, trying my hardest to lend comfort, wrapping her in my arms, holding her close.

"It's okay, my love," Dad calls back, as calm as ever. "This is all a misunderstanding."

I watch on, silently, tears turning my smoky eye to a charcoal mess as my hero is manhandled toward the back seat of an unmarked cruiser. A stocky officer with a menacing buzzcut opens the back door, and I close my eyes, unable to watch any longer.

"Wildflower." My eyes fly open at the sound of my dad's nickname for me. His steely gaze meets mine, infusing me with his courage. "Watch after your mom for me. I'll call."

After he was hauled away, Mom and I were coolly informed that anything purchased by him in the last five years was hereby considered seized as evidence—including our home and my mother's car. I'd never been more thankful that my own vehicle was a sweet-sixteen gift from my grandparents— halle-fucking-lujah.

It was almost a full twenty-four hours before we heard from him, and now we're verging on hour fifty. *He should have called by now, dammit!* Finally, at the half hour mark, my cell phone rings. I swipe across the screen to answer so quickly I almost decline the call. "Hello?" I whisper, clutching the phone to my ear.

"You have a collect call from Ken Kellan, an inmate

at the King County Jail, a Mississippi State Correctional Facility. To accept the charges for this call, press three—"

I yank the phone away from my ear and open the keypad, all but drilling my finger into the screen. The operator continues on with her spiel, explaining the charges and reminding me that the call is being recorded; none of it matters, though, as long as I get to talk to my dad.

There's a slight pause, and then the voice I've been anxiously waiting to hear filters through the line. "Stacia."

"Dad!" I cry. "How are you? Is everything okay? What's going on?"

"Calm down, wildflower," he soothes, though how he can sound so calm is beyond me. "Is your mom there?"

"Yeah, she's here."

"Good. Put me on speaker." Crossing the small room to sit by Mom, I do as he says. "I saw the judge today."

A million words race from my brain to the tip of my tongue, but I hold them in, waiting to see if my mom is going to take point. When after a few moments she remains silent, I speak up. "What did he say?"

"Well, I got good news and bad."

Inhaling deeply, I say, "Good first."

"Good is they set my bail."

"Dad! That's amazing! What is the bad?"

He sighs, and in that one heavy breath, I hear all of the stress and worry he's been trying to hide. "It's high, wildflower." He rattles off a figure large enough to make even a prince pause. But it's his next words that have my heart dropping straight to my gut. "Cash—it's cash only."

"What? Why?"

"Why's the sky blue?" Dad asks, sounding resigned. But fuck that. My dad is a good man—an innocent man—and there's no way in hell I'm going to let him rot in a jail cell over crimes he didn't commit.

"This… I… we'll figure it out," I say, infusing every bit of strength and determination I possess into my words.

"You're a good girl, Stacia."

I smile through my tears. "Because you and Mom raised me that way."

We chat for a few more minutes—well, Dad and I do, Mom just sits there, as silent and broken as ever—making a tentative plan until Dad says he has to go. It pains me to hang up, worry for him weighing on me like a wet blanket. But I shake it off—I have too much to get done if I want to see my dad bonded out. And since worrying away our problems isn't an option, I've got to get proactive.

Which means a list. I need to make a list. Writing shit down equals getting shit done. At least, for me it does. From my spot on the edge of the bed, I lean forward and wiggle open the single drawer of the rickety bedside table. All of the usual suspects are there: a Gideon Bible, a list of television channels, a whopping two takeout menus, along with a notepad and pen—*bingo!*

I snag what I need and shove the drawer shut before moving to the chair in the corner. It rocks a smidge, thanks to one leg being shorter than the rest, but I'm so focused on the task at hand, I hardly notice.

1. Call Dad's lawyer about bond, etc.

2. *Call bondsman.*
3. *Call grandma.*
4. *Call AJ.*
5. *Call work.*
6. *Make money.*

My list may seem arbitrary to most, but the vague bullet points are more than enough to keep me focused. I make quick work of leaving a message for Dad's attorney, following it up with an email, as well, just to be safe.

After crossing task one off of my list, I dial up my grandparents. To be honest, I'm kind of dreading this call—while I know Mom needs the support, I'm worried they'll assume the worst.

"Stacia, dear, what a treat." My grandmother's voice rings through the line.

"Hey, Gramma." I can't fake a cheery tone for her.

"What's got you down?"

I suck in a lungful of air and break the news. "Dad was arrested." A sharp gasp is my only reply, and I rush to add, "But he didn't do it. I know my dad, and he's innocent."

Finally, after the world's longest stretch of silence, she asks, "On what charges?"

"Embezzlement."

"Where are you and your mother?"

"A motel," I whisper, emotion clogging my throat. "The house was seized as evidence."

"Well, that won't do, will it?" I hear scuffling as though something is covering the microphone on her end, followed by Gramma hollering "Haaaaank!" The two of them exchange words too quiet for me to hear. After a few minutes of whispering, Gramma returns. "We'll be there by five."

"Are you sure?" I ask hesitantly, not wanting to look my gift horse in the mouth.

"Why wouldn't I be?"

"I-I don't know…" I trail off. "I was worried you—"

Gramma cuts me off with an indignant scoff. "Stacia Iris Kellan. If you think for one minute I'm going to abandon you and your mother, you've got another thing coming. I may not always see eye-to-eye with Ken or agree with his choices—innocent or not—but he's my daughter's husband and your father. Family is everything."

God love my grandmother. She and my grandfather aren't wealthy by any stretch of the imagination. Nope, they're your average blue collar, middle class work-hard-for-what-you-got kind of family, and far too proud to accept any handouts from my parents. They instilled those same values in my mother, and I know from many a story that Dad had to work hard to woo her, because flashing his old-money status didn't do a damn thing for her.

I know coming here will be a strain on them, but once this all gets sorted out, I'll make sure they're reimbursed for every single expense they incur and more. Because like she said: *family is everything.*

It's only after I end the call that I realize without our home, my grandparents have nowhere to stay. But, Gramma's nothing if not resourceful—honestly, I probably get at least fifty percent of my badassery from her—she says it's in our DNA, a trait that all Harrison women possess. I can almost guarantee she was on her ancient-ass desktop computer booking an Airbnb. God love her, she's the perfect mix of old and new—incredibly set in her ways yet still able to learn new tricks.

I'm not going to even attempt the bondsman without speaking to Dad's lawyer, so I tell my mom I'm going to step outside, and I dial my bestie. Thank fuck, she answers on the first ring.

"Babe! I've been dying, waiting on you. Are you okay?"

The genuine concern in her tone gets me, and I sniffle before replying. "They took the house."

"Come over."

I want so badly to, but… "Mom needs me. I don't think I can leave her alone right now."

Her sad sigh comes through loud and clear, telling me a million different things—that she hates this for me; that she wishes she could be here, that she could help. "I hear ya. Well, the invitation stands—not that you need an invite. Mi casa es su casa, bitch."

I grin a little. "Thanks, babe."

"So, what are y'all gonna do about the house?"

"Fuck if I know. My grandparents will be here in an hour or so, and we will figure it out."

"If you need somewhere to stay, holler at me."

How did I get so lucky to have her as my ride-or-die? "Will do. I'd better go check on Mom."

"'Kay. Love you."

"You, too." I end the call and head back into the motel room, only to find Mom quietly crying into her hands. I rush to her and wrap her in my arms. "Are you okay?" I ask dumbly, because obviously she fucking isn't.

"I...I just..." Another round of sobs wrack her small body, and I squeeze her tighter to me.

"Shh. It will be okay, Mom. He'll be out soon. I promise."

"He's my whole world," she whispers, and my heart breaks. I can't imagine experiencing the kind of all-encompassing love my mother has for my dad. She meant it one-thousand percent when she said he's her whole world.

Their love story is anything but typical—she was a waitress in a little diner the next town over, and he was a hotshot football player with a rich-boy attitude. That is, until he met her. One Friday night, he and some of his teammates stumbled into the diner after an away game. Riding high on their big win, they were being total assholes and giving the staff a hard time. But the second Dad saw Mom, he was smitten. Love at first sight, he calls it, but she wouldn't even give him the time of day. He started going to the diner every day after practice, always asking for her section, ordering a stack of pancakes, a slice of pecan pie, and a glass of milk. Each afternoon, he asked her to join him, and finally, after three months, his persistence paid off, and she slid into the booth across from him. The rest, as they say, was history.

I can hardly fathom what it's like, having a love so great. Hell, the closest I've come to being in love is orgasming—I mean, you've got to love a man who knows what he's doing in the bedroom just a little, right?

Two hours later, Mom and I are on our way to the little cottage Gramma rented indefinitely—emphasis on the word little. And I don't mean that in a snobby way; truly, for all its charm, there's simply not enough room for the four of us in the five-hundred-square-foot space. But we'll make the best of it—*we have to, right?*

Another hour passes, and making the best of it we are not. My mom is still a catatonic mess sitting ramrod straight on the blue tartan loveseat, Grampa is grumbling and mumbling under his breath about everything under the sun from the wingback chair in the corner, and Gramma is a nervous wreck—though, seeing her daughter like this must be hard.

Finally, Gramma snaps. "Matilda Louise Kellan!" Mom's eyes widen as they snap to her mother's. I shouldn't laugh—it's completely inappropriate—but something about hearing my own mother get three-named has the giggles breaking free. However, a frosty glare from my grandmother silences me.

"Sorry," I mumble, my cheeks burning.

Gramma nods, crossing the room to sit next to Mom on the loveseat. "Matilda, I know this is hard. I know Ken is your everything. But you need to listen and listen well. Shutting down is not an option. It doesn't help your husband any. It doesn't help your daughter, who is struggling, too. And it certainly isn't benefiting you in any way."

Mom sucks in a shuddering breath and nods. "I know," she whispers, her voice hoarse from disuse. "I know."

Gramma lays a hand on Mom's knee in an effort to comfort her. "You gotta buck up, Tildy Lou. You can't go falling to pieces at a time like this. Us Harrison women come from stronger stock than that."

"What do I do?" Mom asks, sounding so utterly broken that my lashes brim with unshed tears.

"We need to figure out bail," I say, inserting myself into the conversation.

"How much is it?" Grampa asks, following my suit.

I rattle off the number Dad told me, causing all three of them to blanch. "Cash only," I add, the words feeling like cotton in my mouth.

"We… we don't have that kind of cash on hand," Mom whispers. "Not with our accounts frozen."

"We'll figure it out. I'll figure it out," I vow, knowing in my heart of hearts I'll do anything to raise that money.

Gramma and Grampa exchange an indecipherable look before he returns to his muttering—God love him. "Well, there's nothing we can do tonight," my grandmother says as she stands from the loveseat. "Stacia, why don't you be a dear and run out and grab us some dinner? Pizza, chicken, something. I've got a twenty in my wallet."

"Yes, ma'am," I reply, knowing damn well I'm not going to spend her money.

I hit up a chain pizza place that's known for its five-dollar deals, grabbing us two pizzas, an order of breadsticks, and a two-liter of soda. It's by no means a healthy dinner, but it's comfort food, plain and simple, which is exactly what we need.

By the time I make it back to the cottage, it's dark outside. We crowd around the small oak dining table and chow down on the ooey-cheesy-goodness as if it's our last meal. However, once dinner is over, a whole new problem presents itself—sleeping arrangements.

Obviously, my grandparents laid claim to the bedroom, which leaves the loveseat for my mother and the floor for me. Unwilling to be the squeaky wheel, I grab a pillow and blanket from the linen closet and make myself a nest. Mind you, I'm wide-the-fuck-awake, but it's eight o'clock and the older adults are tired.

I resign myself to playing on my phone until sleep claims me. Finally, around nine, my eyelids begin to droop. Which is precisely when my grandpa starts snoring. Right hand to the Bible, it sounds like a logger is in the bedroom, falling an entire forest. Never in my life have I ever heard someone snore like that, and with every wall-rattling exhale, my drowsiness slips away.

I return my attention to my phone, pinning makeup looks I want to try, hoping like hell that he'll eventually roll over and stop—though, he's been sawing logs for over an hour now, so, it's not looking likely.

Eventually, my exhaustion wins out, and my eyes slip closed. I'm in that delicious space between sleep and awake when the sound of sniffles penetrates my dreams. It takes me a minute to place it—Mom's crying again.

I block out her soft whimpers as best as I can, but it's no use. Between her crying and Grampa's snoring, sleep is so far out of my reach it's laughable.

Finally, I can't take it any longer. This just isn't going to work. I rise from the floor, my back already stiff from lying on the hard surface, and stash my bedding in the laundry room.

I pass back through the living room, pausing at the

couch to let my mom know I'm leaving. "I'm going to AJ's."

Through the dark, I see her nod, the nearly imperceptible movement shredding my tattered heart a little more. Kneeling beside her, I press a kiss to her tear-stained cheek. "Love you, Mom."

"Love you, too," comes her quiet reply before I slip out the front door.

CHAPTER 4
STACIA

I text AJ, letting her know I'm on the way over before cranking the ignition and backing out of the driveway. The drive passes in a blur, my exhaustion weighing heavily on me.

AJ's apartment is in the heart of Cottonwood's downtown area. While our town is small, it's bustling, especially the nightlife. People assume our city is a sleepy little place, but with most of the population having more money than God and a college campus, Cottonwood probably sleeps as much as the Big Apple.

Luck is on my side when I see a parking spot directly across the street from AJ's building—an old factory turned into prime luxury living. There's six units in total, and while the industrial chic thing is one-hundred-and-ten percent my bestie's style, it doesn't call to me. Despite my vibrant red hair, tattoos, and piercings, I'm a total sucker for that Joanna Gaines look. *Cliché, I know.*

Bustling or not, Cottonwood is safe, so I take my time heading into her building. Instead of jaywalking, I stroll down to the crosswalk at the end of the block, relishing in the way the heavy, damp air clings to my skin, allowing me to pretend it's what is weighing me down instead of my sadness.

All too soon, I'm across the threshold and in the lobby. A quick elevator ride to the second floor, and I find myself knocking on my best friend's door.

Despite the late hour, AJ greets me fully dressed with bright eyes. "You okay?" she asks, pulling the door back to allow me entry.

"Yeah." I shake my head. "No."

She wraps me in a tight hug. "C'mon. We had taco fries for dinner, and something told me to save you some."

Fuck. Yes. At least this horrendous day will end on a good note.

As I venture toward the kitchen, the sound of male voices—plural—greets me. Turning the corner, I see Brock and West posted up at the kitchen island, both sipping from bottles of beer.

"Boys," AJ calls, "look who decided to join us!"

Both men tip their chins toward me in greeting. "Hey," I say, trying my hardest not to ogle West. It doesn't matter one iota that he and I have hooked up—only once, and not even beyond a little heavy petting—that man gets my vagina revving like a Ford GT on the start line at a drag race. He's just so… hot. And funny. And pretty nice. Lord knows he was fucking ace in helping Brock and AJ get together.

Trekking through the kitchen to the fridge, I help myself to a beer of my own. I pop the top on the lip of the counter and bring the frosty bottle to my lips, relishing the slide of the cool liquid down my throat.

"Thanks for letting me come by," I say, wiping the back of my hand across my mouth.

AJ pins me with a hard look. "You're always welcome here. Now, come sit and let me feed you."

I quirk a brow at her matronly behavior, wondering what gives. "Uh, sure," I reply, claiming the stool next to West.

He knocks his knee into mine, simultaneously awakening a whole swarm of butterflies in my belly while grabbing my attention. "You good?" he asks, his voice deliciously deep.

Him knowing means one of two things: either the happy couple here told him what's going on, or gossip is already making the rounds. My guess is gossip—Lord knows these people trade in other people's misery like it's the most valuable commodity there is, and being the first to know the inside scoop puts you at the top of the ladder, so to speak.

I shrug and bring my bottle back to my lips, polishing it off in two gulps. "I'm fine, I guess."

His warm stare heats me from the inside out. "Let me know if you—"

"Taco fries!" AJ sings, cutting off whatever West was about to say. Which is probably for the best, because pretty much the only thing he could do to help get my mind off of things is *get me off*, and once AJ and Brock got serious, I vowed to never go there with him. The last thing our little friend group needs is awkwardness between the two of us if one of us was to somehow catch feelings for the other.

Not that I truly think either of us would; relationships and sex are one of those things West and I see eye-to-eye on. We both firmly agree on the commitment-free lifestyle, both more into pleasure versus the pain—unless it's of the ass-smacking and hair-pulling variety, thank you very much—that relationships inevitably bring.

***

"I think I'm gonna call it a night," I announce on a yawn, my belly full and eyelids drooping.

"Sure, of course. Your room's ready for you." I can't help but grin at my bestie. And then, her words hit, and I'm all-out beaming. My. Room. We weren't allowed to take much of anything when they seized our home, but I have an entire bedroom full of things here still. Halle-fucking-lujah.

Pushing away from the island, I deposit my plate in the sink and hug AJ's neck before retreating down the hall toward my room—well, really it's the guest room, but the closet is full of my shit, and that makes it mostly mine.

I nearly weep as I step into the room; swear to God, the futon in here has never looked more appealing than it does now. Between the motel bed's lumpy, questionable bed, and the cottage floor, this may as well be a five-star hotel mattress.

After nudging the door closed, I strip down to my T-shirt and panties and climb into the bed and plug my phone into charge. I worry sleep won't come easy, but wrapped in the covers, burrito style, I drift off in no time at all.

All too soon, the sun rises, bringing with it a fresh wave of anxiety. Even though I slept for at least six hours, I feel like I pulled an all-nighter. Couple all of that with the fact that I'm so not a morning person, and well, yeah, it adds up to one grumpy redhead. Artificial or not, us redheads are a fiery bunch on a good day, and something tells me today will *not* be good.

A quick glance at my phone screen tells me it's barely past six, making it highly unlikely for anyone else to be awake. As much as I'd like to go back to sleep, once I'm up… I'm up. Which means I need two things, stat— piping hot coffee and a steaming hot shower.

Not wanting to wake AJ or Brock, I pad quietly across the hall and into the guest bath. I open the shower door and turn the faucet dial as hot as it can go, stripping out of my panties and shirt as I wait for the water to warm.

Finally, when steam fills the room, I step in, pulling the heavy sheet of glass closed behind me. I take my time, letting the nearly scalding water and luxurious soap wash away some of my worries.

Once I'm shampooed, conditioned, and scrubbed thoroughly, I shut off the water and step out. The frigid air meets my wet body, causing chill bumps to dot my skin.

I grab the towel from the hook and wrap it around myself just as the bathroom door flies open. A silent scream builds and I nearly drop my towel as a shirtless West saunters in. "Oh!" I gasp when I catch a glimpse of the impressive erection tenting the front of his sweats. "My God. What are you doing here?"

He grins lazily, his blue eyes raking over my body has my nipples tightening in a way that has nothing to do with the cold. "In the bathroom or here in general?" His voice is a sultry drawl—all rasp and gravel. *God, why is he so hot?* I'm so caught up in staring at him that I don't even realize he replied.

He steps closer, invading my personal space as if it doesn't even exist. "Stacia." He runs the knuckle of his index finger beneath my chin, bringing my eyes to his. "Are you okay?"

I shake off my weird lusty haze and step back. "I'm fine," I reply tersely, hating how off my game this shit with Dad has me. I've never been the kind of girl to get tongue-tied in the company of a good-looking man—hell, I've had this particular man's tongue down my throat and hands on my breasts and have never once faltered in his presence. Now, here I am acting like a virginal schoolgirl with a crush. *Get it together, Stacia!*

"Fine. You're fine?" he asks, brow quirked, and I nod. "Well, my mother may not have ever taught me much that was useful in life, but something she did teach me is that when a woman says she's *fine*, she's anything but." He steps closer again, eating up the minuscule space I managed to put between us. "So, I'm gonna ask again, are you okay?"

My shoulders sag, and tears cling to my lashes. "Honestly? No. Not really. My mom's a mess—basically a zombie at this point. My grandparents are in town to help, but they can't really afford to stay. The Feds seized most of our assets, including the house. My dad's bond is astronomical and cash only, and I just… I can't catch my fucking breath. It's like I'm barely treading water, and the waves are just getting bigger and bigger, and at any second I know a massive swell is going to break and pull me out to the depths, where I'll surely drown."

Before I even have a chance to be humiliated by my massive overshare, West wraps his corded arms around me and pulls me into his warm, muscled chest, my tears painting his skin. Usually, I would balk at looking so weak, but fuck, I need this. This link, this connection, this… primal sort of comfort.

We stay locked in our embrace until my eyes dry and my breathing evens out. "It's gonna be okay, Stacia."

I pull back and eye him skeptically.

With the back of his hand, West brushes my damp hair out of my face. "I don't know how, but it will be. You're a warrior, and I know you'll figure this out. Plus, you've got backup. AJ would go to the fucking moon and back for you—which means you've got Brock and me by default. You're not alone, so let the people who care about you help."

His words send a little zing of hope through me, and I offer him a weak smile. "Thanks, West."

"Anytime." His teeth graze his lower lip as he slides his eyes over me one last time. "I'll just use Brock's bathroom."

And just like that, he's gone, leaving me alone to work through the confusing maelstrom of emotions currently wreaking havoc on my system. How I can feel utterly helpless and so damn turned on all at once is beyond me.

CHAPTER 5
STACIA

By the time I'm back in my room, my galloping heart has finally slowed to a canter. Never in my life has a man gotten me so worked up by doing so little. Stress and lack of caffeine—that's what I'm chalking it up to. Because, seriously, I've known West Larson for years, and while he's always been able to get my panties a little wet, he's never made me dick-dumb. And just now, in the bathroom, that's exactly what I was.

I opt to dress for comfort over cuteness, drawing on a pair of baggy sweats with cuffed ankles and a loose-fitting cropped tee, sans bra, before slipping my cell phone into my pocket and setting out toward the kitchen in search of coffee.

There's no sign of West—or AJ and Brock for that matter—but judging from the smell of freshly brewed goodness wafting my way and the telltale completion gurgle, someone just made a fresh pot of coffee. "Thank you, whoever you are," I murmur softly as I snag a mug from the cabinet. Filling it to the halfway mark, I top off the steaming liquid with a healthy pour of hazelnut creamer.

"Why don't you have a little coffee with your cream?" West asks from behind me, sending my heart leaping right out of my chest.

"Jesus! You scared me." I spin to face him. "You shouldn't sneak up on people."

"Wasn't sneaking," he says, holding up his hands in a show of innocence.

"Whatever." I roll my eyes and move past him to the island bar.

He's still only wearing his gray sweats—*drool*—and I can't help but admire the sinewy muscles of his back as he fixes himself a cup of coffee before joining me.

"The happy couple is up," he says before taking a sip. "Should be out any minute."

I nod, too busy mentally going over the remaining items on my to-do list. I still need to reach out to my work, Dad's lawyer, and the bail bondsman—*gah, talk about words I never thought I'd say.*

West and I are sipping our coffee in companionable silence when AJ and Brock join us. I try not to notice the pep in Brock's step or my friend's freshly fucked hair, but it's no use.

Especially when Brock comes up behind her at the coffeepot and smacks her ass before nuzzling his face into her neck. "Love you, firecracker," he murmurs before turning to address us. "Sleep well?"

West and I both nod and I add, "Definitely slept better on the futon than I would have on the floor."

AJ quirks a brow. "The floor?"

I drop my gaze to my half-empty cup to try and hide my burning cheeks. "Uh, yeah. The cottage my grandparents are renting is like the size of your living room and kitchen combined."

All three of them cringe. "Babe, that won't work long-term," AJ says, topping off my mug—God love her, she knows exactly how I like it: a one-to-one coffee and cream ratio to start, but only coffee on the refills.

I offer her a grateful smile and a shrug. "One day at a time, right?"

AJ drums her purple painted nails on the bar top. "You could stay here," she says, but I don't miss the look Brock sends her way. Truly, I can't say I blame him; they're basically still newlyweds, with only a year of marriage under their belt. If I were in their shoes, I wouldn't want some freeloader crashing with me either.

"No, I couldn't impose on y'all like that."

She looks as though she wants to argue, but Brock sidles up behind her to whisper in her ear, a hand planted firmly on each of her hips, holding her body to his. The two of them are such a juxtaposition, what with his clean-cut, classic style and her currently teal-colored hair and a plethora of tattoos. Looking at them, you wouldn't think they would work, but my God, they really do. Aside from my parents, I don't think I've ever seen a couple more in love than they are.

"What… what are you gonna do then?" she asks.

I run my hands through my mostly dry hair. "I don't know. Maybe find a cheap room to rent or something."

This time it's Brock bristling. "What if you end up living with a psychopath who wants to kill you, stretch your skin over your bones to make a canvas, and paint it with your blood?"

Well, that was vivid. I roll my lips inward in an attempt to contain my laughter, but it's no use. A snort breaks free. "Dramatic, much? This is Cottonwood. I think the last murder here was like… a hundred years ago or some shit."

"Actually, it was last year," West offers, unhelpfully.

I pin him with a glare. "Regardless. That's a chance I'll have to take. Because, let me tell y'all, sleeping on the floor for… however long this shit takes… is not a viable option."

"Oh!" AJ yells excitedly, bouncing on her toes. "Oh! I have a great idea!"

Something tells me this will not *be a great idea.*

"Let's hear it," I say, hesitantly.

"You could live with West!"

CHAPTER 6

WEST

"She could what now?" I ask, my gaze darting up to meet Abby Jane's. Her deep brown eyes are full of mischief, and I don't like it.

"Yes! It's perfect, really."

I shift uncomfortably on the barstool. "How do you figure?"

She bats her long lashes at me. "Well, now that Brock lives here, you're all alone. Gosh, you have, what, three extra bedrooms?"

"One's my office."

AJ grins. "That still leaves two free."

I look to my cousin for help, but the bastard is smirking at me like this is the best thing he's ever witnessed. Probably because he's fully aware just how much having a woman live with me would cramp my style—especially if I'm going to be knocking someone up within the next year.

"I don't know," I hedge, but the little blue-haired she-demon plows on like I didn't even speak.

"It's really a win-win. What do you think?" she asks

Stacia, leading me to realize that she hasn't said a word about this hare-brained plan.

"I… uh. Um, well." She blows out a heavy breath. "It doesn't seem like something West is interested in."

My cousin's wife pins me with a hard glare. "West. Surely you could offer up your spare room to a friend in need for a while?" *Damn, this girl is good at a guilt trip.*

I turn to look at the woman in question as she shakes her head in refusal. I immediately take notice of her furrowed brow and slumped shoulders. Stacia looks so fucking defeated that something in me breaks.

"Don't worry about it," Stacia murmurs at the same time I say, "Sure. Why not?"

AJ fist pumps the air before doing a little shimmy that leads into jazz hands, showboating like she just scored a game-winning touchdown *and* the extra fucking point.

"I knew you'd come around," she says triumphantly before hooking her fingers into the collar of Brock's white T-shirt. "C'mon, Jockstrap, let's leave them to hammer out the details."

My cousin lights up like a kid on Christmas morning, knowing full well he's about to get laid for the second time this morning.

At the sound of their bedroom door closing, Stacia leaps into action. "I'll be fine. You do not have to let me stay with you. Seriously, West. You know AJ, she gets an idea and she's…"

"Like a dog with a bone," I supply, and we both sport knowing grins.

"Yeah, that." She rises from her stool to carry her mug to the sink, and my eyes drop to her ass. Never would've said baggy, ratty sweats were sexy, but the way hers cling to her ass, combined with the image of her wrapped in that tiny towel have me feeling some kind of way—*horny, it has me horny.*

It doesn't help that I've been thinking about her tits for the last year or so, ever since our little back seat hookup at the river when Brock and AJ were figuring their shit out. *Perky and high, tipped with tight rosy nipples, mmm*—my mouth waters at the thought.

"West? Are you listening?"

Nope, I was too busy being visited by the ghost of make-out sessions past. "Sorry, come again?" I can't help but snigger at my phrasing, because hot damn, I'd love to make Stacia Kellan come again—and again and again.

"I was saying you really don't have to let me stay with you. It's not a big deal."

Her words are saying one thing, but her kicked-puppy tone is saying another. "Oh, yeah? Then what are you gonna do?"

She shrugs, trying for nonchalant, but I can see straight through her false bravado. "Get a sleeping bag? Sleep in my car? Rent a room? The possibilities are endless."

I shake my head at her. *Stubborn, sexy spitfire.* "Or, you could just rent my room?"

"You're only offering because you feel like you have to. I don't want to cause you any problems, and I'm sure as shit not a charity case."

"Listen, you have pride; I can respect that. But you need help right now, and I'm—begrudgingly—willing to lend it."

She whirls around to face me, her brown eyes flashing with anger. "I don't want or need your *begrudging* help."

I'm about to rebuff her again when she stomps out of the kitchen and down the hall to the guest room, where she promptly slams the door.

I trail after her, rapping my knuckles against the woodgrain. "Stacia," I call out but she doesn't reply. "C'mon." I try the knob, but she locked it.

Shit. If I don't figure out a way to fix this, Abby Jane will never ever let me hear the end of it. However, as much as I want to press the issue, I'm smart enough to know that pushing her right now will not result in favorable results. So, I do the only thing I can—retreat to the living room to wait her out. And hey, if I slip in a game of Madden or two, no harm, no foul, right? Plus, it's not like I have anything else to do today.

CHAPTER 7
STACIA

As much as it pains me to admit it, West is right. The only thing stopping me from agreeing to move in with him is my pride. It might have been different if he wouldn't have been so openly opposed to it when AJ suggested it—not that I blame him, because what hot, single guy would want some chick crashing at his place and cramping his style? None, that's how many, absolutely none.

The temptation to cave and agree to stay with him sits heavily on my chest—and I'm talking elephant heavy. Which is why I need a distraction.

It's edging on eight o'clock, which means Gramma will be up. She was probably up before I was, but I was taught—by her—that calling someone before a certain time was considered uncouth. Although, I think our extenuating circumstances would maybe buy me a pass.

I slip my phone from my pocket and dial her number. "Your mother said you're at a friend's house," she says in way of greeting.

"Yes, ma'am. I hope that's okay."

"You're a grown woman, Stacia Iris." She clucks her tongue. "Truth be told, I wouldn't want to sleep on no floor either."

"How's Mom?"

"She's cradling a cup of coffee, staring at the wall," Gramma sighs. "I don't know what to do for her; I worry she'll be like this until Ken is home…"

And if we don't get him home soon, she may just stay this way. Her unspoken words ring through my mind as if she'd spoken them aloud.

"I'm working on it, Gramma."

"I know you are, dear. Harrison women get shit done."

My lips tip up in a grin. "That we do, Gramma. That we do. I'll check in later. Love you."

"Love you, too," she replies, and I end the call.

Feeling renewed, I tread back out to the living area in search of a pen and paper.

Secretly, I'm hoping West isn't still here. But those hopes are quickly dashed on the rocks, as he's deep into some video game with Brock on the couch. *Huh. Guess he and AJ opted for a quickie for round two.*

I hear commotion in the kitchen and follow it, knowing I'll find my best friend in there whipping up some concoction for us to eat. "You all good?" she asks when I enter.

"Meh."

"Did you and West get everything sorted?"

Not wanting to deflate her optimism, I shrug noncommittally. She eyes me skeptically but doesn't pick. "Wanna help me make breakfast?"

I laugh. "Uh, no. I can't cook, and you know it."

"Luckily, heating a Toaster Strudel doesn't require much talent."

Scoffing, I say, "Well, I don't think Gretchen Weiners' father, the inventor of Toaster Strudel, would be too pleased with this."

We both dissolve into a fit of giggles. "What's so funny?" Brock hollers from the couch.

"*Mean Girls* things," AJ calls back, making me grin, because I know she's made him watch the movie at least a hundred times.

A few minutes later, we carry a plate of flaky, frosted, strawberry and cream cheese goodness out to the guys. "Courtesy of Stacia's badass toaster-ing skills and the Weiners family," AJ announces, placing the plate down onto the table with exaggerated flourish.

West shakes his head. "I don't get why women are so obsessed with that damn movie."

I roll my eyes at him, feeling personally attacked. "You'd have to watch it to get it."

He rolls his right back. "Girl, I've seen that movie more times than I can count, and let me tell you, the only upside is Miss Lohan. *Mmm.* She was in her prime for that one."

"Riiight, sure." I snatch a strudel off the plate.

I start to lower myself down onto the cushion next to West, but he kicks his feet up onto it, blocking me. I glare, but he simply shrugs and says, "'You can't sit with us.'"

A cheesy grin splits my cheeks. "That's too easy. Everyone knows that line." I nudge his feet off of the couch and claim my seat.

Brock chimes in, "You don't even go here!" making us all laugh. AJ quotes the iconic line about Wednesday and wearing pink. But I'm still waiting on Mr. Sexy Chest to wow me.

"It's okay if it's too hard," I offer with a smarmy smile, giving him an out.

"Don't count me out yet. I'm trying to pick a good one."

"More like trying to buy yourself some time. It's okay, West. Not everyone can be a *Mean Girls* aficionado."

He doesn't bother replying, taking his out, and conversation between AJ, Brock, and myself picks up. "I have a few phone calls I need to make," I say, standing to excuse myself. "I'll be back."

"'Kay, babe," AJ says, snuggling into Brock who simply nods with a smile. West catches my gaze, a smile playing on his sinful lips. "Grool."

"Grool?" I ask, wondering what on earth he's saying.

"Yeah. 'I meant to say great but then I started to say cool.'"

That's all it takes for me to lose it. I'm damn near doubled over laughing. "Oh. Oh my God." I wipe the tears from my eyes. "That was amazing."

West winks. "I've heard that a time or two."

"Don't flatter yourself, dude. You're more of a Shane than an Aaron," I quip as I saunter back toward the guest room.

"Girl, please. I'm Aaron Samuels and Glen Coco all rolled into one!" West hollers to my retreating back, making my smile grow even broader, because he's right —he's totally an Aaron, and forget four candy canes, he'd probably get like thirty.

In the guest room, I grab the notepad and pen I pilfered earlier before flopping down onto the bed to call Dad's attorney.

"McMasters and McLean, this is Meagan speaking. How may I help you?"

A sudden bout of nerves hits me, rippling up my belly like a swarm of butterflies taking flight. Clearing my throat, I say, "Um, hi. This is Stacia Kellan, I was hoping to speak with Mr. McMasters in… in regard to my father, Ken Kellan."

When nothing but silence meets my request, I add, "They've worked together for years."

"Oh, yes, of course. I'm pretty sure Mr. McMasters is with a client, but I can patch you through to his voice mail, if you'd like?"

I'd love nothing more than to scream, *no, that's not at all what I'd like, Meagan,* but that won't help. Instead, I settle with, "Yes, thank you."

"Great," she coos, and I can almost see the placating this-is-my-customer-service-smile on her face. "I'm going to connect you now."

Annoying elevator music fills the speaker for a beat before the answering machine kicks on. After the beep, I leave a quick message, asking him to return my call as soon as possible. *Fingers crossed and all that shit, right?*

Up next is my job. Maren, the owner of the studio I work at, knows what's going on, and she's been crazy understanding and supportive—even going as far as shifting my bookings around to give me the week off while still offering to pay me. She's a total goddess. "Beauty Box, how can we make you beautiful today?"

"Hey, Joy, it's Stacia. Is Maren around?"

"Yup, she just finished up a trial run on a potential

bride. Let me grab her." Joy—our lash and brow expert—places me on hold.

A few minutes later, my boss greets me. "Stacia, what's good, girl?"

I sigh. "Not much. Which is why I'm calling."

"Lord help me, you better not be quitting."

I chuckle darkly. "Uh, no. I was actually hoping to expand my hours."

"Hmm, expand them how? Your book stays stacked."

"I don't know—maybe some after-hours clients or on-site clients? Honestly, I'll take anything at this point."

"You know I've got you, girl. We will talk more when you're back next week, okay? Right now, you just worry about your dad."

A little of the weight clinging to my chest lifts. "Thanks, M, you're the best."

"Don't I know it. We'll see you Tuesday. Keep me posted."

"Will do."

Right as I hang up with her, another call comes through. "Hello?"

"Stacia? It's Dan McMasters."

Oh, sweet Jesus, maybe things are looking up! "Good morning, hi! How are you, sir?"

"Good, good. It's a real shame about your dad."

Something about his tone sets my nerves on edge. "He's innocent, sir."

McMasters mutters something that sounds a hell of a lot like *that's what they all say* before clearly adding, "That is the way the courts operate—innocent until proven guilty."

"They gave him bond, but it's cash only. Wh-what do we do?"

"Stacia, I'm going to be frank with you. While your father and I have worked together harmoniously for many years, my firm isn't the kind that represents… criminals. I'd be happy to make a few recommendations, maybe even make some calls for you, but that's *all* I can do."

My eyes fill with tears that overflow, trailing down my cheeks and rolling off my chin. "But… he's… innocent."

"Be that as it may, I'm afraid there's nothing I can do for you; our firm just isn't equipped to handle this type of scandal."

It takes my all not to tell this jackass how I really feel. After a semi-calming deep breath, I settle on, "Well, it's a shame you feel that way, Mr. McMasters. I'd also like to remind you that our *family* can't particularly handle this scandal either; especially when those meant to support us tuck tail and run. You have a nice day now," I say, my voice hitching at the end.

As I sit and stew, my quiet crying morphs into full-blown, body-wracking sobs. An indecipherable amount of time and tears later, AJ comes into the room. "Oh, babe." She drops down onto the futon next to me and draws her arms around me. "What's going on?"

Through a sniffle, I ask, "Aside from my entire world crumbling?"

She hugs me tighter, silently offering me her strength, and while it helps, it doesn't *really* help. Too bad hugs don't magically turn into oodles of money and ace legal counsel.

CHAPTER 8
WEST

As lame is it fucking sounds, the air seems less charged without Stacia's presence; while the majority of the morning has passed quickly, these last fifteen minutes seem like they were dipped in molasses. Even down in spirit, the girl's a fucking force to be reckoned with.

"What did y'all work out about her moving in?" Abby Jane asks, and I cringe.

"We're still nailing down the specifics," I say, keeping it vague.

My asshole cousin snorts out a laugh. "AKA she told you to kick rocks, and you're worried my little firecracker is gonna tear you a new one for fucking it up."

I scoff. "That's *not* what happened."

AJ raises a brow at me. "Then what happened?"

"I… she… we're working on it."

AJ flashes an icy glare my way. "See that you do. My girl, she's hardheaded and prideful, but has the biggest heart and the softest soul. She'd sooner drown than ask for help. So, I'm asking for her. Please?"

All of the breath in my lungs whooshes out of me. *The guilt, man.* "Already on it. Promise."

She and my cousin exchange a look. "Good. I'm gonna go check on her; she's been back there a while."

Brock keeps his eyes on his wife's ass as she heads down the hall. The minute she's out of sight, I mime cracking a whip. "Whip-pih-cha!"

"Shut the fuck up," he mutters, checking the time on his smartwatch. "You'll be there one day."

"Nah."

"Yeah, definitely." Brock smirks. "Who knows, maybe you'll find a baby mama with a heart of gold?"

I shoot him a scathing look. "I don't see how you don't have some archaic hoop to jump through."

Brock shrugs. "I told them to fuck right off. There's nothing they could offer me that could make me say otherwise, either. Plus, they already know I don't give a fuck; proved as much when everything went down with Abby Jane. I haven't even talked to my dad, or anyone else from that side of the family other than you, since the engagement party from hell. Swear to God, it's like our entire family is made up of psychopaths—aside from Mimi Jean, God rest her soul. But y'all were closer than she and I ever were."

"Must be nice." I roll my eyes, feeling every bit as petulant as I'm acting.

"You better believe it." He cracks his neck and shakes out his shoulders. "I gotta hit the shower—I have a client at the driving range in an hour."

"Sweet. I'll see myself out."

Brock heads back to his bedroom, and I start gathering up the mess from our breakfast. I may be a rich, entitled asshole, but no one will ever say I'm a less than stellar guest.

Once the dishes are loaded into the dishwasher and the coffeepot is rinsed, I throw on yesterday's shirt and set off down the hall to let Abby Jane and Stacia know I'm heading out. As I approach the partially opened door, the sound of soft whimpering meets my ears. *Fuck.* Female tears are basically my Achilles heel.

I knock my knuckles against the door, pushing it open. The sight that meets me hits me like a roundhouse to the throat—Stacia is bawling her eyes out as Abby Jane cradles her, stroking her hand up and down her back and whispering words of comfort.

For some reason, seeing Stacia so visibly upset has my inner-caveman firing on all cylinders. My body aches to pull her close. My heart feels as if little fissures are running through it with each sniffle. My brain is practically shouting for me to go to her. I can't explain the how or the why of it, but in this moment, she's all I can see. Her pain is so all-encompassing it is blanketing everything in the room.

Unable to help myself, I move toward the pair, lowering myself to the edge of the bed. "You okay?" I ask and instantly want to kick my own ass. Of course she's not okay—hence the motherfucking tears.

Stacia rolls her head to look at me, her gorgeous brown eyes ringed red and wet from crying. "No." That's all she says—that one single, solitary word—and my heart breaks for her. In the years I've known Stacia Kellan, not once have I ever seen her cry. She's tough, a fucking warrior princess—*she's definitely Xena-level hot.*

Taking a deep breath, I reach out and loop a strand of her vibrant red hair around my index finger, the silky strands sliding over my skin. "Move in with me?" I ask, knowing two things: one: this has the potential to blow up in my face, and two: I'm a total asshole for coming at her with this when her defenses are already down.

"West Larson!" AJ hisses, releasing her friend and sitting upright, ready to lay into me. *Can't win with her, can I?*

Stacia sits up as well, pulling her knees to her chest. "No, it's okay. Maybe… maybe I should." She wipes her tears, and as her hands fall away, her gaze hardens. "But I'm not a fucking charity case."

I hold up my hands. "Listen, I know you don't want a handout or anything. We can work out an agreement, and I'll have Colton, my lawyer, draft up a contract to make sure everything is fair and we're both protected."

The two women exchange a glance. AJ nods, and Stacia turns to me. "Yeah, okay." She exhales deeply, some of the stress leaving her body. "Let's do it."

"Well, I'll let you two work it out," Abby Jane says, a victorious smile dancing on her lips, daring to break free. "Stacia, call me later." She stands and exits the room, leaving the two of us to talk.

"You wanna come and see the house?"

"Yeah." Stacia gets to her feet, stretching her arms over her head as she goes. The motion raises the already cropped hemline of her top even higher, revealing a mouthwatering patch of smooth, ink-adorned flesh that I'd love to taste. "Let's go."

My eyes move from her bare skin to hers, only to find her smirking at me. From sad to sassy, this girl is a fucking mystery.

CHAPTER 9
STACIA

s West and I head out, I can't help but wonder if I'm making an epic mistake in moving in with him. It'll be fine—two adults who are obviously sexually attracted to one another shouldn't have any issues cohabitating, right?

A dark laugh slips out as I look back on the absurdity of the last few days.

"What's so funny?" West asks as we wait for the elevator.

"Nothing. Everything." I wrap my arms around myself. "When did life get so messy?"

A *ding* fills the empty hall; the metal doors slide open, and we file into the elevator car. West reaches out and hits the button for our floor. "Life's always been a mess, it's just we aren't as attuned to it when it isn't our mess."

I nudge my shoulder into his. "Look at you, all wise and shit."

"I'm more than good looks, you know?" He winks and I grin, feeling a little bit lighter. We step out into the lobby, heading for the doors. "You wanna ride with me or follow?"

Logically, I know it makes more sense for me to follow him, but I don't want to be alone. "I'll ride with you, if that's okay?"

West reaches out and takes my hand in his. "It is. I wouldn't have offered if it wasn't—that's not my style." He gives my fingers a little squeeze before releasing them, and while I'll never admit it out loud, it sends a little thrill through me. "C'mon, I'm just across the street."

His car, while admittedly douchey, is a hell of a thing to look at—a work of art comprised of aluminum and carbon fiber. "Can I drive?" I ask, rubbing my hands together like an evil genius who just hatched a plan.

West appraises me for a moment before laughing. "That'd be a hell no."

"Why?"

"This car's got a lot of power." He leans back against the passenger door, smirking.

"Yup, sure does."

"And you think you can handle it?"

Scoffing, I say, "I know I can." One of the many things AJ and I bonded over when we became friends was our love of cars; while she prefers old American muscle, I lust over supercars. Either way, she and I both like to go fast—*really fucking fast.* "Don't tell me you're one of those misogynistic assholes that think women can't drive?"

"Not at all. I'm just territorial about my car." A calculating glint shines in his blue eyes. "Give me one good reason I should let you behind the wheel of my baby."

"I've wanted to drive one of these ever since it

completed a lap of the Nürburgring Nordschleife track in just over seven minutes. You do realize you own the seventh fastest street legal vehicle, right?" I step into him, pressing my front to his, my hands roaming over the hard planes of his chest. "No lie, the thought of handling it gets my panties…"

I trail off, and West gulps, sliding his arms around me, tugging me impossibly closer. "Gets your panties what?" His voice is rough and gritty, rubbing over my libido the same way a stubbled jaw would my skin.

Bringing my lips to his ear, I whisper, "Wet. It gets them wet."

"Fuck," he groans, every bit of his longing plain for me to hear—and feel, judging by the bulge pressing into my belly. "She's all yours."

I step back from him, a smug, victorious smile plastered on my face. "I knew you'd come around."

I stride to the driver's side as he sinks down into the passenger seat. The buttery leather feels like heaven as I run my fingers over it in appreciation. I push the start button, and the beastly V8 biturbo engine growls in a show of pure power.

"You know how to get there?" West asks apprehensively.

"Um. No." We usually all meet up somewhere or chill at AJ and Brock's place.

He taps on the nav-screen, programming the GPS for *home*. I check my mirrors before shifting into gear and pulling out onto the street. Given that it's midmorning on a weekday, there's hardly any traffic, so I gun it, pressing the pedal to the floor, laughing as I expertly navigate the quiet streets.

I make it to West's house a full two minutes sooner

than his GPS calculated. "Well?" I ask, feeling and sounding smug as fuck.

West rubs his hand over his crotch. "Not gonna lie. You can fucking drive—and it's sexy as hell."

Now it's me who's winking. "Your house is… unexpected." And by unexpected, I mean stunning—and so *not* where I pictured him living. I always assumed he lived in one of the high-rise condos uptown or near AJ and Brock downtown, but here we are, in the suburbs, parked in front of a jaw-dropping Mediterranean contemporary.

The white brick is perfectly complemented by shades of gray, and the robin's egg-blue front door is so damn cheery and inviting I can't help but smile.

West rubs a hand over the back of his neck, his eyes dropping to the lawn—which is perfectly manicured. "Yeah, uh…"

"What? I don't mean it in a bad way. I just assumed you were more of a bachelor pad kind of guy."

Without meeting my eyes, he says, "It's near my grandmother's place, and I got it for a steal."

My tingling Spidey senses tell me there's more to the situation, but I don't push; it's obvious he doesn't want to talk about it. "Thanks for letting me drive. I… needed that."

"You can drive her anytime," he says, heading for the door.

"Really?" I ask, following behind him like an eager puppy.

He sighs. "Yeah. You know how to handle her. Now, come on, and I'll give you the grand tour."

"I love that show!" I practically shout.

He turns and stares. "What?"

"Nothing."

"You're an odd one. C'mon." West keys in the code, granting us access. "This is the living room, if you were wondering," he says, gesturing to the large, well-kept space.

The inside of West's not-so-humble abode, with its gray walls, thick white trim, and dark hardwood floors, is every bit as gorgeous as the outside. It literally looks like something fresh out of a magazine, which is kind of ridiculous for a twenty-four-year-old man.

Truly, I was prepared for beer bottles and pizza boxes, not custom-made furniture and coffee table books.

He leads me further into the house, taking me through a gleaming, well-appointed kitchen and massive dining room. He points out the laundry room and a half-bath as well, but I'm far too busy gazing at the hot tub in the backyard. Noticing where my attention is, he nudges me, a lecherous smile playing on his plump lips. "Ah, yes. Many a good night has been spent out there."

I pretend to stick my finger down my throat. "Ugh. Gag me."

"Whatever. You're just jelly it wasn't you."

I shake my head back and forth, but deep down, I think we both know I'm full of shit. "You couldn't pay me to get in that germ-infested cesspool now that I know it's your personal little fuck-tub."

West throws his head back, laughing like I've just told the best punchline to the best joke ever. "What's that shit Shakespeare said… something about a lady protesting too much?"

I punch his chest. "Ow!" I yank my hand back,

cradling my knuckles. "Are you wearing a suit of armor or something?"

"Nah, I'm just that solid." He wags his brows. "C'mon, I'll show you my room."

"Um, no. I have no desire to see your sex den."

He shoots me another self-satisfied look, like he loves the fact that I might just be jealous. *Keyword: might.* "Nooo." He tugs me forward. "My bedroom is my oasis. My escape."

I look at him in disbelief. "You've never fucked a girl in your bed?"

"Nope."

"Bull." I don't believe it. There's simply no way.

West shrugs, completely uncaring. "It's a fact. Your lack of belief doesn't negate the truth. Now, come on."

His room is on the first floor and is done up to match the rest of the house. He has a few pieces of art hung over his bed and a chair in the corner. His massive king-sized bed is adorned with a fluffy comforter that looks comfortable enough that Sleeping Beauty would've begged for five more minutes of shut eye. "My bathroom is en suite, and all of the upstairs rooms have their own as well."

We breeze past his office and the first guest room until we reach the door at the end of the hall. "This is where you'll be."

I open the door and venture into my new room. It's bright and airy with light walls and big picture windows. There's a full-sized bed centered on the far wall with a handmade quilt covering it. The closet is plenty big and the bathroom even has a tub. All in all, it's my own little slice of heaven.

Whirling around, I surprise both of us by throwing

my arms around his middle, hugging him. "Thank you. Truly, thank you."

He shrugs off my gratitude. "Not a problem. Mi casa es su casa—literally, after Colton draws up the paperwork. Why don't I let you rest for a minute while I call him?"

Smiling like a fool, I nod. "That sounds good."

He turns and exits the room, leaving me alone. Not wanting to waste a single second, I shimmy out of my sweats and dive under the thick quilt, sleep claiming me the second my head hits the pillow.

CHAPTER 10
WEST

Back downstairs, I dial Colton; he answers on the first ring. "Hey."

"So," I hedge. "I did a thing."

He sighs heavily. "What kind of thing? An I-knocked-someone-up kind of thing?"

I stifle a laugh—barely. "I'm good, but I'm not that good. No."

"Thank God, because that's something we will need to discuss further."

Even though he can't see my eyes, I bat my lashes. "Aw, Colt, I had no idea you were so interested in my sex life."

"Shut the fuck up and tell me what you did."

I grab a bottle of water from the fridge, crack the top, and take a long pull. "Ooh, all business, then? Okay. I asked Stacia Kellan to move in with me." My declaration is met with nothing but stone-cold silence. A silence so prolonged that I shift uncomfortably on my feet, placing my bottle down onto the island. "Well?"

"Sorry, I'm just...flabbergasted. You do realize that—

if all goes according to plan—you'll be a father in a year?"

"I do."

Colton heaves out a sigh, as if I'm being intentionally frustrating. "Okay. And you also realize said child will need a bedroom within your home?"

"Yeah, I'm still not seeing the issue. There's a whole 'nother guest room." I drain the last of my water and toss the bottle into my recycling bin.

"And you think whoever you... procreate with... will be okay with some strange woman sharing a space with their child?"

I huff in annoyance. "Kid'll be half mine."

"West!" Colton snaps, letting me know he's not playing.

"Whatever. Add it to the list of shit we need to talk about. I need you to come by and draft up a rental agreement for Stacia."

"I swear to God, I'm going to be gray before thirty and every single strand will be because of you."

"Damn straight," I say proudly, ending the call.

Twenty minutes later, Colton lets himself into my house. "West!" he calls out from the entry.

"Kitchen!" I holler back, grabbing two bottles of water.

He looks around the kitchen as if he's expecting someone to jump out at him at any moment. "Where is she?"

"Her room." My voice is flat.

"Right. Because... okay. Let's talk." He swings his

satchel up onto the island, retrieving a notebook and fountain pen from inside it. "We need to lay out her monthly rent cost, what bills she will help with, a rental term, as well as a list of ground rules."

"You really think we need all of that?"

He looks at me like I'm an idiot. "You and your own cousin had all of that. Why on earth would you not need it with some random woman?"

I balk. "She's not random. I've known Stacia every bit as long as I've known AJ."

Colton hisses out a sigh, rubbing his temples. "Anyway. Rent—how much? Half?"

Knowing there's no way in hell she could front half of the monthly mortgage, I hesitate. I'm walking a fine line between helping her and pissing off Colton. "Actually... I was thinking maybe no rent, and she can just help out with the bills and groceries?"

"What?" Colton tosses his pen down, his frustration with me and this predicament clearly evident in the thin line of his lips and the hard glare he's aiming my way. "Why on earth would you do that?"

"Dude." I lean forward onto the island, propping both of my elbows on the cold slab of quartz. "Did you not hear me say Stacia *Kellan* when we spoke earlier?" I stress her last name.

"I don't care if she's a goddamn Kennedy—"

I cut him off. "Her dad's in jail; their assets are frozen. She needs the help; I'm offering it, end of discussion."

Colton picks up his pen, poising the tip over his notebook. "Fine," he grits out, "have it your way. Which bills would you like to split with her?"

I do a quick catalog of my monthlies. "Let's do the internet, utilities, and groceries."

"Great," Colton mutters, his tone clearly implying just how *not* great he's finding this. "How long will she be staying here?"

"I can't really answer that. I'll let you ask her."

"Wonderful. Ground rules?"

"No parties without prior consent. No smoking. No pets. No…hmm. What else? Oh! No hookups!" A satisfied grin pulls at my lips as I pick at the label on my water bottle.

"You realize you'll need to abide by these as well?"

I hold my arms out wide. "So?"

"So, no hookups for you either. Might be tough since you're trying to have a baby."

I dismiss him with a brush of my hand. "Nah. That still leaves my car, her car, her place, hotel rooms. The possibilities are endless."

Colton stares at me. I'm pretty sure he's about ready to deck me between the eyes and walk away. Luckily, he's been my friend longer than he's been my lawyer. Still, I can't help but to goad him.

"Your sex life must be hella boring if you only lay it down in bed, man."

His fingers clench his pen so tightly his grip is white-knuckle. "Not even going there, West."

"Listen, it's okay to be vanilla. No judging. I'm sure there's a sweet, equally vanilla lady out there somewhere just waiting for you to wow her with your missionary, lights-off prowess."

He drops the pen again, clenching both fists at his sides. "Why? Why are we friends?"

"Because I'm fucking awesome," I tout and just like that the tension melts.

"Keep telling yourself that."

"Every morning in the mirror." I take a gulp of my water. "Ready to meet her?"

"As ready as I'm gonna be." He stands. "Please Lord, don't let this blow up in our faces," he mutters, making the motion of a cross in front of his chest before following me up the stairs.

I knock on her door lightly, but she doesn't reply. "Stacia?" I call her name, knocking again.

"Hmm?" she calls back, and I take it as my cue to enter.

I stop dead in my tracks when I see her on the bed, tangled up in my Mimi Jean's quilt. Her pants are nowhere to be seen and her shirt has scrunched up beneath her bust. She's showing off more skin than she's covering. My mouth feels like it's been stuffed with cotton balls as I take her in—she looks like a fucking goddess, laid out on display. My hands ache to touch her, but I don't, because that'd be pervy as hell. Everyone knows consent is sexy.

Colton clears his throat, simultaneously breaking my trance and waking her. Stacia's eyes fly open. "Oh my God!" she shrieks, covering herself as quickly as possible. "What in the hell?"

"Shit!" Colton covers his eyes. "Sorry!"

I, however, am not such a gentleman and keep my blues locked firmly on her, my brow lifted in challenge. "I asked Colton over to draft up a rental agreement. So, throw some pants on—or don't—and let's get to it."

Stacia huffs. "Aren't you gonna give me some privacy?"

I widen my stance and cross my arms over my chest. "Didn't plan on it. I walk around in my boxers all the time; I don't plan on changing that just because you're living here. I'm not doing the whole eggshells thing. Take me as I am."

She stares at me for a beat before laughing. "Sure, okay." She pushes the quilt all the way off and stands, her long, lean legs on full display. "Let me just get dressed." She turns her back to me, and my eyes instantly fall to her ass—her very bare, smooth, bounce a quarter off of it, tight ass. I bow my head in thanks to the G-string gods above.

I groan audibly when she bends to step into her sweats. There's nothing but thin silk covering the promised land between her thighs. "Fuck."

"This is cool, right?" the she-devil murmurs as she stands and shimmies her pants up. "No eggshells, right?"

I gulp. "Riiiight."

Stacia grins and winks. "Great. Let's go talk." She sashays right past both me and Colton, out the door. "C'mon, boys."

The three of us set off down the stairs back toward the kitchen; Colton shoots me incredulous looks and glares every step of the way.

In the kitchen, Stacia hops up onto the island, and I can't help but notice it leaves her at the perfect height for someone—me—to step between her legs and show her a good time. "You got any coffee?" she asks, swinging her feet.

"Um, yeah." I nod my head toward my Nespresso machine.

"Sweet!" She hops down and struts over, making

herself right at home as she fills the water reservoir and browses my different capsule options. I keep a keen eye on her, fascinated with how easily she moves about my kitchen—like she belongs here. And don't even get me started on the deep satisfaction that strums through my chest when she selects my favorite—Arpeggio. "Y'all want any?" she asks, pressing the brew button.

Colton and I both say yes, and without batting a lash, she whips up two more. "Y'all want cream or sugar? Not that I know where you keep anything."

I grab the creamer from the fridge and the sugar bowl from its place on the counter. "Here ya go." The three of us doctor our coffees to taste before gathering around the island.

"So, what's the deal?" she asks.

Colton appraises her with a cold stare. "The deal is, West has asked that in lieu of you paying rent, for you to cover the internet bill, a portion of the utilities, and half of the groceries."

I can see it, so clearly, her desire to argue. Her pride is begging her to reject my offer, but luckily, her sensibility wins out. "Great," she bites out.

"There are some rules," Colton adds, before relaying them all to her. "Are these terms acceptable?"

Stacia hesitates, only for a second, though. "They're perfect."

"That just leaves one last thing. How long will you be staying?"

Stacia rears back, and I kind of want to smack him. "I, um. Well." Her eyes glisten, and my gut churns. "Just um—three months should be enough time to be able to afford somewhere on my own. Is that okay?"

I fucking hate the vulnerability in her voice. This

woman is a fucking queen and should bow to no one, and I kind of hate my best friend for knocking her crown askew. "You stay as long as you need," I tell her firmly, not caring one bit that I'll soon be facing Colton's ire.

"West—" he starts, but Stacia cuts him off.

"Three months. Put it in writing. I'd hate to overstay my welcome." She polishes off her espresso before carting her mug to the sink to rinse it out. "Just let me know when the contract is ready, and I'll sign it. Until then, I'll be in my room." She turns and flees before either of us can respond.

CHAPTER 11
STACIA

pause halfway up the stairs, my chest heaving. I knew this was a bad idea. But desperation is the mother of all bad ideas, and as much as I hate to admit it, I'm a little desperate.

As I try and catch my breath, the sound of their masculine voices reaches me. "Way to be a fucking asshole."

"My job isn't to be nice; it's to watch out for your best interests."

"Maybe sometimes my best interests aren't the most important thing."

Colton's resounding sigh reverberates through my body, causing a painful ache in my heart. "Far be it from me to try to stop your death on your cross."

I know I should retreat the rest of the way to my room, but I'm rooted to the spot, eavesdropping on a conversation fully not meant for my ears.

"Be a little more dramatic, Colt." The clanking of dishes being thrown into the sink punctuates his words. "I'm not being a martyr; I'm not dying on a cross or falling on a sword. I just… want to help out a friend. I know I'd want someone to be there for me if I was in her shoes. Right now, I need you to be my friend and not my lawyer. Think you can handle that?"

West's decree is met with a silence that is so prolonged, I consider slinking the rest of the way up the steps. That is, until Colton says, "Yeah, man. I've got your back."

Their footsteps sound, alerting me to the fact that they're heading my way. I scamper up the remaining steps as quickly and quietly as possible, all but dive bombing into my room.

I throw myself down onto the bed and take a few deep breaths, trying to calm my racing heart.

Their footsteps sound in the hall, and for a second I worry they know I was listening. I grab my phone, trying to act nonchalant in case they bust up in my room like before, but a door opens and shuts down the hall. *Thank God.*

My relief at not being caught listening in is a palpable thing, and with my heart no longer in my throat, I dial up my mom. She doesn't answer, so I try my grandmother instead.

"Stacia, dear, did you speak to the lawyer?"

I hate knowing I'm about to let my grandma down, but I'm not going to lie to her either. "It's not good. The short of it is, they're not willing to risk scandal to represent him."

"Well, shit," Gramma curses, sounding as disgusted as I feel.

"It's gonna be okay. I talked to my boss, she is gonna give me extra hours, and I found somewhere to stay so y'all won't be crowded. I'm gonna figure this out—I'm going to make sure Dad comes home."

She sniffles. "This shouldn't be your weight to bear."

"Regardless, it is. I know my dad; I know his heart. He's innocent, and the thought of him rotting away in a cell makes me sick."

"You're a strong young woman. I'll keep working on your mom, and if we hear from Ken, I'll let you know—same for you."

"Yes, ma'am. I love you." She echoes back the sentiment, and I end the call.

It's only then that I realize I'm trapped here. Trapped with literally none of my stuff. As fun as driving West's Mercedes was, I'm having serious regrets. And seeing as he's locked away with Colton the asshole, I'm truly stuck here.

Shit.

Maybe AJ will come and get me? My fingers fly across my screen as I send her a text.

Me: 911.

AJ: What's up?

Me: Can you come get me?

AJ: Um yes. Where are you?

Me: …West's.

AJ: !!! I'm on my way, but be prepared to answer questions.

Me: Yeah, sure. Just let me know when you're here.

The next five minutes feel like the longest of my life, but finally her text comes through telling me she's idling at the curb. I slide my feet into my shoes and creep quietly down the stairs and out the front door, not wanting to deal with either of the overbearing alpha men in the house.

I slide into the passenger seat of her badass matte black '69 Chevelle. The thing is a fucking beast, and for a split second, I worry West will recognize it. But I cast my misplaced worry aside—who cares if he knows I left? I live there now, and I'm free to come and go as I please.

"So?" AJ asks once we reach the cross street.

"Ugh. It's nothing, really. I rode over here with West, and he's currently busy with his guard dog of a lawyer. I need to pack some things and didn't want to bother them. Simple as that."

She cuts her eyes toward me. "Simple as that, you say?"

"Yup." I refuse to give an inch, because that would mean examining the feelings slithering through my system far too closely for my own liking.

"Hmm." She taps her nails on the wheel. "If you say so. Why don't we grab lunch before heading back to mine?"

"Only if we can get something greasy and incredibly bad for us."

AJ beams. "Mickey D's, here we come."

I throw my head back, running my fingers through my red locks. "Ugh, yes. I would bathe in their sweet 'n sour if I could."

"Yes, girl, yes." Her stomach grumbles, almost as if on cue, and the two of us dissolve into a fit of giggles.

Ten Chicken McNuggets, a medium fry, and two tubs of sweet-n-sour sauce later, AJ and I are back at her place sorting through the assortment of items I'd left in her guest room over the years.

It used to be a running joke between the two of us that I'd grab my shit to take home next time, but now, I'm so grateful that next time never came, because I'd literally have nothing save for the clothes on my back.

But in the sanctuary of AJ and Brock's spare bedroom, I have a closetful of clothes, spare makeup and brushes, panties and a bra or two, and at least four pairs of shoes. I even found a little muslin sack filled with a few pairs of earrings and a necklace. *Hell. Yes.*

AJ pulls up some music on her phone, blasting some old school Blink-182 while she sends out emails for the nonprofit she works for and I pack my stuff into a duffle bag. Mark Hoppus is crooning about Friday nights and cologne when my phone starts buzzing on the floor next to me.

Glancing down, I see West's name and number flashing across the screen. "Hello," I say, keeping my voice even.

"Where are you?" he asks, sounding mildly panicked. "Are you okay?"

"I'm fine, West."

"Where are you?" he asks again.

"I'm back at AJ's."

"Why? Are you staying with her now? Shit. This is all Colton's fault." He starts muttering under his breath, and I can't help the little zip of happiness that moves through me at his concern.

"Chill. I just came to get my stuff."

"But how'd you get there? You… you didn't walk, did you?"

"Dude. AJ came and picked me up. I'm fine. I'll be back in a little bit."

A breath whooshes out of him. "And you're not mad?"

"At you? Nope. I think your friend's a grade-A jerk, though."

"Yeah, he, uh… he can be. But once you get to know him, he's a really good guy."

I snort. Good looking? Sure. Even I can admit that his lean, muscled physique, dirty blond hair, chiseled jaw, and piercing eyes are an appealing combination. Too bad his personality takes him down from a ten to a two. But… whatevs. "I'll take your word for it."

"Okay. You'll be home for dinner?" he asks, his voice tinged with something that sounds a lot like hopefulness.

So, naturally, I have to mess with him. "Depends. Whatcha making? Fair warning, I can't cook."

"Eh, it's not my strong suit either, but I make a mean grilled cheese. I'll even throw a can of tomato soup on the stove."

"Campbell's?"

"As if I'd get any other."

"Deal. See you soon." I end the call with a huge, cheek-splitting, cheesy grin.

AJ wastes no time, pouncing like a lioness. "Don't you look happy?" she sings.

Not willing to give an inch, I reply, "Well, all things considered, I'm not unhappy."

"Ugh!" She throws a sweater at me, and I snatch it out of the air, fold it, and place it into my bag. "I hate you sometimes."

"No, you don't. You love me. You couldn't live without me. I am the fucking Gina to your Spencer," I say, referencing two of our favorite book characters.

"True, true. But I swear to you now, if my future children ever ask me about truffle butter, I will die. D–I–E, die."

We both crack up, laughing nearly as hard as we did when we read it the first time. God, I love our little two-gal book club.

Once all of my stuff is packed up, we stand and survey the room. "Gah! It looks so… empty," AJ declares.

"Right? Maybe y'all should have a baby!" I say, only half joking.

AJ rears back. "Whoa, hey—no." She shakes her head vehemently. "I mean, one day, but not yet. We've only been married a year, and I think we wanna enjoy each other a little more."

I check her hip with mine. "Putting in those practice hours, huh?"

Her cheeks pinken. "Yeah, that."

"No shame in your game, girl. No need to act coy—I know you. You liked fucking before Brock, and you absolutely love it with him. Need I remind you of the tubing trip? Y'all were so busy getting it on you almost missed the trolley back!"

"You're one to talk!" AJ hoots. "Because I'm pretty sure I vividly recall stumbling upon you grinding all over West's lap in the back seat of Brock's truck, titties out and all, while y'all waited on us!"

Judging by the warmth engulfing my face, my cheeks have to be as red as my hair. "Yeah, well, shut up."

"For real, though, are you gonna be okay with him sleeping right down the hall?"

"He's downstairs," I counter lamely. AJ tilts her head,

studying me. "You know how I feel about stairs; dude might as well be at the base of Everest."

"You're insane."

"Insanely awesome." I heft my bag up onto my shoulder. "I'll call you tomorrow."

"I know you will. And this weekend, let's brunch."

"Mmm. I could def go for some Benny's."

My bestie laughs and draws me into an awkward side hug, thanks to my duffle. "It's a date."

CHAPTER 12
WEST

Ever since Colton left and I realized Stacia wasn't here, I've been on pins and needles. Honestly, I don't even know why, but the thought of her suddenly not living here made me feel ten shades of crazy. Which *is* crazy, since she hasn't even moved in yet.

"Jesus." I check the clock for what feels like the fifty-billionth time. Maybe it's time for something stronger than water. I help myself to a beer from my fridge, something local, brewed in small batches. I twist off the cap and take a long pull, sighing as the hoppy brew slides down my throat.

When the clock strikes four-thirty, I go ahead and start buttering slices of bread for our grilled cheese. Once I have eight slices prepped and ready to go, I heat my pan and get to cooking.

Stacia walks in just as I go to flip the third sandwich. "Honey, I'm home," she calls out, and for reasons I'm not willing to examine in depth—or at all—it sends a little pulse of happiness straight to my heart.

"Wanna grab me a soup can from the pantry?"

She walks into the kitchen and plops her bag onto the floor. "Sure. But… where's the pantry?"

"Guess my tour was lacking, huh?" I nod my head to the left. "It's the door on the left before the laundry room."

"You pointed out all of the important things."

I warm the soup on the stove, adding milk instead of water, which blows Stacia's mind. Once everything is ready, I plate it up and grab myself a new beer. "You want one?" I ask, and Stacia eagerly accepts.

"So, you really can't cook anything other than grilled cheese?"

"I am also a scrambled egg master. Hmm, what else… I can make ramen noodles that are out of this world, and what might be the best PB-and-J in the entire state."

Stacia laughs, just like I wanted her to, and the sound soothes some wayward part of my soul that only seems to exist in her presence. "It seems like such a shame for this pretty kitchen to go to waste."

I glance around, taking in the space through her eyes. From my custom cabinets to the Sub-Zero appliances, this kitchen is any chef's wet dream. "It came with the house," I say, and she laughs again. "Plus, that big-ass fridge holds a shit-ton of drinks and takeout. Did I mention I'm fucking great at ordering takeout?"

The gorgeous redhead lifts her bottle in a toast to mine. "Now, that's something we have in common!"

"I'm sure you're tired of talking about this, but how is everything going?"

And just like that, Stacia deflates. "It's… really rough. I know this sounds incredibly first world, but it's like my entire life was ripped away in the blink of an eye, and processing it has been really hard. Add in this bullshit with Dad's lawyer, and I just… feel kind of hopeless."

"What's going on with his lawyer?"

She turns to me with fire blazing in her eyes. "The pompous jackass said he couldn't risk the scandal of representing him. Never mind the fact that Dad has been his loyal client for as long as I can remember."

"Shit, Stacia. That blows."

"Tell me about it," she laments, burying her face in her hands. "Feels like we're being fucked by the long dick of the law."

An idea dances on the periphery of my mind—*maybe I could ask Colton to help her out.* But just as quickly as it appeared, it vanishes. I mean, even if I could get—coerce—him to agree to it, she would never accept his help. Those two are straight-up oil and water; I don't think I've ever seen two people clash right off the bat like the two of them did.

"You know what you need?"

"What?"

"A distraction. Let's watch a movie."

Stacia licks her lips. "I did notice some popcorn in your pantry."

"Why don't you pop it, and I'll pick out something to watch?"

"Ooh, you're asking me to place a lot of trust in you, Mr. Larson."

I blanch. "That's my dad, and he's a jackass. But, we're roomies now… so, c'mon, let me pick."

"Fine! But you better not mess this up. I would hate for our first movie night to be our last."

Not wasting a second, I sprint to the living room.

Television on, and Prime opened, I wrack my brain for the perfect movie. Finally, as the microwave dings, the perfect movie pops into my head.

Stacia enters the room right as the first notes of *Too Hot to Stop* by the Bay-Kays starts playing. "Oh my God! *Superbad!* I love this movie."

I grin. "I figured as much."

"How?" she demands, tossing a handful of buttery popped kernels into her mouth.

"You almost verbatim quoted it a minute ago. *The long dick of the law...* sound familiar?"

She smacks her palm into her forehead. "Good ear. Now, pipe down."

We both fall quiet as Jonah Hill's character calls Michael Cera's to discuss the Vag-tastic Voyage. We've just reached the part where a drunk Seth passes out and accidentally headbutts Jules.

"Did you know they say fuck one hundred and eighty-six times in this movie?" Stacia blurts out randomly. "Which is insane, because it's only one hundred and thirteen minutes long; that's literally more than one F-bomb a minute!"

I stare at her for a second like she's an alien. And hell, maybe she is; what other woman loves and knows fast cars, drinks beer, openly admits to not being able to cook, and can quote movies like a boss, all while looking fine as fuck? I know I can only think of one.

Sputtering, I ask, "How do you know this shit?"

Stacia shrugs and draws her feet up under her, the motion moving her a little closer to me. "I don't know. My brain is a whole cache of semi-useless information. But I kick ass at trivia!"

"We'll have to go out and play sometime."

"Sounds goo—" A yawn cuts her off, and we both fall back into an easy quiet as the movie plays on.

Toward the end of the movie, Stacia nods off and her head tips onto my shoulder. It pains me to move her, but I know sleeping sitting up is not an option—not if I don't want to be in a world of pain tomorrow.

Carefully, I ease out from beneath her and cradle her sleeping form in my arms. The trip up the steps is a little more daunting, but I manage to make it to her room, where I deposit her into her bed. With the quilt tucked around her as she sleeps peacefully, I'm struck by how fucking gorgeous she is in this moment—makeup free, dolled down, totally natural. Her red hair fans around her like a fiery halo, and though it's not the first time I've thought it, I can't help but wonder what it'd feel like if she was mine.

And I don't mean for a night, but for long-term—months, years, forever. While I've always said I'd never settle down, if I ever did, Stacia's the exact kind of girl I'd want to do it with.

Maybe it's the whole opposites attract thing, with her bright hair, inked skin, and piercings and me being a clean cut, everyday kind of guy. Or maybe it's just that she's a fucking good person, with insides every bit as stunning as her outer shell. Fuck if I know—other than the fact that the girl's been under my skin ever since I laid eyes on her that night at Quixote's.

It's probably pretty pathetic that I still even think about that night. It was well over a year ago, and we didn't even speak. While my cousin was hyper-fixated on Abby Jane and their weird little love-disguised-as-hate thing, all I saw was her.

She was so damn alluring—different than any other

woman I'd ever been with. She was wearing blue lipstick, for Christ's sake. And even though she wasn't the woman I took home with me that night, she's definitely the one I thought about as I came.

Finally, I lean down and feather a kiss across her forehead before retreating downstairs to my bed. The urge to rub one out to memories of the way she danced that night in her black leather miniskirt tempts me. Add in the details of our hot and heavy make-out session that happened a few weeks later, and I'm harder than I've ever been. But I refuse to beat my dick to thoughts of her while she sleeps under my roof—at least on her first night here.

CHAPTER 13
STACIA

've settled into living with West far easier than I thought I would have. He and I... we just gel, like we've been living together for years and years instead of a week.

Unfortunately, my successful cohabitation is pretty much the only good thing in my life right about now.

My dad is still in jail—and judging from his down-trodden tone, Ken Kellan is not suited for life on the inside. And don't even get me started on Mom. She pretty much never leaves the couch in the rental cottage, and I'm pretty sure my grandparents are at their wit's end with her.

The pressure to bring Dad home is weighing on me heavier and heavier every passing day, but I'm stuck. *So fucking stuck.* I've even started searching for a second job, and while a few listings look semi-promising, none of them are going to bring in enough extra money for me to pay a retainer to a lawyer—much less to post Dad's bond.

Not to mention, today's the day I have to let Maren

know I've been looking for other jobs. She has a firm non-compete in place, but I should be okay, seeing as I'm looking at desk jobs and retail. Hopefully she gets it and isn't upset. *Fingers crossed.*

Tired of my downtrodden and mopey thoughts, I crank the music in my car, drowning my anger and hopelessness in some Brand New. By the time I make it to work, I've played half of the album; I don't feel any better, though. I drain the last dregs of my coffee—*here's to fake smiles and hoping making people pretty does the trick.*

"Hey, girl, hey!" Joy greets as I enter the studio. Her infectious smile lifts my spirits a little. "Maren added a bride to your book after lunch—she's having her bridals done, and her original girl came down with the flu."

"Yes!" I do a little happy dance. "Not that I'm celebrating someone being sick, but more money is always a good thing."

"Yeah, girl. Plus, if you end up wowing her, and she books her actual wedding with you, I think she said she has like eight girls in her party that will all need their makeup done as well."

"She'll book." I sound cocky, but it's called confidence when you have the skills to back it up, right?

Joy updates me on the rest of my day—two expectant mothers, a woman who is announcing her retirement, and a handful of date night-ers. Oh, and my bride.

I head back to my station and start prepping my supplies. Even though we don't technically open for another twenty minutes, there's a sort of energy flowing through the space, the kind that amps you up and renews your kickass attitude. Or maybe that's just the Billie Eilish Maren has pumping through the speakers. Either way, I'm ready.

Six hours later, I'm dead on my feet, but… the bride booked me not only for her wedding but for her engagement pictures, shower, and rehearsal dinner, as well. *Cha-ching.*

"Maren," I say as I pass her to finish cleaning my brushes. "Can we talk really quick?"

"Sure." She pops a bubble with the gum she's always chewing. "Come find me in the back when you're done."

After stowing away my brushes, wiping down my station, and cleaning my mirror, I head off in search of Maren. "Hey," I say, as I walk into the breakroom where she's playing on her phone.

She places it on the table, screen down. "What's up?"

I suck in a deep breath and bite the bullet. "First, I wanna thank you for the extra appointments."

She arches a perfectly sculpted brow at me. "Uh-huh. You're welcome."

"But I still need to make more money, so I'm looking for a second job. I wanted to be totally transparent with you, and I promise it won't interfere with my time here or breach my non-compete."

"Did you think I was gonna be mad?" Maren asks, sounding almost a little hurt.

"No. Yes. Maybe. Everything feels so topsy-turvy right now for me that I don't know up from down."

"I hate this for you."

I shrug. "Maybe I'll land a part-time job that pays crazy good?" She casts a dubious look my way. "Hey, a girl can hope."

"You know," she says, pausing dramatically. "If you really need funds, I might know of something."

Eagerly, I pull the free chair closer to her before plopping down into it. "Tell me more—everything. Tell me everything."

She clasps my hands in hers. "You'll have to keep an open mind."

"As long as you're not suggesting prostitution or stripping."

Maren rolls her neck. "Not exactly." I start to protest, but she stops me. "Hear me out! There's this app called Virtual Kitty. It's like… I can't really explain it."

"Try," I deadpan, just desperate enough to stick around for what she has to say.

"So, it's like a porn app. But like… gah! Okay, let me just show it to you." Maren grabs her phone, unlocks it, and passes it to me. "Click here."

I tap the icon, and the entire screen goes black before a little animated cat pops up, followed by the words *'pick your kitty, watch her purr.'*

Mildly intrigued, I tap the *enter* button. The screen immediately fills with what looks like a grid of social media-ish profiles—all women. Tatted up, pierced, stunning women. Beneath each picture is a username, along with a series of symbols and abbreviations. I notice some women have a camera, while others have a video camera or a microphone, followed by things like DP, BBC, BBW, CFNM. Literally, the only thing there that makes sense to me is SOLO; the rest is gibberish.

"What in the hell does all of this mean?" I ask, a little overwhelmed.

Maren peeks over at the screen. "Oh! Those are the types of videos they do. DP is double penetration; BBC is big black—"

"Got it!" I shout, feeling like a freaking prude, which I'm certainly not. I watch as much porn as any other twenty-something-year-old woman with a healthy sexual appetite, but I've never paid attention to stuff like that. I just click what looks good and suits my mood, get off, and get out.

However, my brain keeps going back to solo. "And solo is…"

Grinning, Maren explains, "It's exactly what it sounds like. The woman all by herself. Masturbation, strip teases, showers, that kind of stuff."

"And there's no guy or sex or anything?"

"Nope, not with solo. Some girls even just do dirty pictures."

"Huh." My mind is reeling, and as much as I hate to admit it, thoughts are wheeling around and around in my brain. Things like how much do these women make —how much is enough for me to…

"Well, I've got a hot date tonight." Maren pops up from the table, derailing my runaway train of thought. "Wanna do my makeup before you go?"

"Um, yes!" I say, freshly cleaned brushes be damned, because Maren hardly lets anyone make her up. As cheesy as it sounds, it's an honor that she asked me.

***

The following morning, I wake to a text from AJ, asking if I'm down for a mani-pedi after we hit up Benny's. My natural inclination is to say *hell yeah, girl, and let's hit the mall* but that was *before*. Now, instead of feeling excited, a lead weight sits in my gut.

With trembling fingers, I log into my bank account app and check my balance. While it's not necessarily a number to frown at, I know it won't get me far now that

I'm not living under my parents' roof—not that they can call it theirs anymore.

As spoiled as it makes me sound, I need to learn to budget and fast.

As I head downstairs and make some coffee, I do a quick tally, estimating what I'll owe West for this month as well as the next. Add in gas, my cell phone, and car insurance, and yeah, things are tight.

ME

I think I can only swing brunch today if that's cool.

AJ

Why don't we just do each other's nails?

"What's got you smiling?" West questions, joining me at the island in nothing more than a pair of low-slung sweats.

I turn my dopey grin his way and gasp. Holy-dick-print, Batman.

He chuckles and palms his morning wood. "I'd apologize, but it's a natural reaction."

Finding my voice, I say, "Noooo. No need to apologize. Everything is great. Fine. Perfect."

West chuckles and flexes his hips so that his sizable erection virtually leers at me. "You keep staring at him, and he's gonna think you want sausage for breakfast."

I tear my eyes away from his groin as we both guffaw at the utter absurdity of what he just said. "Damn, dude. You spit game like that, it's a wonder women aren't beating down your front door!"

A scoff passes his highly kissable lips. "Please. You

know firsthand exactly how much game I have. As I recall, it landed you in my lap in Brock's back seat."

I roll my eyes even as I feel my cheeks heat. "Once, and you didn't even get to seal the deal."

He steps closer to me. "Only because Brock and Abby Jane came back. If they'd have been thirty—hell, *ten* minutes later, I guarantee, I'd have had you writhing in pleasure and chanting my name like a sacred prayer."

I laugh him off, unwilling to admit that my panties pretty much just burst into flames.

He moves away, and while I feel like I can breathe again, my body misses his closeness. "For real though, what's got you smiling so early?"

"Uh, it's after nine. But, I have plans with AJ today. Is it cool for her to come over later?"

West eyes me oddly. "You live here. You don't have to ask permission for your best friend to visit."

"Right. Yeah. Sorry."

He presses the brew button and tosses a wink my way. "No problem. Oh, before I forget, Colton is supposed to bring the contract by for you to sign. I know we should have done it last week, but he's been working on some big case and we fell to the wayside."

I scrunch my nose. "I'm shocked. I figured protecting little, old, helpless you from big, bad me would be his first priority."

West drains his espresso in one gulp. "As luck would have it, I managed to convince him you weren't an evil shrew."

I do my best witchy cackle, which admittedly is lacking. "That's good. Is he always so…"

"Anal?" West supplies.

"I was gonna say uptight, but sure, let's go with anal."

"It's almost like there's two Coltons—lawyer Colton and normal Colton. When he's in lawyer mode, he can be damn near unbearable, but the fucker is good at what he does. Like, insanely so."

"What kind of—" The sound of my phone ringing cuts me off. "It's AJ. I've gotta get ready. See you later!" I dash up the stairs as I answer her call. "'Sup, bitch?"

"Want me to pick you up?"

My brows tug low at her question. Picking me up is totally out of her way. "Why?"

"Well, Brock is doing lessons at the country club, and I figured I'd surprise him after, so I'll be out your way no matter what."

As much as this feels like a handout, I accept. "Yeah, okay, if you're sure."

"I am. I'm heading that way now."

I check out my reflection in the full-length mirror hanging opposite my bed. From my gnarly bun to my sleep shorts, I'm a full-blown hot mess, completely unfit for venturing out of the house. "Shit, okay. Let me get ready!"

I hang up without giving her the chance to reply and fly through getting ready. Dry shampoo, a braid, brows, a dab of concealer, and a fresh outfit later, and I'm ready to go. Too bad AJ honked to let me know she was here ten minutes ago.

CHAPTER 14
STACIA

"Fuuuuuck, this is so good," I moan as I devour the last of my French toast.

"I know, right?" AJ agrees as she drags her last strip of bacon through the river of syrup on her plate.

While brunch today may be a poor financial decision, it is exactly what my soul needed. Some time to feel normal—like things are the way they've always been—has me feeling almost like my usual self.

"So, what's going on with… everything?" AJ asks, waving her hand in a vague gesture.

Oh, hello reality, how nice of you to crash my brunch. "Things are really… rough."

My best friend frowns. "You know, I could—"

"No." I stop her cold. "Just no."

AJ looks offended by my refusal. "Why?"

"A million reasons."

She crosses her arms over her chest. "Give me one."

I lean in and whisper the amount of Dad's bond. "How's that for starters? And, it's cash only."

"Whoa." She lets out a low whistle. "Well, even still—"

"That's not counting the cost of legal representation. And, not to mention, I don't know how long my grandparents can swing the cost of the Airbnb they're renting. My job literally covers the bare necessities." I laugh bitterly. "There's a limit on what you can legally gift someone, monetarily. It's just too much."

Still unwilling to accept defeat, AJ pushes, "Well, what if Brock and I both—"

I feel bad to keep cutting her off, but it's just not going to happen. "I love you, babe. But, I just can't. The thought of borrowing that kind of money from anyone makes me ill. And who knows if I'll ever be able to pay you back. I can't have that hanging over our friendship. I appreciate you more than you will ever know, and the fact that you're willing to help speaks volumes. No matter which way we spin it, it's too much."

AJ's brow furrows as a dejected sigh escapes her. "Yeah, I guess you're right."

I feel bad for practically pissing all over her effort to help me, but really, it's the only way. "I've been looking for a second job; you'll never guess what Maren suggested."

Baited, she leans in and asks, "What?"

I proceed to tell her about Virtual Kitty, even going as far as showing her the app.

"Are you actually considering this?"

I shrug. In all honesty, I'm torn. I've been obsessively researching the app since last night, and from what I've learned, the *kitties* can make a pretty penny. Even the solo ones. "I...I don't know. From what I've read, the company pays really well. Better even than Pornwheel."

"Oh, wow. PW is legit."

I nod. "So is Virtual Kitty. Except it's an app and not a website. It's almost like... Suicide Babes, Pornwheel, social media, and online dating came together and made a baby. The user gets to pick his kitty based on their personal preferences. Some women only do solo stuff—twerk videos, pole dancing, strip shows, masturbation. Some girls even just dirty talk, sext via the messenger, or post pics."

AJ smirks. "Well, sounds like you've done a lot of research since... last freaking night!"

I shrug, shooting for carefree and breezy, but I'm ninety percent positive I missed my mark. Because really, who takes becoming a porn star—so to speak—lightly? "I figure I need to weigh out all of my options."

"Sounds to me like your mind's already made up."

The bell over the door chimes, saving me from saying anymore. "Sounds to me like we need to settle our bill and skedaddle."

AJ laughs loudly. "Only if you promise to never say skedaddle ever again."

Back at the house—because I've finally started thinking of it as *my* house and not just West's—AJ and I scurry up to my room to do our nails, dark purple for AJ and navy for me. For the next hour and a half, we catch up and laugh until we cry. Turns out spending time with my bestie and feeling carefree for a few hours was exactly what I needed.

Around two, AJ shows herself out, and I dive back into my current read—*Center of Gravity* by K.K. Allen—

and lose myself in the pages of Lex and Theo's breath-taking love story.

I must have fallen asleep at some point, because I wake groggy and disoriented to the sound of male voices outside of my door.

"You need to figure something out," a harsh voice whispers. "The clock is ticking."

"I have plenty of time, Colton," the voice I recognize as West replies.

Ah. That explains the grumpiness. "You really don't. Less than a year, and that's assuming it takes... quickly."

One of them scoffs, presumably West. "Please. I bet it'll be one and done."

Undistinguishable muttering follows before the sound of West's office door opening and closing meets my ears. *Huh. I wonder what that's about?*

The temptation to crawl out of my bed and listen in is strong, but I fight it. I know I'd be pissed if West listened in on one of my private conversations, so as intrigued as I am, I tamp down the urge. Instead, I send a text to Mom and head downstairs to grab a drink.

My intention was to scamper down the steps quiet as a mouse. But, the sound of Colton's barking voice has me rooted in place, as if it's me he's fussing at. "You do realize if you don't make this happen, you'll lose every-thing you hold so fucking dear, right?"

"I..." The resigned tenor of West's voice makes my belly knot. He is usually so upbeat and cocky; hearing him sad makes me want to make his mission mine, just so he'll be happy again. Then again, I've always been a fixer. "I know. I do. I just... how?"

"For as much as I bullshit and joke about it, I can't really go out, snap my fingers, and be done with it—

wham, bam, thank you, ma'am. This is something that will take discretion. Certain criteria will have to be met. This is more than fulfilling the terms of my trust; this is… the rest of my life. And someone else's."

I want to stay and listen, but my gut is swimming with guilt for what I've overheard already. If West wanted me to know what was troubling him, he'd tell me. So, I head down to the kitchen, making myself scarce, like the good roomie I am.

CHAPTER 15
WEST

"I'm gonna crack soon," I growl. Colton eyes me warily from the other side of my desk—as he fucking should. The pressure is getting to me, as is the irony. I need to knock someone up, yet I'm currently as celibate as a monk. I haven't had a dry spell like this since… *ever*.

"I keep telling you, we need to get the ball rolling." The smarmy little asshole leans back in his chair, a stupid smirk tugging at his mouth.

"Fine." I spear my fingers through my hair. "What do we need to do to start?"

"I thought you'd never ask." He leans down and whips out his legal pad. "First we need to narrow down what you're looking for."

"Like… genetically?" I ask.

"That and in general. Keep in mind, whoever you impregnate will be in your life for the foreseeable future."

I cringe, because—*fuck!*—*that sounds awful*. Honestly, I can't think of a single woman who I'd want to be that closely connected to for the rest of forever. *Except for one,* my Benedict Arnold brain shouts.

"Okay." With my thumb and forefinger, I pinch the bridge of my nose as I lean back into my chair. "Let me think."

"Ready when you are." I crack my eyes open, and, sure enough, there's Colton, pen to paper, just waiting on me to talk. Such a fucking choir boy.

"Okay," I say again. "Attractive—for obvious reasons. Well educated. Not a psychopath. A semi-normal family would be nice, too. She needs to be a good person—like morally. A sense of humor would be nice, because something tells me our situation might require it. Honest. She has to be honest, in her motives for agreeing to this and in… co-parenting." I spit the last word out, damn near choking on it.

"Keep going," Colton urges.

"I'd prefer someone patient—parenting is fucking hard enough traditionally. Respectful, empathetic, able to prioritize, and maybe willing to change all of the shit diapers?"

Colton shakes his head. "You're an idiot."

"Oh, and someone with easily accessible medical history. No STDs, obviously. No one that smokes. No current or past substance abuse issues. No criminal record."

"Those are good." He scribbles away. "I'd add willing to sign a contract and possibly an NDA."

"I can't decide if it sounds like I'm selecting a dog or a goddamn mail order bride."

Colton cracks up. "Only you."

"Tell me about it." Every muscle in my body is taut

with tension. "So, how do we find a woman who meets all of these?"

"Well, first, you adjust your expectations—no one is going to meet *all* of it. The answer is obvious though—we hold auditions."

I drop my head to my desk, smacking it against the hard surface a time or two. "How is this my life?"

Colton's laugh—at my expense—only makes me want to bang my head into it again. "Don't get all bent out of shape over it. Plus, aren't you used to auditioning women?"

Slowly, I sit back up, rolling my neck from side-to-side. This right here is why I don't talk much about my work; people love to crack jokes. But Colton knows the full scope of my job, which is why he damn well knows he's being an ass. "That's been outsourced for the last three years."

He smirks, the baiting motherfucker. "Yeah, I know. Seeing you riled up sparks joy in my life."

"Don't you Marie Kondo me."

His smirk ratchets up to a full-on grin. "What? I said you spark joy; I'm keeping you."

"Whatever," I mumble under my breath. "You say that shit like you have a choice."

It's been a week since Colton and I sat down and really got to work on this baby mama bullshit, and he's been hard at work ever since. Where or how he plans on finding women to audition for this is beyond me—and truthfully, I'm not sure I want to know.

I mean, is this some kind of dark web shit? And if it

is, are the women involved in it really the kind I want to parent a child with? My mind races with questions day in and day out, but I keep them to myself. As idiotic as it may be, this is one of those *'ignorance is bliss'* situations.

My phone rings, buzzing loudly against the quartz countertop. "Colton," I say in way of greeting.

"Where are you? I called your office, and Margaret said you were out of the office. Wouldn't say where or when you'd be back, either." He sounds so put out, I can't help but grin.

God love Margaret Wells; she's petite, with pale everything—hair, skin, and eyes. She's thirty-five but doesn't look a day past nineteen. She swears it's some German skin care line, but her wife says it's genetics. Either way, Margaret looks as fragile as a flower, but it's a lie. She has thorns—razor-sharp thorns that she won't hesitate to stick you with.

"Oh, yeah, I'm working from home today."

"Home? Why?"

I pop a capsule into my Nespresso and tap the Lungo button, opting for a larger pour. "Yeah, it's rainy today."

"You say that like it is a justifiable reason to not go into the office."

"It's not?" I ask, the fresh smell of espresso overwhelming my senses.

"Privileged asshole," Colton mutters under his breath. "It was torrential at six, but I still went on my run, yet you couldn't manage to drive to your office in a drizzle?"

I laugh. "To each his own. Now, what's got your panties in a wad?"

"We need to set a date, time, and place. I think I have enough women lined up."

"Let me grab my laptop." I lay the phone back onto the island, tapping the speakerphone button. "Okay. Ready."

"I have ten women lined up to start. All of them match at least seventy percent of your criteria. The one non-negotiable they all agreed to was an NDA as well as being tested prior to the interview."

"Okay, good. Let me pull up my calendar." I click around on my laptop, scanning over emails as my synced schedule loads. "Got it. It looks like any day next week except Tuesday is good."

"Let's do Monday then. Best to get it out of the way, don't you think?"

I'm so consumed with our conversation that I don't even hear her approach. "That should work. Do you think we can do all ten women at once?"

"It'll be rough, and exhausting for sure, but we can handle it. Check your email, I'm sending pict—"

"Um, what?" Stacia asks, cutting Colton off and scaring the shit out of me.

"Fuck! I thought you were at work." I fumble around for my phone, pressing my thumb onto the end call button with far more force than necessary.

She arches a delicate brow. "My car is literally right next to yours in the driveway."

My skin feels too hot and too tight as embarrassment crawls over, under, and through me. Which is stupid; I have nothing to be embarrassed about. I'm doing what I need to do to claim something that should have been mine to start with—something worth this and more to me.

I shrug, trying for casual and unaffected. "Huh. Okay. No work today?"

Stacia shuffles closer, seeming a little hesitant. "Uh, it's a late day since I'm doing the makeup for the cast of a burlesque show."

"Oh, okay, right. Good." I shake off the lingering awkwardness. "I'm just gonna get back to—"

"Arranging your Monday morning orgy with Colton?" Her voice drips with a stinging mixture of sarcasm, uncertainty, jealousy, and disgust.

I have every intention of correcting her, but for some reason, my brain latches onto that jealousy like it's a rope meant to lead me out of the darkness. Not to mention, she flees back upstairs before I can utter a single word.

I swallow down the dregs of my now-cold coffee. *Here's to hoping our living arrangement didn't just become hella awkward.*

CHAPTER 16
STACIA

I race back to my room as if I'm being chased. And I am—by a little green monster called jealousy. My heart pounds as the snippet of the conversation I overheard replays in my head.

Ten women. Surely, I misunderstood, right? There's no way he and Colton have plans to fuck ten women. That's… it's ludicrous.

Back in my room, I pace in front of my bed. My natural inclination is to call AJ, but I don't. Because I know I'd sound crazy if I dialed her ranting and raving about my hotter-than-hell roomie planning a two-on-ten sex-fest. Jesus! I feel like I've got a few screws loose just thinking it.

I need a distraction. Something—anything to get my mind off of what I think I heard.

On instinct, I find myself researching Virtual Kitty. Apparently, it was created by someone from Mississippi, which is kind of cool. I tried searching out the owner's name, but everything comes back to a company called Easton Incorporated. However, many websites mention that the developer was only nineteen when he launched VK. I'm pretty sure when I was nineteen, I was more concerned with boys and partying, but we can't all be overachievers.

The more I look into this company, though, the more I feel at ease about submitting myself as a kitty. Hell, they even offer benefits for the women after a year of steady uploads. I'm pretty sure that's not the norm in the porn industry, but what do I know?

Before I lose my nerve, I text AJ.

ME

Hey, are you free today?

AJ

Yeah...

I quickly text her my plans and ask her to meet me in two hours. Like the true ride-or-die she is, she agrees.

After a quick shower, I braid my damp hair and throw on a pair of cutoffs and an old concert T-shirt. I leave my face makeup free, knowing I'm going to need a more dramatic look later today.

I grab my purse and slowly tiptoe down the stairs, listening for West. I hate that I feel so out of sorts with him. It's like hearing his conversation this morning gave way to a part of my brain I didn't even know existed. And if I'm being honest, it's not a part I like. I feel petty and insecure and jealous, and I fucking hate it.

Especially because I have zero right to feel that way. West is my friend. Nothing more. Sure, he's the hottest guy I know. And yeah, our long-time-ago hookup left me wanting more, but I've always managed just fine seeing him with other women since. Maybe it's because

I'm in a dry spell? All I know is these feelings need to scram, because ain't nobody got time for that.

Everything downstairs seems quiet, so I creep into the kitchen in search of a cold drink and something to eat. I'm bent over, rummaging through the fridge drawers, when my plans to avoid the master of the house are dashed to hell and back.

"Lookin' good in those shorts," West says from behind me, causing me to jump and knock my head on the shelf.

"Gah!" I yelp, rubbing the back of my head as I straighten and whirl to face him. "You shouldn't sneak up on people."

West cocks his head. "Wasn't sneaking. What are you up to today?"

With my quest for food long forgotten, I shut the refrigerator door and put a little distance between us. "Hanging out with AJ," I say, hoping he won't ask to tag along.

"And after?" he asks.

"Um." I don't finish the thought. Because *taking sexy pictures of myself to submit to a porn app* is not something he needs to know about. "Just... stuff."

His gaze sharpens, working over me as if he's using X-ray vision to see all of my secrets. *Thank fuck that's not a real thing.* "Okay, then, don't tell me."

He steps a little closer, invading my personal space, and picks up the end of my braid. "I like this." He wraps the strands around his fist and tugs a little, and I stumble farther into him. "I like it a lot."

I fling his hand off of me and step back, hating how our proximity sent my heart racing. "It's just a braid," I deadpan, pleased when my voice comes out even and not breathy, because Jesus-H-Christ, when he yanked on my hair like that, all I wanted to do was say *yes please, more please.*

He shrugs. "Do you work on Monday?"

My heart plummets, and my libido dies a fast death. "Why?" I ask, but I already know.

"Colton and I just need the house for a few hours."

I cross my arms over my chest. "I'm sorry, what?"

West sighs. "It's not what you think."

"Really? Because it sounds to me like you're asking me to vacate our house for you to have a sex party. Which is bullshit, because we have a no hookups rule."

"Actually." West steps into me again. "You haven't signed the rental agreement yet, so…"

Red tinges my vision. "Then give me a pen."

I expect him to retort with some smartass comment, but instead he slides open the top drawer of the island and snags a manila folder and a pen. "Here you go."

I scrawl my name at the bottom and pass it back to him. "There. Find somewhere else to"—I wave my hand in the air—"do whatever."

His kissable lips tip up. "I'll let Colton know we need to arrange for a new location."

A hurt I can't explain wraps itself around me, whispering into my ear how foolish I am. Unable to look him in the eye, I nod, grab my purse, and flee.

"Are you sure about this?" AJ asks as we walk into what is usually the happiest place on earth—otherwise known as Target.

What a loaded question—one that washes away my

trivial West-worries. "Yes," I say. And I am. But, also, I'm not. It's complicated, but I feel like it's what I *need* to do to help my family.

The last few times I heard from Dad, he's sounded worse and worse. Never in my life have I heard him sound so hopeless. At the start of this shit, he was positive and ready to fight. Now, he seems resigned and depressed, and I hate it.

I hate hearing him hurt. I hate seeing my mother withering away. I hate that my grandparents are digging themselves deeper and deeper into debt.

Most of all, I hate that I feel like I'm out of options. Sure, I'm looking for a more traditional second job, but I still need more. I could probably even get a small personal loan—emphasis on the word small. But Virtual Kitty not only pays well, they pay fast.

"If you say so," AJ hedges, as if she's waiting on me to change my mind.

"Positive." I grab her hand. "C'mon, I think the tripods are this way."

"Gah! Who knew there'd be so many?" she asks, staring at the display.

"Right?" Finally, I settle on a short one with bendy legs that can wrap around things. "This should work!"

We check out, hit up the Starbucks, and go our separate ways. The entire drive home, I say a prayer that West isn't there. I'm honestly not sure I can deal with seeing him right now.

It seems as though luck is on my side when West's car is absent from the driveway when I get home. I fly up to my room and get to work, not wasting a precious second. Mostly because I don't want to lose my nerve, but also because I have no clue when he'll be back.

In my bathroom, I carefully paint my face. Once I'm contoured to perfection with a heavy smoky eye and candy-apple red lips, I step back into my room to get dressed—well, undressed.

I opt for black lace, knowing it will make my body art, lips, and hair pop.

It takes me longer than I thought to get the tripod, phone, lighting, and the angle of my body just right—let me just say, no woman should have to see those types of outtakes of her own body.

Once I find my groove, I manage to capture several appealing poses. However, I know if I want to catch their attention, I need to up my game.

I strip down to nude and carefully arrange myself so I'm exposed but not actually baring myself. I snap a few shots and then toss on my robe.

After I email myself the photos, I set to work, scrolling through the photos, deciding which to delete and which to submit. "Whoa!" I breathe out, shocked when one of the nude ones appears on my screen. I don't just look good, I look… amazing. Confident and sexy. Empowered.

I'm lying prone on the bed, with my right leg extended over the footboard and the left pulled up and bent at the knee so that my foot rests on my right leg. My back is delicately arched, emphasizing the swell of my ass and the dip in my waist. The entire side of my left breast—nip and all—is exposed, along with the swirling, colorful art that decorates my body. My left arm is propping me up and my right hand is tangled in my hair as I smirk at the camera with my chin tipped up defiantly. The light is hitting me just right; I look like a goddamn queen, fearless and ready to conquer.

It shows a little more than I intended for it to, but… it's a money shot if I've ever seen one, and I know it will secure me a spot with VK.

Before I can second-guess it or talk myself out of it, I toggle over to their submissions page and fill out the form. I read over the terms and conditions one last time, attach my best shots, and send it off.

A knock sounds at my door right as a little rainbow cat icon pops up, letting me know my submission is pending. "Yeah?"

The door opens, and West steps in. "What—" His eyes take in the state of my room—black lingerie on the floor, me clad in only my robe, the screen of my laptop. "What are you doing?"

Frantically, I exit the window, only for a popup to appear thanking me for applying. "Nothing. Why? You?"

He scans the space again. "Uh." He clears his throat and shifts on his feet. "Movie night?" His voice is tight, like he's asking to be polite and not because he wants to.

Fuck. My. Life.

CHAPTER 17
WEST

hy is the Virtual Kitty site pulled up on her laptop? Why is there lingerie—incredibly fucking sexy lingerie—on her floor? Why are the covers all mussed up? Why is she painted up like a doll? A million questions and scenarios flit through my mind.

Originally, I came up to ask her to join me downstairs for some pizza and a movie—an olive branch, of sorts. Things are tense between us, and I hate it.

But now… now I have questions, and they need answers, so when she turns me down with a smile faker than the red hue of her hair, I'm a man on a mission.

To add insult to injury, the vision of her in that tiny, barely-there robe is pretty much burned into my retinas. The thought of sliding my hands beneath the lapels to explore her smooth, creamy skin has my dick twitching beneath my navy sweats.

My curiosity trumps my arousal, however, and I lock myself away in my office, pull up the site, and enter my credentials. Within two seconds, I'm in the admin-only area, scrolling through submissions. *Jesus, there's a lot.* Finally, a familiar headshot catches my eye, and I click the link.

Name: Stacia Iris Kellan

Preferred username: Defiant_Queen

Preferences: Solo, pics, chat

I scroll a little lower, and her submission photos begin to load. A twinge of guilt pinches my heart for looking at these without her consent. Then again, Virtual Kitty is my fucking company. She gave her consent when she uploaded them. With that in mind, I hold fast.

The first image is her headshot: she's facing the camera straight on, smirking naughtily. The second is a full-body shot of her wrapped only in black lace. She looks like a naughty present—one I'd fucking love to unwrap. The third image is her from the back, looking over her shoulder at the camera, biting her lip.

The fourth picture though—*goddamn!* It has me up and out of my chair, erection and good sense be damned.

I barge into her room, ready for… I don't fucking know what. But my skin is electric, and my blood feels fuzzy in my veins.

"The hell—can I help you?" Stacia asks, sitting on the edge of her bed, still wearing only her robe, looking perturbed.

Stalking toward her, I'm an apex predator with prey in its sights. "Yeah, you can," I say before stepping between her legs and claiming her lips with my own.

I half expect her to shove me away and cuss me out, so imagine my shock when she tugs me down on top of her and locks her legs around my waist, grinding into me.

Our kiss isn't sweet or tender; it's rude and devoid of all pleasantries. We're a combustible combination of lips, teeth, and tongue as each of us airs our frustrations with our bodies.

I tangle my hands in her hair. She scratches her nails down my back. I grind my erection into her. She bites down on my bottom lip damn near hard enough to draw blood. It's an erotic push and pull as we lose ourselves in each other's bodies until we're nothing more than a mass of panting, writhing limbs.

Finally, she pulls back. I can't help but stare at her messy hair, flushed cheeks, and swollen lips. She looks like a sex goddess come to life, and I'm all too willing to lay myself at her altar.

"What in the fuck just happened?" Stacia asks, not bothering to right her robe.

"You wanna tell me about Virtual Kitty?" I stay cradled between her legs, with a hand on either side of her face, arms extended to hold me above her.

She sputters. "Wh-what?"

I shift closer, and my erection brushes against the apex of her thighs. We both moan. "You heard me. I saw your application."

This catches her attention. "You what?" she shrieks, trying like hell to get out from under me.

I pin her—though she could easily escape if she wanted to—and drop my lips to her ear. "That's right, Defiant Queen," I whisper. "I know all about your dirty little secret."

"H-how?"

I draw back so I can see her face when I let this bomb drop. "I own it. Virtual Kitty is mine."

"No. No, it's not." She shakes her head. "It's owned by a company… Easton Incorporated."

I grin. "That's right. Easton. Weston. It's all mine."

"You had no right!"

"What part of *it's my company* don't you get? I have every right." She lifts her chin defiantly and I can't help but to kiss along her jaw. "So, you wanna do porn? Be a good little kitty? Want me to make you purr?"

"Oh, fuck you!" But there's no bite to her words. If anything, she sounds turned-the-hell-on. The way she arches her back and rubs her tits against my chest only confirms it.

"I'm trying," I grit out before claiming her lips again.

Stacia's hands blaze a trail up my chest, shoving my shirt up and out of the way. I break our kiss just long enough to pull it over my head and toss it to the floor.

She kisses her way down my neck, stopping to nip at my collarbones, all the while rubbing herself on my dick. My sweatpants have to go. Stacia must agree, because her hands make quick work of shoving them, and my boxers, down my hips.

I kick them to the floor and mimic her earlier movements, kissing my way down her neck, parting her robe as I go. Instead of her collarbones, I suck one tight, rosy nipple into my mouth as my hand pulls and plucks at the other.

"I need you inside of me," she whimpers, digging her nails into my ass.

Without hesitation, I shift the black silk of her robe to the side, line myself up at her entrance, and thrust home.

We fuck the same way we kissed—rough and with utter abandon. There are no limits as I plunge into her, making sure to hit her sweet spot with every stroke.

"You feel so fucking good," I groan, meaning it with every fiber of my being. Being inside of Stacia feels so good, I swear I'd live there, forever, in her pleasure.

All too soon, she's chanting my name and shattering into a million pieces beneath me. "West, oh, God, West!" She milks my dick for all it's worth, and before she's even finished climaxing, I'm right behind her, pressing into her for all I'm worth, my body heaving against her slick skin.

I collapse, rolling off of her as I go. "Goddamn." My voice is rough, even to my own ears.

"Ditto," Stacia murmurs. A swell of masculine pride thrums through me at her satisfied, lazy tone.

We lie here for a few minutes, basking in our post-sex glow. Unfortunately, all good things have to come to an end.

"Oh, shit. We didn't use a condom," Stacia blurts out, her sultry and satiated tone replaced with worry.

I gulp. Colton is gonna kill me if she ends up pregnant. "Fuck. I'm… I'm sorry. Are you… protected?" My gut sinks when she doesn't immediately assure me. "Stacia?"

"No," she whispers.

"You're not on birth control?"

"Um, when Dad was arrested and they froze his accounts, our insurance was canceled for non-payment, so I…I couldn't refill."

Shit. "Come here." I tug her into my arms, cradling her to my side with her head on my chest. "It's okay."

She mutters something unintelligible before asking, "What's today?"

I rattle off the date and wait.

"We… should be okay. Mostly. I think."

"You think?"

She nods, her silky hair tickling my chest. "Yeah. I mean, I'm like… seventy-six percent positive."

I hold her a little tighter to me. "I'll take those odds."

Something niggles at the back of my brain, forming a dark thought that whispers in my ear—*if she is pregnant, you gain access to your trust with time to spare.* But I shake it off; Stacia's so much more to me than a means to an end. Though, I can't help but wonder if she'd be willing.

"So, what now?" she asks, moving away from me.

As she sits up, her entire body on display, the old adage *'I hate to see you go, but I love to watch you leave'* comes to mind. "Wait a fucking minute. Is… is your snatch bedazzled?" I ask, my eyes honed in on the sparkling gemstones peeking out through her neatly trimmed curls.

Stacia snorts out a laugh. "It's pierced."

"Well, hot damn. If I'd have known that—"

"You'd have what?" she asks playfully.

"I'd have pre-gamed a little more instead of skipping right to the main event."

She shrugs. "I'd say next time, but this should probably be a one-time thing, right?"

It's on the tip of my tongue to agree with her, but instead I find myself saying, "Maybe. Meet me at my office tomorrow at nine—I have a proposition for you."

Her eyes widen comically. "You… you want me to join your orgy?"

I shake my head. "It's not an orgy, Stacia. Just be there at nine, and I'll explain everything."

A sigh escapes her. "I… sure, okay."

Mentally, I fist pump. "So, about that pizza and movie?"

She nibbles on her plump lower lip. "Uh. Let me shower first?"

"I'll order while you do—meat lovers?"

"You know it. With ranch, please."

I lean in as if to kiss her, but think better of it. "Sounds good. Come down whenever you're ready."

CHAPTER 18
STACIA

itting next to West last night on the couch after he delivered the best orgasm of my life was nothing short of pure torture. Every single time he shifted, his hand would brush my thigh, and a flurry of tingles would zip through me.

Don't even get me started on the fucking sex scene in the movie. I don't know what we were thinking watching *Forgetting Sarah Marshall*, but regrets were had.

Oh, and the fact that he's the owner of Virtual Kitty—talk about a total mindfuck. I've spent the last thirteen hours fluctuating between outrage at not knowing and desire as I remember the way his body felt moving inside of mine.

I'd venture to say West Larson and I are the walking definition of *it's complicated*.

And now, this morning, I'm standing buck-ass naked in front of my closet, debating what on earth to wear to this weird not-orgy meeting.

It's at his office, so I should probably dress up. I settle on a black bodycon dress. It's tea length with lace trim and long sleeves. Sexy, yet elegant. I slide my feet into my royal blue velvet peep-toe pumps—the very same ones I was wearing the first time I ever laid eyes on West. How fitting.

At eight forty-five a.m. on the dot, I leave the house and drive over. Nerves rattle my stomach the entire way as I wonder what on earth this could be about. *Oh, God. What if it's a live audition for VK? What if he's expecting me to have sex with someone or pleasure myself while he watches?*

My panic builds until finally, I tell my inner worry-monger to shut up. "West wouldn't do that," I say aloud, speaking it into existence. As soon as the words leave my lips, a calm washes over me. Because deep down, I know that's not why he's called me here.

So, the question remains—*why?*

My GPS guides me to the uptown area, full of high-rises—well, high for Mississippi—and parking garages. "You have arrived at your destination," the mechanical voice tells me as I approach a gleaming glass building. There are signs directing me where to park and I follow them, parking on the third level.

From there, I wind through row after row of parked cars until I find the elevator. Inside, there's a directory listing the names and floors. Easton Inc. is at the very top.

Nerves war with the calm I found on the drive over as the elevator car climbs. My hands are clammy and a single bead of sweat works its way down the back of my dress.

I wipe my hands on the front of my dress just as the door opens, revealing to me a stunning lobby. Glass outer walls make you feel as if you're standing in the clouds. Everything in the space is modern and sleek, from the polished concrete floors to the polished navy reception desk and inviting cream-colored chairs. Hell, there's even a gold chandelier dripping in crystals hanging over the center of the room.

"Oh, hello," a honeyed voice greets me. "May I help you?"

I glance up to see a tall, thin woman waltz into the room. She's pale, but in that stunning Snow White sort of way, only her hair is blonde and her eyes are the palest blue I've ever seen. Simply put, she's a knockout and belongs on a runway, not in an office, even one as pretty as this.

"Yes, I have an appointment with Wes—Mr. Larson— at nine."

"Stacia?" she asks, glancing down at something on her side of the tall desk.

"That's me."

"Great. He's not quite ready, but if you'd like to have a seat right over there, I'll let you know when he is."

I nod and traipse over to the closest chair, sinking down into it, sighing as the cushion forms around me.

"Would you like coffee while you wait?"

My mouth waters at the thought. "Yes, please."

She asks how I take it and smiles when I tell her half coffee and half cream.

I slide my phone out of my bag as she heads off to wherever their coffee machine is. I send a quick text to Mom and one to AJ before aimlessly scrolling through social media.

The lobby is so quiet that I damn near throw my phone across the room when the sound of raised voices penetrates silence. "Have you lost your goddamn mind?" Colton barks, sounding angrier than I've ever heard.

"It's a good idea and you know it!" West shouts back.

I have a feeling neither of them realize they have an audience.

"It's a train wreck waiting to happen!"

Something slams in the distance. "It's perfect. She meets nearly every box on my list—"

"You need to think about this! If things go south—"

"They won't!" West roars. "If she agrees, this is the perfect solution. I'll meet the provisions of my trust and she—"

"She what?" Colton asks. "What's in it for her?"

Silence follows, and I can't help but wonder if they're talking about me.

West speaks again, and though this time his voice is softer, it still carries. "If she agrees, we can skip the auditions. If I can convince her to say yes, to help me…" He trails off, leaving the thought unfinished. "We already know there's chemistry there, which makes everything easier. I…I asked her to come by."

"When?" Colton barks just as the receptionist returns, coffee in hand.

"Oh my," she murmurs. "Let me go deal with them. I'll let them know you're here, too."

She scampers around the wall behind the desk, down a hallway I didn't even know existed. "Your nine o'clock is here," she says primly, "and you two idiots have given her quite the show."

Two masculine groans trickle into the space, and I chuckle.

Blondie returns. "Mr. Larson will see you now." I stand. "Oh, I'm Margaret, by the way; it's nice to meet you." We shake hands, and she guides me back to West's office.

If I thought the lobby was grand, it has nothing on this space. An oversized desk takes up most of the far wall, with floor-to-ceiling bookshelves making up another. There's a gold bar cart in the corner and a stunning navy blue velvet sofa dead center, and tying it all together is a massive sheep-skin rug.

West is at the bar cart, decanter in hand, while Colton is on the couch, rubbing his temples.

"Have fun," Margaret whispers before heading back out to her post.

When neither man says anything, I do. "So, what's this about?"

"Nothing, it's a mistake," Colton barks.

"It's not a mistake. She's perfect."

"It's a goddamn travesty," Colton replies, his tone all vinegar.

"Um, excuse me. I am right fucking here, and one of you better start talking."

The two men exchange a meaningful look. "Okay," West starts. Colton shakes his head, but West pays him no mind. "My grandfather passed away recently—"

"I'm so sorry," I interrupt.

He waves a dismissive hand. "He was a miserable, manipulative old bastard who makes Brock's dad look almost saintly." I recoil, because Everett Larson is a monster. "As I was saying, he passed away and left my Mimi Jean's estate to me, along with some accounts."

A beat of silence passes, and I just know whatever he's about to say will be huge.

"In order to gain access to these things, there are

conditions that must be met, and I only have a year to do so."

Ohhh. I've read books like this. "What? You need a wife? I'll do it."

Both men stare at me like I've lost my marbles, and maybe I have. I mean, I'm about to start doing porn and just offered myself to marry my roommate. *I think I need a drink.*

West drains his glass and pours himself another. "Actually, I don't need a wife."

"What do you need then?" I ask, shifting on my feet.

Colton mutters something under his breath.

"A womb. I need a womb."

I reel back. "You need a what now?"

"The trust says he must produce an heir before he turns twenty-five."

I'm still not computing. "What?"

"A baby. I have to have a baby."

My gears start spinning again—in overtime. "You goddamn asshole! You... you did this on purpose! You knew!" Tears fill my eyes and panic claws at my chest. "You knew!"

West approaches me, drink in hand. "I swear, it's not what you're thinking."

"And what is she thinking, West?" Colton asks, rising from the couch.

My vision swims as the men close in on me. I snatch West's drink from his hand, gulp it down, and shove the glass back into his hands. "I...I thought. You. We... I thought." I can't seem to string together a coherent sentence for the life of me, but that's probably because it currently feels like everything I know is crumbling around me and I'm trapped in the ruins.

"Stacia." West says my name softly, but I'm not falling for it.

"Answer me this: did you intentionally not use a condom?"

"No!" West shouts simultaneously to Colton yelling, "What?"

My heart is racing and I feel faint. I need to get out of here. My gut says to trust him and to listen, but my brain says there's too much evidence stacked against him.

The murderous look in Colton's eyes isn't helping either. So, I do the only thing I can think of.

I run.

CHAPTER 19
WEST

"I hate to say I—"

"I swear to fucking God, Colton, if you say I told you so, I'll lose my shit."

He holds up his hands in mock surrender. "I'm just saying; this thing had train wreck written all over it."

"No. It doesn't," I state petulantly. I know I'm right. I know Stacia is the perfect baby mama. She is the definition of low-key. She's fucking gorgeous. She's smart, driven, talented, tenacious. I know she doesn't have any health issues and that she isn't crazy. Sure, what's happening with her dad is unfortunate, but she is adamant he's innocent. Maybe it makes me a fool, but I believe her. "She's perfect."

Colton pinches the bridge of his nose and exhales slowly through clenched teeth. "You're chasing a pipe dream. I get that she's hot and you apparently fucked her already—without a condom, I might add. But she's not it, man. You saw how badly she just reacted."

"Yeah, because she thinks I fucking played her. She thinks I tried knocking her up *intentionally* without *consent.* Any woman in their right mind would react badly to that, dumbass."

"Only dumbass here is you. In what universe is arranging a pregnancy with your roommate and friend a good plan?"

I stare at him blankly. "In all of them. Think about it; she already lives with me—check. She is someone I trust. And I know having her be a part of the rest of my life won't be a hardship."

Colton sighs. "Fine. Maybe you're right. But, she's probably on her way home to pack her shit and leave. So." He shrugs. "You might wanna go after her."

Shit. He's right. I grab my keys from my desk. "Close up for me," I call over my shoulder, never giving him a chance to argue.

I probably break about every traffic law on the way home, and by the looks of it, I somehow managed to beat her. How, I don't know, but I'm not going to complain.

Inside, I park myself on the couch so that when she comes in, I can catch her.

Minutes pass, and she doesn't show. So, I call her; she sends me straight to voice mail. *Fuck—I'm well and truly in the doghouse.* Desperate, I text her.

ME

> Stacia, it's not what you think. Where are you?

Twice.

ME

> Let's just talk. Please give me the chance to explain.

But still, she doesn't answer. And she's had plenty of time to come home, so my guess is she's not coming back, at least not today.

Anxiety and guilt churn in my gut as I dial one last time. Still, nothing. I feel like a crazy-ass stalker, but the thought of her being alone and upset, especially because of something I did… it fucking rattles me all the way down to my soul.

Unable to sit and wait, I head back out to my car, dialing Brock on the way. "You done fucked up, man," he answers, confirming my suspicions as to where Stacia is.

"It's a misunderstanding."

"I'm sure it—" There's a scuffle before a new voice comes through the line.

"Listen here, you little dick weasel." Abby Jane is in full-on guard dog mode, and while I love that Stacia has such a fiercely loyal friend, I really hate being on the receiving end of her anger. "Stacia doesn't want to talk to you. She doesn't want to see you. She doesn't even want to hear your name. I mean, really! I thought I knew you—but you're a no good, heartless prick, and you can fuck. Right. Off. Oh, and in case you were wondering, you're no longer welcome here."

She hangs up before I can reply, and when I call back, it goes straight to voice mail. However, a grin fights its way free, because now I know for sure where she is, and there's nothing—not even a feisty, blue-haired pixie— that's going to stand in my way.

The entire drive to Brock and AJ's place, I hype myself up. With every turn, I tell myself she'll listen. At each stop sign, I convince myself that she has to see things my way. And at the stoplights? There I fool myself into believing that maybe she's already over it and laughing it up with AJ. *Yeah, no, I know that's a load of shit. I'm not completely delusional.*

A stream of doubt begins to trickle down from my subconscious on the elevator ride up. And as I knock on the door, I worry I'm making a mistake.

"Jockstrap, grab your wallet!" The door opens. "The pizza—*what the fuck are you doing here?*"

"Don't slam the door!" I yell, wedging my foot between the door and frame.

"I told you—you're not welcome here."

"Please." My shoulders slump. "Just... let me talk to her. If she tells me to leave, I will. I'm begging you, Abby Jane. Please."

She must hear the truth in my words, because instead of telling me off or stomping on my foot, AJ opens the door, allowing me to enter. "If she doesn't want to see you or asks you to leave, you're out of here, got it?" I nod. "Good. Wait here."

I hover near the door, nerves blasting through my system like a rocket launching into space, as I wait to see what Stacia decides. Finally, after what feels like three lifetimes, both she and AJ emerge from the hallway.

"Stacia—"

"You have fifteen minutes." AJ nods to the couch. "Use them wisely."

We each grab an opposite end of the couch. Stacia's eyes are watery, and her cheeks splotchy. "Are you okay?" I ask lamely.

She huffs. "What do you think?"

"I…I swear this is a massive misunderstanding. Will you hear me out? Please?"

"I'm here, aren't I?"

I take a deep breath. "Stacia, what happened between us last night was not planned or premeditated at all. I didn't seek you out with the intention of fucking you. I would never—and I mean never—disrespect you or any other woman by trying to trap them with a pregnancy.

"And yes, I realize that sounds like a load of shit, given the circumstances. I swear on my life—my health, my business, my Mimi Jean's grave—what happened between us was legit. I was so caught up in the moment —in you—that protection didn't even cross my mind. All I could think about was how you'd sound with me inside you.

"I know you feel deceived, but that was never my intention. I respect the hell out of you and wouldn't lie to you like that. Please. Please believe me."

Stacia releases a shuddery breath. "I—I have some questions."

I scoot a little closer. "Anything."

"Ten women… why were you and Colton…?"

She leaves her sentence unfinished, but I know what she's asking. "We were interviewing potential baby mamas."

Stacia sucks in a sharp breath. "You really didn't plan it? Or at least plan to ask me?"

"Honestly, no. The thought didn't even occur to me until after we'd already fucked."

"You're… clean, right?" she asks, ducking her head before rushing to add, "I totally am. I was checked at my last gyno appointment. It was four months ago, but I haven't been with anyone except you since."

"Clean as a whistle."

She looks relieved, and honestly, I am, too.

Stacia shifts uncomfortably, and I know the big question is coming. "Explain why you… *need*… to have a baby?"

"You already know, from everything Brock and AJ went through, the Larson clan aren't exactly… sane. Or cuddly. Or kind. Except my Mimi Jean. She was the best part of my childhood. If it weren't for her, I probably wouldn't be here."

Stacia's face softens a fraction. "What do you mean?"

"My parents liked the *idea* of having a kid. All of their friends were doing it, so they did, too. But the actuality of it was not for them. They had a nanny until my mother caught Dad fucking her; after that, she refused to hire another and I was left to fend for myself. If I wanted food, I found it; I lived off of Goldfish crackers and Cheerios. I drank water from the bathtub faucet. I literally never left the house unless it was for a special occasion. I was a prop. Brought out and put on display when needed, then tucked away and forgotten."

Stacia's eyes are wide and glassy, but she doesn't interrupt.

"Eventually, I lost so much weight that my Mimi Jean started asking questions—ones my parents couldn't answer. She demanded right there on the spot for them to let me live with her—and they agreed, as long as I still was present when needed, to play the part of a loving son. Isn't that some shit?" My voice breaks a little as the tidal wave of their abandonment crashes over me. Even still, it hurts. The fact that they could just give me away so easily—even if it was for the best—fucking hurts.

"Anyway, Mimi Jean took me in, no questions asked. Her husband—my dad's Dad—wasn't happy about it, but he loved her and tolerated me. Well, at least until I was around sixteen. She passed away the day after my birthday, and he didn't waste a second shipping me back home. He couldn't stand being in their house without her, but couldn't bear to get rid of it either, so he sealed it up and moved. Those eleven years were the best of my life. Every single childhood toy, photograph, and memory is tied up in my Mimi Jean's estate.

"When he died, he left the estate to me in a trust. But the only way I can access it is if I have a baby before my next birthday. So yes, while I desperately need an heir, I would never force it onto anyone—especially you."

In an unexpected but oh-so-needed move, Stacia reaches over and takes my hand. Her thumb brushes over the top, soothing the storm raging inside of me. "I...I don't know what to say, West."

I look up from our joined hands, locking my stare onto hers. "Say you believe me. That you forgive me. That you'll come home."

"I do believe you," she whispers, her voice shaky. "And there's nothing to forgive."

As corny as it sounds, my heart soars. "Really?"

She squeezes my hand. "Yeah, really."

"So, you'll come home?"

"Yeah, West, I will. But I won't have your baby."

"You sure?" I ask, laying on the charm.

Her newly found grin falters for a second. "Yeah, like seventy-six percent positive."

My first genuine smile of the day peeks. I answer her now the same way I did last night. "I'll take those odds."

CHAPTER 20
STACIA

t's been two weeks since the whole baby mama debacle went down and life with West ever since has been… *interesting*. He ended up not going forward with any of his interviews. Turns out he's pretty much dead set on cajoling me into agreeing to be more than just his roommate—he wants me as his wombmate.

On my first night back, he treated us to a catered five-star dinner, which was a definite step up from our usual diet of takeout and college-esque type cuisine—aka Ramen and Uncrustables.

The following morning, he brought me coffee in bed with a note reading: *if you were my baby mama, this would be your daily wake-up call.* I thanked him and sent him on his way, and despite my refusal, he still brings me a piping mug of goodness every morning.

The past two Wednesdays, he's had flowers sent to Beauty Box. Oh, and not just for me, but a bouquet for each of my coworkers as well. Apparently Joy is a little traitor who's easily swayed by a sexy voice and veiny forearms. The truth is, I can't even blame her, because

West's muscular, ropey arms are a freaking drool-worthy work of art.

Oh, and he even had dinner delivered to the studio one night when we were there late working on a group of ladies who came in to get prettied up for their friend's fiftieth birthday.

Last night, we did our usual dinner and a movie, and the conniving bastard snuck in a foot rub toward the end. At first, I was like, *jackpot!* But then he started shooting me sly glances that said *I'd do this nightly if you let me knock you up.* Once I caught on, I yanked both of my feet out of his lap and moved to the far end of the couch. He pouted like a scolded puppy for the rest of the movie, which kind of made me smile.

Now, the weekend is upon us, and I'm shockingly off. Which is actually a blessing, as I have super important plans at noon. *Fingers crossed.* For obvious reasons, things with Virtual Kitty didn't pan out. West tried offering me a corporate job with them, but I know it was out of some sort of misplaced guilt because the only thing I'd be qualified to do in that office is fetch coffee.

"Knock, knock," West calls out before stepping into my bedroom. Clad in only his boxers with my coffee in hand, he looks as though he was sent by the fertility goddess herself to test my steadfastness.

Judging from the way my ovaries are screaming, it's working. Luckily, my brain is stronger and far more sensible.

"Got any plans today?" he asks, taking a seat on the edge of my bed.

"I have a job interview," I murmur, inhaling the delicious aroma of my espresso mingling with West's spicy scent. The two combined are basically an aphrodisiac; clearly the universe is testing me.

He scratches the back of his neck and the temperature in the room seems to skyrocket. *When did the simple action of itch relief start turning me on?* "Oh, yeah? Where at?"

"A place out in Dusk River," I say, referencing the next town over.

West eyes me, taking in the thin material of my sleep top. My nipples pebble under his heated gaze, something he undoubtedly notices if his smirk is anything to go by. He licks his lower lip, following the motion with his teeth, and I just about throw myself at him. Thank God he speaks before I have the chance. "Good luck."

"Thanks."

He stands and heads to the door, but instead of leaving, he lingers.

"Did you need something else?" I ask.

"Let me take you to dinner. Tonight."

He doesn't ask; he tells. Which is the only plausible explanation for why I find myself nodding, agreeing.

"Great. Six o'clock. Dress sexy."

By the time my better judgment kicks in, he's long gone, and I'm in danger of being late for my interview if I don't haul my ass out of bed and into the shower.

I arrive at Buck and Lesli with twenty minutes to spare. While working in a restaurant isn't exactly at the top of my list—or anywhere on it, if I'm being honest—the pay posted in the job listing was too much for me to pass up.

Hopefully it's not too good to be true.

The outside of the building doesn't give much away. It's your typical steakhouse, comprised of an appealing mixture of stone and glass. It looks chic and inviting. The only thing that gives me pause is the sign: Buck and Lesli Steakhouse Plus. What on earth is the plus for?

At fifteen til, I step out of my car and inspect my appearance in the reflection of my driver's side door. My black pencil skirt is still lint-free, and my striped blouse is mostly unwrinkled. All in all, I look presentable and professional. Dare I say, hire-able? I sure as hell hope so.

The inside is your typical modern steakhouse. Polished concrete floors give way to dark-colored walls —save for the ones accented in the same stone from the exterior. The ceilings are tall, and the chandeliers are extravagant. A large, curved partition conceals most of the dining room from view, but I take a quick peek. Generously sized booths, with plush leather benches— the kind that curve around the table in a half moon— make for a highly luxurious dinner spot. *Maybe that's what the plus is for… to let people know this isn't your ordinary cowboy-style big-chain steakhouse?*

A hostess in a low—and I mean *very* low—cut top stands behind a massive wood and stone podium. "Welcome to Buck and Lesli, how can I help you today?"

Her voice drips with sugar, the genuine kind, and it immediately sets me at ease. If everyone here's as nice as she is, then I'll get on just fine. "Hi, I'm Stacia. I have an interview at noon."

Her green eyes glitter as she takes me in. "I'm Cari." She extends a hand my way. "It's nice to meet you."

"Thanks, you, too."

She eyes me for a moment longer and smiles. "Oh,

yeah. I think they'll like you. C'mon, I'll take you back to the office."

Her statement strikes me as odd, but I follow along all the same. She leads me to the back of the restaurant, stopping in front of a matte black door that blends into the wall so well I would have completely missed it on my own.

Cari knocks and then turns to me. "Keep your chin up. Smile. Don't let him rattle you—no matter what he says or asks, be confident."

"Uh, thanks?" *I think.* Unaffected by my less than stellar gratitude, Cari smiles brightly and sashays back toward the hostess stand.

"Come in," calls a gruff voice from behind the door. I shoulder it open and step into the dimly lit office. It takes my eyes a second to adjust, but when they do, I'm a little taken aback.

Gone is the polished, chic space of the steakhouse dining room, and in its place is quite possibly the seediest office I've ever seen. Black walls give way to black floors, and there's a thin layer of smoke lingering in the air. A cluttered black desk is positioned a few feet in front of the far wall, and behind it sits the largest man I've ever seen. He's tall and wide—strapping really—with a severe haircut and a massive beard, but his kind eyes temper his otherwise intimidating appearance.

"Can I help you?" he asks. He sounds like he eats gravel for breakfast, lunch, and dinner.

"Hi, yes. I'm Stacia Kellan. I have an interview at noon."

He checks something on his desk; though what, is hard to tell because there's literally book on top of book. "Great. Take a seat."

I do.

"Name's Buck." He doesn't offer me a hand to shake, and I'm kind of okay with it, because he'd probably crush every bone in my hand with a single squeeze.

"Is there a Lesli?" I ask before I can think better of it.

His eyes spark, and his entire face comes alive. "There is. Lesli will join us in just a bit." He glances at his desk again and then back at me, his mustache twitching. "Gotta make sure you're worth meeting before she comes in."

I can't tell if he's joking, so I say nothing at all.

"Your application doesn't show any serving history."

"That's correct."

"What's fifteen twenty-five from forty-six fifty?"

Oh. Math. Easy. "Thirty-one twenty-five," I say, cocking my head to the side. "Why?"

"Gotta make sure you can do basic math." I nod, because that makes sense. "You comfortable serving men?"

I start to scrunch my nose, *because what a weird question*, but Cari's earlier words ring back to me and I hold his gaze. "Why wouldn't I?"

"Ain't my place to judge." Buck lifts his shoulders and lets them fall. "How about if they get a little handsy? We have a no tolerance policy, but..."

"I mean, I'd rather not be fondled by patrons, but I wouldn't shank anyone with the cutlery."

Buck's facial hair twitches in what I think might be a smile. "You know how to walk in heels?"

"I do."

"You comfortable showing a little skin?"

These questions are getting a little weird, but I press on. "I'm confident in my body."

"Tattoos or piercings?"

I quirk a brow at him. He sighs.

"How many of each?"

"Too many tattoos to count. Piercings: ears, septum, nostril, nipples, and..." I trail off, not particularly wanting to disclose my clit ring. "...Other places."

Buck nods knowingly. "Lemme call Lesli." He picks up a phone from somewhere on his desk and taps around on the screen. "Come on back," he rumbles into it. *Here's to hoping that meeting Lesli is a good thing.*

A few seconds later, an incredibly petite—both in shape and stature—woman walks into the room. Her skin is a deep golden bronze, and her platinum blonde locks hang clear to her ass. She's decked out in a sparkly pink mini dress and sky-high matching stripper heels.

She walks right past me—as graceful as a gazelle, which in seven-inch heels is hella impressive—toward Buck and flings herself down onto his lap.

He wraps his meaty arms around her number-two-pencil-thin waist. One bear-paw hand completely covers her ass and the other wraps around her shoulder, hiding it from view. They kiss as though they've been separated for ages. I feel like such a voyeur watching them, but he has to have at least eighteen inches on her in height and is easily four times as wide. Honestly, I'm wondering how they even have sex—because looking at the two of them, he is the very definition of *does not fit.*

The two are veering toward pornographic when I clear my throat. Buck and Lesli break apart slowly, as if the loss of full-body contact will kill them.

Once Lesli is back on her feet, she tugs her dress down and straightens it before fluffing her hair and reapplying her lipstick. She obviously has practice, because she applies the vibrant shade perfectly without a mirror.

"Buck here thinks you might be a good fit," she says, skipping over small-talk and pleasantries. "But I've got a few questions of my own."

"Ask away," I say, trying my best to not sound as weirded out as I am—which is a lot. This interview is just... weird. Like, weirder than applying for porn weird.

"Bra size?"

My eyes widen. If I had to guess, I'd say they're as big as saucers. "Thirty-four C."

Lesli's gaze flicks down to my breast and she nods. "Sequins or tassels?"

What the fuck? "Uh, sequins."

"Leather or lace?"

I laugh through my nose and shift in my seat. "Leather?"

"You sure?" she asks, her tone whip sharp. "We don't have time for wishy-washy employees. You're either all in and ready to commit or you can head on down the road to TGI Fridays." You wouldn't think a little pixie-sized woman could be so scary, but Lesli with her hands on her hips, fierce eyes, and scowling Botox'd lips is intimidating as hell. All four-foot-eight of her.

"Leather. I'm certain." Even if I have no clue what she's asking me, I know I prefer leather to lace. Lace is thick and hot and completely unbreathable. Oh, and scratchy, too. The only place I like lace is on curtains or a pillowcase.

"Tallest heel you can walk in?"

"Four inches."

"I suppose that's decent."

She goes on to ask a few more questions—*can I dance? Am I comfortable flirting a little with the patrons? Do I have any bartending experience? Do I want any?*—before finally offering me employment.

Something in my gut tells me I'm missing something big, but my brain is too caught up on the pay to care. I know most waitresses survive on their tips, but Buck and Lesli appear to pay their employees quite generously.

I know I should probably be wary, but let's be real—I was willing to do porn; waitressing should be a cake-walk in comparison. So, I readily agree, scrawl my name at the bottom of the employment agreement and agree to show up Monday night for training.

CHAPTER 21
WEST

The day passes in a blur of seemingly unending paperwork. Contracts, listings, and more. Not to mention, I am working on a few new ideas to branch Virtual Kitty out. The current focus of VK is women—what can I say? It was the brainchild of my horny, smart, and well-funded teen-self.

However, older and wiser—and even better funded—I firmly believe it is time to be a little more inclusive and open up channels for broader tastes.

Unfortunately, that means paperwork, lots of fucking paperwork, and for every contract Colton and I read through, another three appear in its place. Page after page of redundant legal-ese.

"This is mind-numbing," Colton groans, stretching his arms over his head.

I shoot him a wry grin. "As a lawyer, isn't mind-numbing paperwork kind of your thing?"

"Furthering my point," he drawls, rising from his chair. "If I'm bored, that's saying something."

"Truth."

"Early dinner?" he asks, checking his watch, which prompts me to glance down at mine. It's nearly five.

"No can do. I'm taking Stacia out tonight."

Colton sighs. "You're still barking up that tree?"

"Woof!" I grin crookedly.

"Damn fool," he mutters, packing his things away.

"There's something there, man. I know it. And I'd be remiss not to explore it. Plus, Mimi Jean always said the best things are worth the battle."

"And you think sticking your dick in her and impregnating her falls into that category?"

Visions of our romp in her bed flit through my mind—the way she lit up beneath me, the sound of her breathy moans, the way she gave as good as she got, how fucking combustible we were. Add in the fact that she's just a down-ass-chick, and yeah, she definitely falls into that category.

I tell Colton so, too. "Yeah, man. Honestly, at this point, she's the only woman I can see having my kid." And it's true, too—I can fucking picture her artfully inked belly swollen with my baby so clearly. It's honestly kind of hot to imagine.

The weight of my words settles over the both of us, though the true meaning of them doesn't hit me until much later.

I freshen up at the office before heading to the house to grab Stacia, hoping like hell she took me at my word when I told her to dress sexy. Then again, she could wear a burlap sack and I'd still probably pop a chub; she's just that hot.

Knocking on my own front door is a little weird, but I want this date to be as date-like as possible. Which means waiting on the porch for my girl—not that she's mine.

But she could be, my brain shouts.

A moment or two later, the door swings open, and I fucking swallow my tongue at the sight of her, a vision in red. Her Jessica Rabbit-red hair is styled in that way designed to make a man think of sex, and her lips are painted a shade or two darker than her shining locks.

As I drag my hungry eyes over her, I find myself noticing things about her that I've never paid attention to on a woman before. Like the way her long, sooty lashes nearly touch her brows and the way her brown eyes seem to glimmer with specks of gold.

She has her bull ring—as I like to call it—flipped up, but the hoop on her nostril glints, a little red stone winking at me from its center.

Her red dress fits as though she was poured into it. With spaghetti-thin straps, the top resembles a bra with a V between the cups, showing off her ample—and bite-able—cleavage. From there, the fabric sweeps down her body, clinging to her like a second skin, ending mid-thigh.

The look is wrapped up with matching red heels. She's all curves and confidence as I lick my lips, helping myself to a second serving, dragging my eyes back up to hers. I pause at the soft curve of her belly, visible through the stretchy, clingy material of her dress, and I can't help but wonder if her panties are red as well.

She clears her throat, and I find my words. "You look fucking decadent."

She laughs through her nose. "Decadent?"

I step closer, skimming my hands over her hips, pulling her into me. "Good enough to eat." My voice is low, wolfish, hungry.

She inhales a stuttered breath and puts a little distance between us. "Ready?"

I give her one last once-over. "More than." I offer her my arm and she takes it as I walk her to my car and help her into the passenger seat.

"Where are we going?" Stacia asks as I drive us out of town. All I offer in reply is a tight-lipped smile. When I veer onto the interstate on-ramp, she asks again. "Seriously, West. Where?"

"Shh," I murmur as I reach for the volume dial on the stereo. "Just let me surprise you."

Shockingly, she nods and settles back into her seat as I crank the volume, flooding the small space with music.

An hour later, we've reached our first destination of the night—dinner. I park and kill the engine before coming around to open her door. "Hope you're hungry," I tell her as I press my palm to the small of her back, guiding her to the entrance.

"Always." On cue her stomach rumbles as I open the door for us, holding it to allow her to pass. "Oh my God," she moans as we step into the cozy space. "It smells like heaven."

She's not wrong either. The scent of sizzling garlic, roasted tomatoes, and fresh basil cling to the air. Stacia takes in the space as I speak to the hostess, who quickly whisks us back to our table.

Over delicious and crusty rosemary bread, Stacia and I swap stories of our childhoods. The difference in our respective upbringings strikes me; hers was happy and relatively normal, whereas mine was a literal shitshow.

Our conversation pauses when our main courses are delivered, and we lose ourselves to the delicious and authentic Italian flavors.

"Oh, shit," I start as our plates are cleared. "I'm such a jackass. How was your interview?"

She beams. "I got the job!"

My heart pinches at the thought of seeing her less. *What the… weird.* "Oh, yeah? Tell me about it?"

"It's… I'll be waitressing." She shrugs.

"Nothing wrong with that." I hold her eyes, blue locked on brown, conveying my sincerity. "Not a single thing."

"Thanks. I know that, it's just… everything feels so… heavy."

I'm half-tempted to tell her I'll solve all of her money problems if she'd just have my baby, but that seems sleazy, and if—when—she agrees to this, I want it to be on her terms and not because I manipulated her into it. "I can't even imagine. Hopefully tonight we can take your mind off of everything for a while."

Dessert—a shared slice of cheesecake with a fresh raspberry compote—is placed before us, along with two cappuccinos. Stacia spoons off a small bite and wiggles in her seat. "Fuck! That is to die for."

"Glad you approve."

"Question, though." She licks a drop of sauce from her spoon. "As amazing as this place is, why did we go so far out of town for dinner?"

I wink and set my card on the edge of the table for the server. "You'll see."

After the bill is settled, we head back to the car and I open her door first, like the gentleman I am. Once she is seated, I lean against the open door, unlooping my tie and tugging it off. "Wh-what are you doing?" she asks, looking up at me with wide eyes.

"You'll see," I say again. "Just not yet." Before she can protest, I bend down into her space and secure my tie around her eyes, effectively blindfolding her.

"West Larson!"

Cupping the back of her head, I feather a kiss to her forehead. "You trust me, beautiful?" She nods as I trail my knuckles over her shimmering cheekbone. "Good. We'll be there shortly."

I rush behind the wheel, start the ignition, and head off toward our final destination, hoping she loves it as much as I think she will, especially seeing as I paid a shit-ton to go after-hours.

Fifteen minutes later, we arrive. A tremor of nerves works its way through me. While I'm ninety-nine-point-nine percent positive this will be a home run, there's still that small, tenth-of-a-percent chance she'll hate it.

"Are we here?" she asks, reaching for her blindfold.

Reaching out, I intercept her hand, holding it in mine. *Fuck, her skin is soft. So soft.* "Hang on."

I come around and help her out and up. She sniffs the air, and I grin. "Any ideas?" I ask.

"Smells like motor oil, gas, and burned rubber."

Is it weird that her knowing that kind of turns me on? Probably so, seeing as before her I didn't know shit about cars. Hell, I still don't. I picked out my Mercedes AMG GT-R because it looked sick, went fast, and I knew my parents would hate it.

I crowd her from behind, wrapping her in my arms

with my hands resting low on her stomach. The position is intimate, and before I can stop it, I'm envisioning us just like this, only in my mind, she looks as if she's swallowed a basketball. *Shit.*

Skimming my nose up her neck and my hands up her sides, I gently tug on the tail of my tie, letting the blindfold fall away. "Surprise," I whisper before pressing a kiss to that sexy-as-hell space where her neck and shoulder meet.

Stacia freezes. "West." My name a prayer on her luscious red lips.

"Yeah?"

"Is this for real?"

"As real as you and me."

"There is no you and me," she whispers, and while the words send a little zip of sadness through me, I know what she means.

Without thinking about it too much, I say the first thing that comes to mind. "But there could be." She whirls to face me, her eyes wide and lips parted. Not wanting my weird sentimentality to ruin her night, I add, "Now, let's go drive some fast cars!"

I start off without her, leaving her slightly stunned. "C'mon, Stacia! Don't you know if you're not first, you're last?"

At that, she hurries after me. "Lord baby Jesus in a ghost manger, I love that movie!"

A stupid smile splits my cheeks, because I just *knew* she'd get the reference.

As we enter the building separating the parking lot from the track, a thought suddenly strikes me. "Are you gonna be able to drive in those?" I glance down to her heels that would look so good digging into my back or wrapped around my shoulders.

Her eyes lower as well, and she blinks twice before looking back my way. "Yup. Not a problem."

The gentleman working behind the counter comes out. "You sure?" he asks, reaffirming my concerns.

Stacia scoffs. "One-thousand percent. I've been driving in heels since before I could even legally drive."

We both look at her with our brows lifted.

She rolls her eyes. "Give me the paperwork I need to sign, and I'll prove it."

"Now hold on," the employee says. "I don't know if this—"

"It's fine..." I glance down to his name tag. "...Jed. I personally will cover any incidentals if something goes awry."

"I need to call the owner."

I gesture for him to go ahead and pull Stacia to the side. "Don't make me put my money where my mouth is."

She grins wickedly. "I can think of much better places for your mouth to be."

Fuuuuuck. I'm about to tell her, in great detail, all of the places I'd like to put it, but Jed returns. "I don't like it, but the owner gave the all-clear. Paperwork's on the counter."

Stacia squeals and darts over, initialing and signing as needed. I follow suit, and Jed leads us out to the track, where a line of brightly colored exotic supercars wait. Ferraris, Lambos, McLarens, Porsches, and more.

Stacia approaches the cars, stopping to admire each one, and looking at her standing with them, she could easily be the hot chick on the car rag cover. She's literally a walking wet dream.

"Which one do I get to drive?" she asks, her voice breathy, almost as if she's turned on, which fucking turns me on.

"Whichever you want," I tell her, and without a lick of hesitation, she marches over to a matte black McLaren with vibrant red accents. "This one. Oh, God, please this one."

"Why that one?" I ask, secretly loving her enthusiasm.

She trails her fingertips over the door and sighs. "A V8 with twin turbos with seven-hundred-and-ten horses under the hood and zero-to-sixty in less than three seconds." She shivers. "This car is fucking sex on four wheels."

Both Jed and I barely suppress groans because, this fucking woman, she's sex in heels. And a total badass. The walking embodiment of the *full package*. She... she's kind of perfect.

Jed regains his composure before I do. "Let me grab the keys." He heads back to the office, and I saunter over to Stacia. She pivots back to face the car, admiring it while I admire her.

"It's so beautiful," she murmurs.

I step up behind her, caging her against the sleek body with an arm on either side of her, my palms splayed against the door. I press my lips to her shoulder, moving them up the slope of her neck in an erotic slide. "You're goddamn right."

Something in my tone—probably my reverent need —has her looking back my way over her shoulder. Her eyes glimmer as she stares up at me. "You're so beautiful," I croon before claiming her lips with mine.

I nip at her bottom lip, trying to deepen our kiss. Unfortunately, Jed the cockblock returns, keys in hand, just as she opens for me. I back away from her with great reluctance. Being near her, touching her, is a special kind of high—one I could easily become addicted to if given the chance.

Stacia goes to move past me to claim the keys, but I stop her with a hand to her wrist. "This isn't over." I tug her back into me, kissing her hard and fast. "Far from it."

Slightly dazed, she moves away from me and toward Jed. He hands her the fob. "Track's yours for the next two hours." He glances down to her heels. "Don't... just be... careful. Be careful."

She shoots him a grin. "Sure thing. Careful is my middle name."

Jed huffs and relinquishes the keys. Stacia lowers herself into the McLaren with grace and ease. I, on the other hand, struggle to get in. "Why the fuck is this thing so low?" I grumble under my breath.

"Speed. For speed." Stacia taps the start button and steers us to the start line. "You ready to go fast?"

"Impress me, baby."

She shoots me a shit-eating grin and proceeds to blow my mind—and almost my load—as she expertly flies down the track. She maneuvers the tight turns with ease and hits the straightaways like a speed demon. She drives like a dream, and I can safely say I'll be beating off to the memory of her controlling this beast of a machine, all dolled up in red, looking like pure fucking sex, for a long time to come.

Once our two hours are up, Stacia guides the McLaren back to its spot in the lineup, exits the vehicle, and tosses the keys to an awestruck Jed. As she passes him, she winks and says, "Told ya."

"You ready?" I ask, bringing my hand to the small of her back, guiding her back to the parking lot through an exit gate.

"No. I could easily go another two hours."

I shift, wrapping my arm around her waist, drawing her close. "I'll bring you back."

She stops and spins into me, her arms twining around my neck. "Thank you. This was so thoughtful and amazing. Absolutely the best date I've ever been on."

We both lean in at the same time, drawn to one another. I capture her juicy lower lip and suck on it before she opens for me. I claim her lips the way I'd like to claim her heart: boldly and without any remorse —*wait, what?* I lick and bite, sting and soothe, as I show her just how much I want her, deciding to focus on the physical need I'm feeling for her rather than the emotional. At least for now.

She clings to me, and I hitch one leg up, letting her feel just how much she affects me. We remain lip locked in the parking lot, kissing endlessly, moaning, grinding, and exploring one another's bodies over our clothes like two horny teens.

I'm damn near ready to strip her bare and claim her on the hood of my Mercedes, and judging from the way her nimble fingers are plucking at the buttons of my shirt, Stacia's on board.

That is, until Jed exits the building and clears his

throat—loudly. *Fucking cockblock.* "Y'all have a nice night," he says. "Just take it somewhere else."

Stacia's cheeks pink, and she buries her face in the crook of my neck. "Oh my God!"

I lift a hand in a half-hearted wave. "Will do."

Jed lingers for a minute, presumably to make sure we leave, so I wrap an arm around Stacia's shoulders and guide her the rest of the way to my car, this time with no sexy detours, sadly.

The drive home is quiet. You'd think after getting hot and heavy, it'd be awkward, but it's not. If anything, it's a comfortable sort of silence, one that feels warm and familiar, ridding us of the need to fill the void—because there isn't one.

As I pull into the driveway, I notice Stacia's fallen asleep. And as much as I'd love to pick up where we left off, I'm not about to wake her. With great care, I extract her from the car and carry her upstairs. She must be fucking exhausted, because she doesn't stir, not even a little.

With her laid on her bed, I slip her heels off but leave the rest and tuck her under the fluffy duvet. I linger for a minute, absolutely enraptured by her beauty. I'm not sure when it happened, but at some point, my feelings for her became… *more.*

Suddenly, she's more than my friend. She's more than my roommate. She's more than a hookup. And if I have my way, she'll be my everything.

I lean down and press a soft kiss to the corner of her mouth before heading back down to my room. I have a lot to think about. A lot to plan. A lot to put in motion if I'm going to well and truly make this stunning woman mine.

CHAPTER 22
STACIA

After my magical date with West, the rest of the weekend flew by, and now, all too soon, it's Monday. And while the first day of the work-week typically sucks, this particular Monday sucks extra hard as it crash-lands in a flurry of soul and uterus-crushing cramps. *Just what I need…said no woman ever.*

Except, cramps mean my period is coming, and my period means that mine and West's irresponsible, but oh-so-hot sex didn't leave any lasting consequences. So, actually, yes, this is just what I need, even if it will make training tonight miserable. Plus, it's nothing a hot shower, coffee, and a few Tylenol can't cure.

With the studio being blessedly closed on Mondays, I take it easy, lounging in bed most of the day with a heating pad on my belly. I alternate between reading my latest find—a book about sexy-as-sin pro-baller Lukas Callihan and the fiery redheaded teacher who brings him to his knees—and watching episodes of my favorite cooking show. I may not be able to cook, but I love watching other people do it. It's truly a shame West can't cook, because that man, shirtless in a kitchen, would be fucking lethal. *Maybe it's for the best he isn't competent in the kitchen, seeing as I already want to tear his clothes off and mount him on a daily basis anyway. Especially with how he's been woo-ing me.*

It's like he's put a spell on me that makes my vagina tingle at even the sound of his name. Add in that I have firsthand knowledge at how adept he is between the sheets, and even him doing the most mundane things gets my panties wet. Things like twisting the cap off of a water bottle—*hello, arm porn*—or the way he always brings me a snack when he makes himself one.

At four, I shove all thoughts of the thoughtful, sexy bastard aside and start getting ready for training. I pull my hair up into a high ponytail and curl the ends before doing what I call my everyday-glam makeup routine— light contour and highlight, golden eyes with winged liner, and a glossy nude lip.

Getting dressed presents a small conundrum— neither Buck nor Lesli ever mentioned a dress code. I opt for a pair of black leather high-waisted leggings I nabbed from AJ, pairing them with a black fishnet shirt over a lace bralette, punctuating the look with my favorite blue heels. The outfit may seem a little risqué for work, but based on Cari's outfit, and Lesli asking about leather or lace, I think I'll blend right in.

I arrive at Buck and Lesli's a few minutes early, wanting to stand back and observe the place a little before my official training starts. The parking lot is jam-packed, and it's barely five o'clock. The sight alone gives me hope—if they're this busy on a Monday night, maybe I'll make it after all.

Quickly, I reapply my lipstick and free my hair from

the ponytail, fluffing it so it falls in soft, effortless waves around my face. I check my phone and see a missed call from my grandma. There's no voice mail, though. I fire off a quick text letting her know I'll call her on my break. God love her, she may not know how to text back, but she can open and read messages like a boss.

It strikes me as a little odd that the lobby area is full —*of men*. Cari spots me from behind her podium and smiles widely. "Hey, girl!"

I lift my hand and wriggle my fingers. "Hey!"

"You excited for your first night?"

"Uh, I think."

"We're all a little nervous the first time." Cari winks as a man in a sharp suit approaches, and I shuffle out of the way. She gives him her undivided attention.

He eyes her hungrily before turning to me. "Is her section open?"

"Oh, shoot," Cari pouts, batting her sooty lashes. "Red here is still in training."

Suit-guy's lips thin. "Fine. Max then."

Cari nods. "You got it. I'll let you know when your table is ready, Mr. Cartwright."

He heads off to wait, and I shuffle back over to the podium. "Is he a regular?"

"Every Monday on even months and every third Thursday without fail."

"Whoa. And you remember?"

She shrugs. "What time are you on?"

"Training at six. I figured I'd come early and scope the place out."

Cari wags her brows. "Have fun."

I scurry around the partition and stop dead in my

tracks. "What the fuck?" I breathe out in astonishment as I take in the scene before me.

Tits. Tits every-fucking-where. Waitresses dressed in nothing more than booty shorts, pasties, and heels expertly navigate the bustling dining room, heads held high and trays higher.

"Oh my God." My pulse hammers as the urge to haul ass back to the safety of my car seizes me.

I pivot around, intending to do just that, when Lesli steps out of what seems like thin air. "Stacia, you made it." She checks her sparkling Michael Kors watch. "Early, too. I like it."

"Oh, yeah, um—"

"Let's head back to the office and get started." Lesli loops her arm through mine, setting off toward the concealed door before I can even reply. She's shockingly strong for her size, and if I don't want to end up flat on my ass in front of this very crowded room, my only option is to follow along.

In the privacy of the dark office, Lesli launches right into everything, giving me no time to adjust. "You'll be shadowing Max tonight. It's all pretty straightforward. Flirt a little, but not a lot. Be open, but not available. Take their order, run the trays. Bat your lashes, lick your lips, cash out, collect your tips."

I stare at her, totally slack jawed.

"I recall you saying you prefer sequins and leather." She snatches a bag off of the desk. "Go ahead and get changed. I'll step out and give you a minute."

In the blink of an eye, Lesli's out the door, shutting me inside of the office alone with my mile-a-minute thoughts. Hesitantly, I peek in the bag. A few scraps of fabric lay in the bottom—my uniform. *Oh, Jesus.*

Figuring I have a few minutes, I slide my phone out of my bag and pull up AJ's contact card. My finger is hovering over the green button when an incoming call comes through. It's my grandmother, again. "Hey," I answer, secretly relieved to hear from her. If anyone can give me a little pep, Gramma can.

"Stacia, dear," she greets, and I can tell from her reserved tone she has bad news.

My relief plummets into a pit of fear. "What? Is Dad okay? Is Mom?"

"They're both—" She hesitates then plows ahead. "As fine as they can be given the circumstances."

"Then what?" I ask. It's not like her to beat around the bush.

"Your grandpa and I can't afford the rental anymore. We're going home, and your mom is coming with us."

The fear spreads, filling my veins, numbing my extremities. Sure, they only live an hour away, but here in this moment, we may as well be on opposite sides of the Grand Canyon. "Oh," I whisper, fighting like hell to keep my tears at bay. I knew from the start this would be a strain on them financially, and I'm damn sure not going to make my grandma feel bad for giving her best.

"I understand," I say, steeling my resolve. This job may not be ideal, but I'll make it work. "I picked up a second job. Once I nail down my schedule, I'll come out and visit."

"That's good, Stacia." Gramma's voice is an odd blend of upbeat and melancholy. "Real good."

We end the call, and I blink away my pesky tears. I might have been two seconds from walking out five minutes ago, but now…now I'm going to wiggle my ass into these microscopic leather booty shorts, cover my nipples with some glorified sparkly stickers, and make the fucking best of it, because right now my family needs me more than ever.

Plus, not all that long ago, I was considering doing porn and surely topless waitressing is a better option than porn. *I mean, it has to be—right?*

CHAPTER 23
WEST

t's been a week since Stacia picked up her second job, and it feels like I only see her in passing, like we're nothing more than two ships in the night. I know she's helping her family, but fuck, I miss her. Which is the only explanation for why I'm downstairs attempting to wow her with a home-cooked breakfast instead of getting ready for my much-dreaded standing bimonthly lunch with my dear old dad.

But really, how hard can eggs and bacon be?

Hard. Really hard.

My sad attempt at eggs are stuck to the pan and my bacon is charred beyond recognition.

"What's that smell?" her soft, sleepy voice asks as she pads into the kitchen.

I sigh as her bare legs come into view. "That would be my attempt at making you breakfast."

Swear to God, she swoons. "You tried cooking for me?"

"Try being the keyword."

She saunters closer, her sleep shirt skimming her

thighs. She pops herself up onto the island and draws me between her legs, her fingers tangling in my hair. "A for effort," she whispers before brushing her lips against mine.

I'm not really sure what's happening right now, but Jesus H. Christ, I will attempt three meals a day for her for life if this is the response it gets me.

Sure, we've become more and more affectionate, but we typically straddle that friends-slash-more-than-friends line pretty well, angry sex and car date aside.

But now, as our kiss moves from soft and exploring to five-alarm-fire, I can't help but wonder what brought on this highly welcome change.

Especially when she starts rubbing her panty-clad pussy against my thigh like a cat in heat, pun intended.

As much as I'd love to let this continue and to lose myself in the Mecca that is her body, I can't without talking to her first. I need to know her frame of mind before this goes any farther. So, with great willpower, I pull back.

I keep one arm locked around her middle and cradle her cheek with my free hand. "You okay?" I ask, praying like hell she doesn't think I'm rejecting her.

Stacia blinks and shakes her head. "Oh, wow. Shit." She tries to wriggle free. I step back to give her some space, but not enough to duck and run. "I...I am so sorry. I don't know what came over me. I've just been..." She trails off.

"You've been what?" I ask, gently trying to coax the words from her.

She buries her face in her hands. "Turned on. Like, every little thing revs me up here lately. I'm like a teenaged boy. A stiff wind is enough to make me want to…ugh!"

I bite my lip to hide my grin. "There's no shame in wanting sex."

She pins me with a glare. "I know that. And I'm not ashamed. Just a little embarrassed that I basically tried to dry hump you in the kitchen with the smell of burned bacon wafting in the background."

I step back, and wink, trying to keep things light and easy. "You can dry hump me anytime."

"You ass," she says, but she's laughing and smiling now. *Mission accomplished.*

"Any particular reason you think you're so…randy?" I finish the sentence in my best British accent—ala Austin Powers—and waggle my brows.

"I just had my period." She shrugs, like that explains everything. Hell, maybe it does. Because while I know my way around a woman's body, I don't know shit about its inner workings.

Still, I nod like it makes perfect sense. "You free today?" I ask, changing the subject.

"I was gonna try and visit my mom, actually."

"In town?" I ask, following my question immediately with another. "Do you ever go see your dad?"

She deflates. "Uh, no. To both. Dad refuses to let Mom and me visit; says he doesn't want us to see him like that. And my grandparents couldn't afford the cottage anymore, so they're back home and Mom went with them."

An ache forms in my chest as her brown eyes brim with tears. Before I know it, I find myself asking, "Want some company for the drive?"

"Really?" she asks, twirling a red strand around her

index finger, her tears drying as a breath-stealing smile tips up the corners of her mouth.

"Really, really. I just need to shower and make a quick phone call."

She lets out a happy squeak and hugs me to her again. "Thank you!"

I run my knuckles over her cheekbone. "Don't you know I'd do just about anything for you?" I ask, leaving her, rosy cheeks and all, with those parting words.

In my room, I dial up my dad, mentally prepping for whatever he may throw my way. "Weston," he barks into the phone after the first ring.

"I'm not gonna make it today." I cut the shit and get straight to the point.

Steely silence meets my proclamation followed by a low growl of displeasure. "You must have misspoken, because it sounded like you were canceling."

"Yeah, that's because I am. Something's come up."

"This is a standing reservation, Weston. We—"

I cut him off. "I know, I know. But I think we'll both survive missing just the one." *Hell, if it were up to me, I'd miss them all.* It's not exactly fun to sit across from someone who's supposed to love you unconditionally and listen to them put you down and pick you apart as if they're filleting you with a hot knife, removing flesh from bone. Real talk: the filleting would probably be more enjoyable than lunch with Roland Larson.

"This is unacceptable. Something more important than your own blood? Your family should be—"

I cut him off again. "You're hardly one to talk about

family. I have a friend who needs me, and I'm going to be there for her. Some things are more important than blood—a foreign concept, no doubt. But try hard, maybe you'll get it." I end the call, knowing if we keep going back and forth, three things will inevitably happen: He'll snap. I'll snap. He'll involve my mother, and Jesus Christ, no one on this earth can guilt trip as well as she can.

However, knowing my dad has a penchant for needing the last word, I switch my phone to silent before hopping into the shower.

As the steaming water rains down on me, visions of Stacia creep to the forefront of my mind. Of her spread out on my king-sized bed as I make her thrash and moan with pleasure. Of her crying out my name as I make her come over and over.

Before I know it, I'm stroking my rock-hard dick to thoughts of the sexy-as-hell redhead who shares a roof with me, wondering how I can convince her to share her heart as well.

CHAPTER 24
WEST

A week has passed since Stacia and I drove out to her grandparents' place. Talk about a culture shock—which sounds dumb as hell, seeing as I didn't even leave the state—but it's the only way I can think of to describe it.

With my parents, everything is a grand affair. And I mean *everything*. Be it a random weekday lunch, a birthday, an anniversary, or a wedding, it's going to be at least five courses with a full wait-staff and, nine times out of ten, a valet.

At Stacia's family's house, it was down home, serve yourself in the kitchen and eat it at the table casual. And the food…*goddamn*. While I love Mrs. Zelda's cooking, it doesn't hold a candle to Mrs. Harrison's—I mean, Gramma, since that's what she asked me to call her—meatloaf and mashed potatoes. And don't even get me started on the rolls she made. Long, delicious story short, the woman can fucking cook.

What I really took away from spending time there, though, was what kind of life I want for my kid. I want them to have a home full of life and love, not just material things. I want them to have laughter and memories and pillow forts. I want them to have all of the things my own parents neglected to give me—the things my Mimi Jean tried her best to provide. I want them to feel safe and loved. And fuck me, more than anything else, I want it with Stacia Kellan by my side.

However, she isn't currently anywhere near my side, in any sense. It seems like lately, every time we try and make plans to chill, something comes up. She either gets called in or some completely preventable crisis pops up with Dirk Hellerman—the C.E.O of the company who's recently started courting me in hopes of securing a retail contract with my company. They want an exclusive line of Virtual Kitty merch products in a chain of adult novelty stores they run. Between all of that, we may as well be strangers.

Case in point, last night, we had plans for pizza and a movie that fell through due to the studio having a last-minute booking—a bride was left high and dry when her makeup artist never showed, and Stacia jumped on the opportunity.

And tonight, I have an in-person with Dirk, Lord fucking help me. From our conference calls and emails, I've deduced the dude is a jackass supreme, but his company is stupidly successful, so I'm—mostly—willing to deal with him. At least, until I decide if I want to move forward or not with him; if I do, I'll be passing his ass off to Margaret with zero regrets.

Colton will be tagging along as my counsel and to act as a buffer. Which is kind of ridiculous, seeing as he runs far hotter than I do. But, whatever. His ill-tempered ass is still better than me going it alone.

Especially seeing as Dirk has us meeting at the douchiest joint in three counties. I'm sure he thinks he's being clever—arranging a meeting between a sex toy-slash-adult film company and the owner of a virtual porn empire at a topless steakhouse, but dude missed his mark by a long shot.

Don't get me wrong. I love tits. I love steak. I just don't particularly love random tits bringing me my steak. I haven't even told Colton where we're going yet, because he'll probably have a coronary—and I don't have the time or inclination to baby his ass.

Stacia's working her second job tonight. She's been picking up shifts left and right, working her fine ass into the ground trying to help her dad. I swear to God, I'd bankroll her entire life if she'd let me. But…she won't. Strong, stubborn, sexy woman. Which is all the more reason to go out of my way to do things for her.

Sure, it started off as a way to woo her into having my baby, but it's turned into something…more. Doing shit for her, making her coffee, and rubbing her back, has almost become second nature. There's just something about seeing the smile on her face that sends a zip of pleasure through me.

Which is why instead of dashing out the door to pick up Colton like I should be in order to make our dinner meeting on time, I'm writing out a message in icing across the cookie cake I ordered for her.

Seeing as I'm not a fucking baker, my frosting writing could use work. It's a little lopsided and slanted at an angle. And maybe what should read '*Not as sweet as you*' looks more like '*Hot as sweat as you*', but whatever. It's the thought that counts.

I quickly replace the plastic lid on the container

housing the cake and scrawl out a message on the inside of a card before laying it on the lid, grabbing my keys, and running out the door.

I swing by Colton's place to collect him; he lives in a swanky condo uptown, complete with a doorman and a valet. He's waiting at the curb when I pull up, looking perturbed by my lateness. But in the words of Kanye, he should be honored I even showed up for this fake shit.

Well, not really. Technically, I'm the grateful one—to have him as not only my lawyer, but as my friend and all-around right-hand man.

However, that doesn't mean I'm not going to fuck with him.

I lower the passenger window as I roll to a stop at the curb. "C'mon already, man, we're gonna be late."

Colton scowls darkly, and I crack up. "Asshole," he mutters as he folds his tall frame into my passenger seat.

"Only on days that end in Y."

Colton massages his temples. "You exhaust me." I laugh again, and he punches my arm. "Are you ready for tonight?"

"I think so. I know where I'm not willing to compromise."

"And where's that?" my friend asks, quizzing me like I don't know my own business or ethics.

"No sweatshop productions. No child or slave labor manufacturing. I'd prefer domestic, but will bend as long as he can provide up-to-date insights on the factories and their practices." Colton nods, pleased with my reply.

"Where are we eating?" he asks, as I turn right onto the interstate ramp.

I duck my head, taking care to keep my hands at ten and two on the wheel. "About that…"

"What, West? What?"

"He made reservations without consulting with me. Legit. He called Margaret today with the time and location."

"Where?"

"Buck and Lesli's."

Colton frowns. "That sounds familiar. Why?"

I'm torn between letting him find out for himself and telling him. I waffle for two exits before finally settling on the latter. "It's that topless steakhouse in Dusk River."

Colton whips his head around to look at me. "You're fucking kidding."

"Unfortunately, no."

"That's a mark against doing business with him in my book."

I flick on my blinker and merge onto our exit. "Mine as well. However, I'm at least willing to hear him out, and if I decide not to work with him, I'll do so with a clear conscience."

Colton groans as the building comes into view. "Double. You're doubling my fee for every hour of this shitshow."

I laugh. "Okay, bud. I'll pay you double to eat steak and stare at scantily clad babes."

"You're paying me double to deal with this level of unprofessionalism and for holding my tongue on telling this jackass exactly how I feel about it."

I kill the engine and wink. "Got it. C'mon. The quicker we get in, the quicker we get out."

Colton huffs, but follows all the same.

The two of us walk into the steakhouse side-by-side, a united front, ready to handle anything Dirk could possibly dish out.

The quiet of the parking lot fades away into a cacophony of sound as we step into the building. There's sultry music, raucous laughter, and loud conversation coming at us from every angle. It's a sensational over-load—and not in a good way.

The tall, curvy blonde behind the hostess stand smiles as we approach. "Hey there, gentlemen. Do y'all have reservations this evening?"

"We do. It should be under Hellerman."

Blondie's eyes twinkle. "Oh, lucky you. You're in Red's section."

Colton laughs dryly. "Lucky us."

"Just you wait," she says, winking as she steps out from behind her stand. "Now, if y'all will follow me, I'll take you on back to your table."

The din of noise surges even louder as we step around the partition and into the actual restaurant. The sound of scraping knives and clinking glasses ring through the room.

We weave a path through the room until we're dead center. "Gentlemen!" Dirk stands, greeting us. Whereas Colton and I are both dressed in sharp suits, Dirk looks like he's headed to a luau, wearing khaki, beach-looking pants with a matching partially unbuttoned shirt. "So glad you could make it."

Several members of his team are also seated at the table. Dirk makes quick introductions but a flash of familiar red hair distracts me and I miss most—okay, all—of their names.

It's not until Colton elbows me that I realize both he

and Dirk are sitting. Quickly, I claim my chair, trying to shake off the weird feeling making waves in my gut. "What is your deal?" Colton hisses in my ear, pretending to peruse the menu.

"I...I thought I saw—" I shake my head, dislodging my crazy thoughts. "It doesn't matter."

Colton glares. "You forced me here, be present."

A server decked out in five-inch heels and a barely-there black fishnet mini dress—literally, it only covers her vag and nipples—swings by our table. "Gentlemen," she purrs, her voice low and sultry. "I'm Max, and I'll be grabbing your drink orders real quick while Red finishes up with another party."

She leans forward, placing her ample, shimmering cleavage directly into my line of sight, and while in the past I'd have been all over a fine specimen like her, here and now, she does nothing for me. Nope, these days, it seems the only woman that gets my engine revving is a certain tatted-up redhead with killer curves and a smart mouth I'd love nothing more than to kiss any time I damn well pleased.

"What'll you have, handsome?" she asks me, clicking her pen before deliberately nibbling on the end of it in a way I'm sure most men would find seductive.

As politely and disinterestedly as possible, I order a gin and tonic, my eyes never once straying to check out all of the skin she has on display.

Unruffled, Max moves onto Colton; he, too, orders impassively. I'll give her credit though; she simply smiles and trots off to the bar to place our order. Then again, a girl like her probably isn't ever lonely for long.

Dirk doesn't waste any time launching into why he

thinks I should partner with his company. "West, your proposed product line virtually sells itself."

"Then why do I need you?" I ask pointedly.

The man grins. "I was hoping you'd ask that."

Colton and I glance at one another from our peripheries, likely thinking the same thing—that Dirk Hellerman is full of shit.

"You see, while your product, listed on your site, sells with minimal effort, I want to expand your horizon —and profit margin. In working with me, I can do two major things for you. I can up your production and get your line in front of new consumers."

I signal for Colton to take notes while Dirk and I go back and forth.

"Tell me this, Dirk, is your company LGBTQ friendly?"

The men seated with us exchange looks. "We aren't currently plugged into that market," he says smoothly. But I know what he really means.

"That's a shame, because it's an avenue Virtual Kitty is heavily pursuing."

Dirk starts to speak but a smoky, sultry, and very fucking familiar voice interrupts. "Sorry about that wait, gentlemen." I tilt my head back to look at the woman who sounds so much like my roommate. "The bar is —West!"

A deep growl works its way up my throat as I shove back from the table to stand. My chair screeches across the floor, silencing damn near the entire dining room. "This?" I hiss the word. "This is where you work?"

Colton mutters under his breath at my side, but I pay him no mind. No, my eyes are locked onto Stacia, standing before me in nothing but a pair of skimpy-ass black leather boy-shorts with red glittery hearts covering her nipples.

"Um, yeah," she says softly, her eyes looking anywhere but my face.

I step closer to her, and even in her four-inch heels, I'm still a head taller than her. "This has to be a joke. Tell me you're fucking joking."

Stacia straightens her spine and snaps her gaze to mine. "You are not about to judge me for—"

"For what?" I sneer. "Serving overcooked steaks with a side of tits and ass?"

She crosses her arms over her already perky tits, making them even fuller. It's then I notice every single man at our table—save for Colton—is eating her up with their eyes.

Anger mars my vision. She's fucking mine. No one else should see her like this. Only me.

I whip my suit jacket off and cover her very exposed body with it. She sputters, "What do you think—"

I pay her no mind as I grip her elbow and drag her away from the table. She stumbles in her tall heels, and I scoop her up into my arms. "Privacy, now!" I grit out, because if I have to see one more of these sorry, most likely married motherfuckers check her out, I might snap.

I *know* exactly what they see and how it makes them feel. On a scale of one to ten, Stacia is easily a fifty. And the way her glorified leather underwear hug her hips and ass, combined with her creamy, inked skin and ninety percent of her tits on display, she paints a rather alluring package—one every man in that room is imagining unwrapping, myself included, which only pisses me off more.

I know I have no real claim to her, but I want one. *I need one.* I need this woman to be mine. For this body to be for my eyes, my hands, my mouth…my worship *only*.

With a small tilt of her head, she points me toward a door I never would've noticed on my own. I tow her into what appears to be an office, slamming the door behind us and flicking the lock.

I drop her to her feet and box her against the door with one hand planted beside her head and the other by her waist. "Do…do you know what you fucking do to me?" I moan, well aware of how absolutely crazed I sound.

She blinks back at me with her big, brown, doe eyes, and I snap, lunging for her lips. I show her with my tongue and teeth and pawing hands just what she does to me.

"West," she whimpers. "You're gonna get me fired." Her palms move to my chest, and I tense, sure she's about to shove me away. So imagine my surprise when she tugs me closer, hitching one of her legs around my hip.

I grind myself into her leather-clad heat. "Good."

She parts her lips, possibly to argue, but I seize the moment and bite down on her lower lip. She gasps and claws at my chest as the pressure of my teeth toe the line of pleasure and pain. Drawing her lip into my mouth, I suck away the pain.

Stacia's hands move from my chest to my hair as she lifts her other leg. I palm her ass and pin her to the door. "Do you know?" I ask against her skin.

She shakes her head, her hips still rocking in search of friction and relief for the fire she's ignited in both of us—hell, probably in every man out there, except

Colton. The thought brings my anger right next to my lust in my mind as the two warring emotions duke it out.

"Do you know how it feels to watch other men look at you? To see them lust over you? Do you have any idea how badly I want you?" I spit my questions rapid-fire, never once backing away from her. "Do you know how it makes me feel to see you here, your body on display for other men, when I'm more than willing to take care of you and your every need?"

My words hit their mark, and she shoves me away. "No! No, you don't get to make me feel bad or guilty or ashamed. I'm doing my best to help my family. They need me. I need money. This is—"

"So help me God, if you say the only way—" I shout, completely uncaring that the entire restaurant is most likely getting a closed-door show.

Stacia glares at me with fire in her eyes, gorgeous chest heaving. But before she can speak, someone knocks on the door. "Open up," calls a gruff yet commanding voice.

I move Stacia behind me and swing the door open to reveal a mountain of a man and a hummingbird-sized woman. "Wanna explain to me why you're holed up in *my* office with *my* employee?" the big man asks.

Any other day, I'd probably be intimidated. Hell, I probably should be right now. He could easily snap my neck or call the cops...but right now, all bets are off. "First of all, she's not *your* anything."

The petite woman titters as Stacia practically shoves me out of her way. "Buck, Lesli, I am so-so-so sorry for my *roommate* coming in here and causing such a distur-bance. I assure you both it will never happen again."

"Damn right, it won't," I growl. "You won't be returning."

I'm half expecting her employers to kick my ass out, but instead they exchange a knowing look and sport matching grins.

"You don't get to decide—" Stacia starts, but Lesli cuts her off.

"Head on home. Max will cover your section. We will talk tomorrow."

Stacia stares at the woman, slack jawed. I, however, give her a nod of thanks before scooping my woman back up into my arms and heading for the door.

I slow as we pass my table. "Gentlemen, I'm afraid we will have to pick this up at a later date."

Dirk and company all stare in shock—can't really say I blame them. This is clearly not the outcome *any* of us were expecting.

"Don't worry," Colton calls out after us, his tone completely flat. "I'll find my own way home." *Shit. His fee just tripled.*

As I exit, the hostess calls out with laughter in her voice, "Told you Red was a treat!"

CHAPTER 25
STACIA

I stay mute as West deposits me into the passenger seat of his car, silently mulling over all of the various ways I can kill him if Buck and Lesli fire me.

The entitled little shit truly doesn't *get it*. I *need* this job.

He comes around and flings himself down into the driver's seat and angrily punches a knuckle into the start button.

Once we're on the interstate, I let him fucking have it. "Do you realize you probably just cost me my job?"

He snorts but doesn't otherwise reply.

"I'm glad this is all so amusing to you. That my life falling apart at the seams can—"

"Stop." His voice is gentle but commanding, and for some dumb reason, I listen. "You wanna scream at me? Fine. Wanna yell at me? Fucking go for it. Or, and this is just a thought, you could set your pride aside and let me help you."

I sweep my hands over my outfit—or lack thereof. "Pretty sure I ditched my pride when I took this job."

"Then agreeing to let me help you shouldn't be the humiliation you're advertising."

"Help how?" I ask, fully prepared to turn him down flat.

His grip on the wheel tightens to white-knuckle, but he doesn't speak.

"Listen, pride aside, I'm not willing to take a handout for this. AJ already offered, and I turned her down, too. For starters, the amount of cash I need is astronomical. Like, more than you can legally gift in a year. So, even if you had that kind of cash—"

West cuts me off. "I do."

The arrogance of his reply sends ice into my words. "—I wouldn't feel comfortable being indebted to you like that."

"Hmm," is all he says, and it takes every ounce of my fraying willpower not to chuck my stiletto at him.

The rest of the drive to his house passes in a tense, thick silence. I can't help the sigh of relief that escapes my lips when he pulls into the driveway; I can't wait to hide away in the sanctuary of my room.

"Get showered and change, and then we'll talk," West says, ruining my escape plan.

We both exit the car. "Let's just talk tomorrow."

He keys in the unlock code and opens the door. "You have twenty minutes. A second over and I'll come find you."

I shoulder past him and stomp up the stairs, not willing to test him by arguing.

Exactly fourteen minutes later, I pad downstairs and into the kitchen dressed in a pair of sweats and a tank top, my face scrubbed free of makeup and my hair still dripping.

West slides a mug of coffee my way on the island and says, "I've called your work. Buck is going to send your purse and shit with Colton, and he's going to drive your car back since he rode over with me."

I nod and take a sip. "What happened tonight isn't okay, West."

"Agreed. Though, something tells me we're not on the same page as to why. So, let's agree to disagree."

"Just like that? You want me to move on and be okay with the fact that your little caveman stunt probably just cost me my job?"

He scrubs his hands over his face and for the first time, I notice how stressed he looks—like the entire weight of the world is on his shoulders.

"What…what if I had a solution that could help both of us?" The pitch of his voice is soft, imploring, and I find myself nodding for him to continue. "You need money for your dad's bond and legal counsel and for just life in general. And I need to be able to fulfill the terms of my trust. I know it's crazy, but I really think this could solve both of our problems."

I stare at him. "You…can't be suggesting what I think you are."

He sips his own coffee. "That depends on what you think I'm suggesting, Stacia."

"For me to…to have your baby."

West nods once. "That is exactly what I'm suggesting."

I scoff. "My womb in return for what?"

"As you know, by fulfilling the terms, I gain access to not only my Mimi Jean's house but also a monetary inheritance."

"Good for you," I deadpan.

"Consider it yours."

I balk. "What?"

"The inheritance. It's in a few different accounts. I'll add your name to the account, making it as much yours as mine. You can spend every cent on helping your family."

Jesus. It almost seems too good to be true. When I hesitate still, he tacks on, "And Colton will represent your dad, gratis."

Again, I ask, "What?"

West nods, picking up steam. "Yeah. Yes. Just have my baby, and your financial worries will be over. And it's not a handout," he adds emphatically. "Win-win."

It takes me a minute to find words. Because what he's offering is insane. Then again, I was willing to do porn and was working in a topless steakhouse, so how is this any worse? Other than the fact that a child is a lifetime commitment. And an actual person with actual needs and not something to drag into the hot mess of my life.

"Listen, I appreciate your willingness to help me. And I want to help you, too. But being a single mom at twenty-two doesn't exactly sound like my idea of a good time. Plus, you're my best friend, West—well, one of— and my roommate, and I don't want to ruin either of those relationships by muddying the waters. The very last thing I want for us is to be at one another's throats because I'm stuck at home with our kid, resenting the very air you breathe, while you're out with your latest flavor, living it up."

"It won't be like that, Stacia. I swear it."

"How?" I ask him. "How can you make such a bold promise?"

"Because I fucking love you!" he growls before clamping his lips together. West's eyes are wide with panic, and his breathing is erratic. From the looks of it, his shouted admission surprised him just as much as it did me.

"You love me? What—as a friend?"

He opens his mouth and closes it. Then again, like a fish on dry land.

"West." I whisper his name, and his eyes fly to mine, as if tugged by a string. "You can't possibly mean that."

He shifts closer to me, bringing us toe-to-toe. Cupping my cheeks with his hands, he peers down at me, his blue eyes brimming with emotion. "I mean it," he murmurs. "I didn't realize it until here and now, but I fucking mean it. And even if you don't agree to having a baby with me, I'll still spend my days showing you exactly how I feel."

I try to shake my head, but his hands on my face prohibit the movement. Everything about him screams that he's telling the truth, but at the same time, does believing him make me gullible? Am I so desperate for an easy out that I'm willing to believe that he loves me?

My lips part, but no words come out. His confession seems to have robbed me of my ability to speak. "West." I say his name again, as no other words will form on my tongue.

He shushes me. "You don't have to answer me tonight. Sleep on it; we can talk tomorrow."

"Tomorrow then," I reply softly. It's not even half-past nine, but I feel like I could sleep for days. I'm emotionally exhausted.

West leans down and presses his lips to my forehead in a lingering kiss before we both retreat to our respective bedrooms for the night.

CHAPTER 26
STACIA

or as bone tired as I was last night, sleep sure didn't come easy. I tossed and turned, with the events of last night and dreams of motherhood spinning like a hamster on a wheel.

It's almost like an out-of-body experience. Objectively, I know if this were happening in a book or on a show, I'd be shouting for homegirl to have his baby and to let him love her right. But…this isn't either of those things. It's my life. My *very real* life, where my family—and apparently my heart—are on the line.

The question, at this point, comes down to whether I am even remotely ready to be a mother. Would I be a good mom?

West says he loves me, but I've never been in love. *Liar*, a small dark part of my brain shouts, but I ignore it.

Seriously, is it normal to be twenty-two and to have never loved anyone outside of family and platonic friends? Am I even capable of maternal affection or is that part of me broken?

Frustrated and overwhelmed, I pull the pillow from the other side of the bed over my face and scream into it.

"Rough morning?" West asks, humor tinging his voice as it penetrates my pillow sanctuary.

"Ugh!" I groan, pressing the down-filled cushion harder onto my face.

West chuckles, and the deep timbre zips straight to my clit. The bed dips, and he rips the pillow away and tosses it to the floor. "Brought you something," he says as the scent of fresh espresso fills my nostrils.

My greedy hands reach for the coffee, but halt midway as my even greedier eyes take him in. He's wearing nothing more than a pair of compression boxers and a cocky smile. *The Lord is testing me.*

"Here, let me help," he says, passing me my mug and thankfully not commenting on my gawking.

I take a long sip, feeling infinitesimally more human. At least enough to do more than stare at the hunky, confusing slab of man meat sitting on the edge of my bed.

West watches me over the rim of his own mug, patient as ever as I gulp down my coffee. Once I drain the cup, he takes it and places it on the bedside table. "Sleep well?"

I go for honesty. "Not really."

He winces. "Sorry about that."

"It's not your fault—well, not entirely."

"I hate to lay it on you first thing, but did you think any on my proposition?"

"Uh, it's pretty much all I've thought of."

"Right, right." West reaches over and takes my hand in his.

The sensation of his calloused palm sliding over my

smooth one sends a wave of butterflies dancing in my belly. I'm not sure what it is about this man, but it almost feels like he was custom made just for me. Every single thing about him heightens my senses. From his panty-melting looks, to his intoxicating scent; from his delicious voice, to the way his hands feel so right on me—West Larson gets my blood rushing and my heart racing.

"And?" he asks when I don't elaborate.

I take a deep breath. "And…I…I'll do it."

West stares at me. "You mean it?"

"Yeah," I say, almost not believing it myself. "I mean it."

The second the words leave my mouth, West tackle-hugs me to the mattress, pinning my body beneath his much larger one. Though, instead of feeling smothered or crowded, I feel protected and cherished as he peers down at me with an unmistakable softness in his gaze. "You won't regret this. On my life, Stacia, you won't. I'll cherish you, and this gift you're giving me. I'll love our child and raise him or her by your side."

Tears dot my lashes. "Please don't make promises you don't plan on keeping."

He brushes my messy morning hair out of my face. "I meant what I said last night. I love you. I don't know when my feelings morphed into something more, but they did. I. Love. You. And I'm going to love our child as well—with every ounce of my being, I'll love y'all. And I don't expect you to just take my word for it. I'm going to show you. Day in and day out, I'm going to show you."

My lips tremble as I try and keep my tears at bay. "You're too much," I say as a lone tear falls over.

"Sometimes I worry I won't be enough. You're… you're so full of life and fire and passion, and some days I just feel lucky to be able to bask in your glow. But, Stacia, I don't want to leech your light. I want to add my fuel to your fire; I want you to combust and burn so brightly that nothing can ever stand in your way."

I press my lips to his, the salt of my tears flavoring our kiss. "You're so much more than enough, West. You're…everything."

We stay in my bed kissing and touching and talking until the sun sits high enough in the sky that its light fills my entire bedroom.

"Are you free the rest of the day?" he asks.

"Yeah, I just need to call Lesli and get ready."

"Come find me when you're done, and we'll go see Colton."

I tilt my head to the side. "What? Why?"

His eyes smile back at me. "I said I was going to *show* you. Step one, having Colton draw up a contract making sure you're protected in case, God forbid, things don't work out between us."

I gape, shocked by his honesty.

"Plus, we need to break the news about him working for your dad for free. I'm really looking forward to that one." West hops up from my bed. "Oh, and there's a cookie cake downstairs. I bought it for you."

As sad as it is, my heart pitter-patters at his words. "You got me a cookie cake?"

"Mmhmm. Decorated it myself, too." He leans down and kisses me. "Save me a slice." And with that, he's gone.

My mind is racing as I dial up the steakhouse. To say I'm overwhelmed would be an understatement. It feels like things between West and me are moving at warp speed, but at the same time, it feels like this has been a long time coming.

Obviously, I've had a thing for him since we met, but us moving in together seemed to be a catalyst. It, along with some other variables, brought us together in a way that I don't think would have otherwise happened.

And while, yeah, it's hella unorthodox, maybe we can work?

Jesus, Stacia, slow down. You're having his baby, not wearing his ring, I scold myself, shutting down the craziness stirring in my brain.

"Buck and Lesli's, this is Lesli."

I clear my throat. "It's Stacia, hi."

"I've been waiting to hear from you," she says. I was expecting her to sound mad, but if anything, she sounds…smitten.

"I am so sorry for last night." *God, was it only last night?* "My behavior was highly unprofessional."

"Your boyfriend was mighty upset." Lesli laughs, which surprises me even more.

"He…he's not my—"

Lesli cuts me off. "Let me tell you a story?"

"Uh, sure?" This conversation is not going at all the way I imagined.

"Fifteen years ago, I was twenty-five and a single mom. Buck and I had only met a time or two in passing, through mutual friends and what not. We had chemistry, the works, you know? But I brushed it aside. My kid came first, right?"

"Yeah, right," I agree, seriously confused.

"Anyway, I was working at a seedy little strip club, shaking my ass and twerking on a pole to keep food on the table. One night, a bachelor party came in, and sure enough, Buck was a part of their group. Girl, when he saw me on that stage dressed in nothing more than six-inch heels, a see-through thong, and a smile...he charged it like a bull. Scared the shit out of me when he yanked me down and tossed me over his shoulder."

She laughs lightly before continuing.

"I squirmed and flopped, but his grip never faltered, not even when he smacked my bare ass and barked at me to be still. He marched me right out of that club and took me to his place. This probably sounds crazy to you, but we talked for hours, about anything and everything. I told him about my son and he told me I wouldn't be going back to the strip club. He said I was his and that he'd provide for me and my kid. We've been together ever since."

The line falls quiet as my mind tries to process her insane story. Finally, I say, "I don't mean to be rude, but why did you tell me that?"

"I told you that because the young man that carted you out of my restaurant last night looks at you the exact same way Buck looked at me."

My heart thumps in my chest. "How?" I whisper.

"Like you're something precious, something worth treasuring...like you're his."

I shake my head in denial, even though she obviously can't see me. But...he did say he loved me. *Holy shit, he really does love me!*

We chat a bit longer, and before we end the call she says, "I hate that you won't be with us, the clientele loved you, but you and your man are welcome to stop by anytime."

I thank her, even though I know good and well West

won't darken their doorstep, before ending the call and tossing on some clothes and heading downstairs.

CHAPTER 27
WEST

tacia says she didn't sleep well. *That makes two of us.* All night, sleep eluded me as I obsessed over the fact that I told her I loved her. At first, my declaration shocked me as much as it did her.

"Because I fucking love you!"

As the words settled, I realized they were true. I do love her, and maybe I have for a long time. Only, it's been an ever-changing love. First, I loved Stacia as a friend. But those feelings have grown, multiplied, and now I love her in an entirely foreign way. Which is probably why my own words shocked me so much.

Speaking of shock, I am damn near dying to see the look on Colton's face when we stop by and catch him up. I tap out a text to him, letting him know we'll be by after lunch—I'll give him a little head's up; wouldn't want him to stroke out or anything.

His reply is instant.

COLTON

She didn't murder you in your sleep? I'm shocked.

ME

It gets better.

COLTON

Something tells me we define the word better differently.

ME

If we do, my definition is the right one. See you soon.

I toss my phone down onto my bed and get ready for the day. Fifteen minutes later, I emerge dressed in dark wash jeans and a white button-down with the sleeves rolled, and a pair of brown leather boots on my feet.

When I step into the kitchen, Stacia is seated at the island, looking like a vision as she licks a glob of frosting from her finger. "This cake is yum!" she says after she swallows.

"Glad you like it."

She smiles softly. "The message was cute—once I figured out it was calling me sweet and not sweaty."

"Safe to say cake decorating isn't my forte."

"I know something you're good at," she hedges before pinching off another bite.

"Yeah? What's that?"

"Being good to me. Every day since I've moved in, you've managed to show me how much you care in one small way or another."

As much as it pains me, I blush. *Fuck.* Hearing her say that has me wanting to hop around and beat on my chest in victory. "I'll always show you I care." I come around the island and lay my lips on hers. She opens to me instantly, tasting of sugar and chocolate and something inherently Stacia.

While I could easily drown in her kisses, I draw back, pressing one last soft kiss to her mouth. "C'mon. Let's head out to see Colton."

She smiles. "Lead the way."

"This is so not what I was expecting," Stacia says as we pull up at Colton's office. She's right, too. Looking at Colton, you'd expect him to be in a high-rise or at the very least uptown, but nope. Colton runs his firm out of a small building in the heart of the downtown area. To the left of him is an upscale baby boutique and to the right is a yoga studio. No shit, his front window has a flower box, and his door, which is painted pale purple, has a fucking wreath on it.

"Yeah, it's…" I trail off, not knowing what to say. Colton is…Colton.

We walk inside, and Stacia gasps. The entire office is one large space, and the far wall is comprised of floor-to-ceiling bookshelves. He even has a sliding ladder.

"Oh, good, you're here," Colton says as dry as ever.

"We need a contract drawn up," I retort proudly, knowing he'll know what I mean.

He heaves out a resigned sigh and mentally I shout *I told you so!*

"All right, have a seat."

Stacia and I both sit, and Colton pulls out his legal pad. "Let's do this. Terms and conditions?"

I don't waste any time. "Stacia has agreed to be the

mother of my child," I state, even though he very much knows why we're here. "Since her father's incarceration, she has lost her health insurance. I would like to either have her added to mine or to have a policy purchased in her name at my expense. Also, any medical costs our child may incur will be paid by me as well."

"West!" Stacia exclaims, but I grab her hand and give it a gentle squeeze before continuing.

"I also want it in writing that if our relationship deteriorates, for any reason, that she'll receive a set amount of child support, as well as a small stipend."

"How much?" Colton asks.

I rattle off a sum that makes both of their eyes bulge. "Also, make note that I will cover any childcare costs as well as future schooling and college tuitions."

Colton grits his teeth, and Stacia digs her nails into my hand. "West, this is a lot."

I pay neither of them any mind. "Obviously, I'd like to come to all of the doctors' appointments throughout the course of the pregnancy, and I would very much like to be in the delivery room—assuming that is okay with Stacia." I turn to her. "Is it?"

"Uh, um. Yes." Her voice is a breathy whisper. "Are you sure about all of this?"

"Yeah," Colton says with an edge. "Are you?"

"One-thousand percent."

"Okay, well, if that's it, I'll get a contract typed up for the two of you to sign." Colton starts shifting papers on his desk, most likely searching for the external mouse to his laptop.

"It's not," I tell him, halting his movements.

"What else?"

"I need you to add that the cash inheritance from my

grandparents' will go to Stacia free and clear, and as soon as I gain access, I'll need you to start the paperwork with the bank to have her name added to the accounts."

"Can we speak privately?" Colton asks.

"Oh, and I promised Stacia you'd represent her father. Pro bono, of course."

If Colton were a cartoon character, he'd have steam billowing out of his ears right about now. "Of course." He says the words with a smile, but it's so far from friendly it's not even funny.

"Great. We're gonna grab lunch. Think you can have the contract ready by the time we're done?" I offer him an exaggeratedly sweet smile. "We'll even bring you something back!"

He balls his hands into tight fists—probably to keep himself from punching me. "Quadruple."

"You're the man," I tell him as I stand. "Let's bounce, baby mama."

Stacia laughs. "Did you just…"

I swat her bottom. "Sure did."

"Can I speak to you?" Colton asks. "It'll be brief."

I look from him to Stacia, and she nods encouragingly. "I'll wait out front."

I pull her in for a quick kiss and reclaim my chair. Colton waits for the door to shut behind her. "West, man, are you sure about this?"

"It sounds crazy, I know it. But, Colt, I…I love her, and I'm gonna do right by her."

"Whoa, hold up. Love?"

"Yeah. Love. As in, over the moon, fucking crazy about her."

His usually stern face breaks into a smile. "Good for you. Truly, I'm happy for you. I'll whip up this contract while y'all eat. Oh, and hey, your girl's purse and keys are in my car."

"Thanks, man." I stand again and head for the door.

"Oh, and, West," Colton calls after me. "I'll take three tacos—the ones with the red cabbage and the cotija cheese, extra lime wedges."

I nod. "You got it."

With my hand on the knob, Colton stops me again. "I wasn't joking when I said quadruple."

I toss my head back and laugh as I walk out of his office. *Jackass.*

Outside, I look for Stacia, but she's nowhere to be seen. Until a flash of red catches my eye through the window of the business next door—the baby store.

A self-satisfied smile tugs at my lips as I enter the store. In front of the back wall, there's an oversized counter with two cash registers. Shelves stack the wall behind it, loaded down with a variety of baby trinkets—rattles, brushes, mirrors, cups, pacifiers, and more. To the left, there's a few furniture displays. To the right, there's neatly folded displays of the tiniest clothing I've ever seen, as well as the hottest woman to ever shop for them.

I make my way over to her, loving the sight of her in here. "Found you."

She turns and grins. "Gah. I guess I'm putting the cart before the horse, here, huh?"

I take the small outfit from her and examine it. I'm holding what has to be the smallest sweatshirt known to mankind. It's a golden yellow color with a patchwork rainbow on the front in orange, blue, and a creamy white. Plainly put, it's fucking cute, and I don't care how lame that makes me sound. "Nine months will pass in the blink of an eye."

"You don't think I'm crazy to be in here shopping for a baby we haven't even made yet?"

"Far from it. Honestly, watching you in here, seeing you hold these small-ass clothes…all it does is make me want to take you home and take you straight to bed."

Stacia pretends to clutch her pearls. "You mean you wanna take me to bed without feeding me first? What kind of man are you?"

I give her a wolfish smile. "An insatiable one with the hottest baby mama in the damn world."

She laughs, and the sound is pure magic. "See anything else you like?"

"Only everything. This whole line is to die for."

I glance down to the table, my eyes roving over the various outfits. A pair of sweatpants that coordinate with the top I'm holding catch my eye, and I grab the smallest pair. "Let's get these."

"What? Really?"

"Yeah, really. Our baby's first outfit."

We head to the register where I pay. As the cashier bags up our purchase, Stacia leans in and whispers in my ear, "Now we've really gotta get to work."

"Swear to God," I growl, "the second we get home…"

She grins, heading for the door. "But we've gotta get food for Colton first and sign the contract."

I sweep her into a hug from behind. "Fuck Colton and fuck food; I'll just eat you."

A small, barely audible moan slips past her pink-slicked lips, and it takes my all not to toss her into the front seat and floor it all the way back to our place.

CHAPTER 28
STACIA

West and I grab my purse and keys from Colton's car and stash them, along with our shopping bag, in his before heading down a block to the best little taco truck that ever was.

Technically, they have an actual brick and mortar location on the other side of town as well. The line is long, but fast moving, and well worth the wait.

When it's our turn, West prompts me to go first, and I waste no time ordering three General Tso's tacos—which is super weird for me. I always get spicy beef tacos, hold the lettuce. But something made me ask for these today.

I step aside for West to order—steak for Colton and chicken for him, as well as an order of chips and guac and three glass bottle Cokes. While we wait for our order, he asks, "Are the GTs any good? I've always wanted to try them but never have."

"Uh, I'm not sure, honestly. I've never had them."

West nods. "Adventurous, I like it."

"That's the thing, I'm really not. I am a creature of habit with my food. I rarely try new things."

He looks perplexed. "Then what made you order them today?"

I shrug. "Fuck if I know. Here's to hoping they're good."

Our ticket number is called and West collects our food, passing me the drinks and chips. Side-by-side, we head back to Colton's.

Not shockingly, Colton has transformed his desk into a freaking table, complete with placemats and cutlery. "You eat your tacos with a fork?" I ask, horrified.

He rolls his eyes. "No, the fork is for the meat that drops out."

"That's what the chips are for."

He swipes a Coke from me and pops the top, not bothering to reply. West watches me as I unwrap my first taco. Housed inside of a homemade corn tortilla is steaming hot General Tso's chicken topped with shredded cabbage and cilantro. A lime wedge is bundled into the end of the foil packet as well. "May as well go all in," I murmur, squeezing the lime juice over the top of my taco before bringing it to my lips.

The flavors explode, bursting across my tongue in a symphony. The mix is eclectic and timeless, spicy and citrussy. "Oh-ma-gah. Dis is ahmazin'," I say with my mouth full. Straight up, one bite, and I'm hooked.

"Let me try?" West asks, and I bring my taco to his lips. He groans, no doubt experiencing the same euphoria I just did.

All the while, Colton watches us dispassionately as he chows down on his own food.

I scarf down my remaining two tacos, along with some of the chips and guac, washing it all down with my cane sugar-sweetened Coke. "Mmm. I can totally see this being a pregnancy craving meal."

West beams. "You just say the word, and I'll be here ordering for you. Rain or shine, I'm gonna keep my baby mama happy."

Colton gags. "Let's dial it down a notch, or twenty. Y'all literally decided to do this today. Not to mention, it's sickening to watch. Before I know it, y'all will be wearing coordinating outfits and finishing each other's sentences."

I smirk at him. Going on looks alone, you'd never think he'd be so uptight. But apparently his lean muscled physique, dirty blond hair, chiseled jaw, and piercing green eyes are all a facade to hide the massive stick up his ass.

I go to call him out, but West beats me to it. "Jealous, big man?" *Take that! We already finish each other's thoughts!*

Colton scoffs before dabbing at his mouth with a napkin. "No, not particularly."

"It's okay, if you are," I tell him, testing the waters. He and I had a really rocky start, but he's going to be in my life for a long, long time to come.

"I'm not."

I continue like he didn't reply. "One of these days, some woman is gonna knock you on your ass, and you, too, will be annoyingly smitten."

"Highly unlikely." He rolls his chair back to his printer and grabs a stack of papers from the tray. "Sign these," he says as he rolls back.

West plucks the sheets from his hand and reads over them—twice—before scrawling his name in the desig-nated spots. I go to sign as well, but he stops me. "Read it first."

"But you signed it," I state.

"Right, but I read it first. And now I want you to read it so you know it's everything we discussed—no more, no less, no funny business."

This man. I do as he suggests and read over the contract. It's verbatim from the terms we laid out; I sign on the dotted line and turn to West. "So, is this the part where we fuck?"

West gulps audibly, and Colton shoots out of his chair like something bit his ass. "Not in my fucking office!" he shouts, causing West and I to crack up.

"You're damn right it is." West springs up from his chair and extends a hand down toward me. "Let's go."

I allow him to pluck me up from my seat and into his arms. He skims his nose over my neck, bringing his lips to rest at my ear. "We were rushed last time—frenzied. Today though?" He steps out of the office and into the sunshine. "Today, I'm gonna go slow, take my time, worship every inch of your body. I'm going to show you how good we are together. I'm gonna make you tremble and beg and scream my name over and over again."

My breathing is shallow as his dirty promises fizz through my veins, my core pulsing with desire. "That's pretty big talk, West."

He shifts my weight to one arm and opens the car door, depositing me into the seat.

He wags his brows. "You know what they say about guys with *big talk*, right?"

I smile. "What?"

"Big cock, too."

Laughter bubbles out of me. "No, I'm pretty sure that's not what they say."

He crowds the door and cups his junk. "Maybe so,

but you already know it's true for me. But, I'm all too happy to give you a reminder."

I lick my lips and rub my thighs together. "Then what are you waiting for?"

He flies around to the driver's side and slips behind the wheel in record time. "Buckle up, baby mama."

The ride home passes in a blur of sexual tension and roving hands; by the time we make it back to the house, I'm nearly panting with desire. "Your room or mine?" I ask as we step into the house, immediately feeling idiotic. He made it clear when I moved in that he doesn't…*entertain*…in his bedroom.

He parts his lips to answer, but I rush to beat him. "Never mind. My room is perfect."

I set off for the stairs, making it all the way to the base before two strong arms lock around my middle from behind. With a hard yank, I'm plastered against the broad planes of West's chest. "My room's fine. In fact, I've been fantasizing about seeing your pretty red hair fanned out across my sheets for weeks."

"What?" I ask in disbelief.

"That's right." He skims his hands up from my waist, moving them over the dips of my sides and up to my breasts. He palms them, testing their weight; the sensation of his touch is like a live wire. "This shit with us is new. It's undefined, so I'll break it down real quick for you. You're *mine*. I want you in *my* bed, screaming *my* name, while I do my best to put *my* baby inside you."

I shiver as his words move over me, lighting me up from the inside out. "Then take me to bed."

West spins me to face him and captures my lips in a searing kiss before tossing me over his shoulder. He moves through the house with ease, even with my added weight, which only turns me on more.

In his room, he wastes no time tossing me down onto the center of his feather-soft mattress. Standing above me, he looks down at me with an almost feral heat in his eyes. His fingers move to the buttons of his shirt, popping them one by one as I look on eagerly.

When the last button is undone, he slides the shirt off, letting it drop at his feet. He moves to his belt buckle next, but I rise up to my knees and place my hands over his. "Let me."

His hands fall away, and I work his belt and pants open. I tug the denim down his hips, revealing his very prominent, boxer-covered erection.

Impatient, he knocks my hands away and finishes stripping so that he stands before me naked and proud —a statue of strength and virility meant to be worshiped —and worship him I will.

The second he moves toward me, I spring forward and take him into my mouth, sucking and licking, reveling in his guttural groans. "Fuck, Stacia, baby. Fuck!" He fists my hair and guides himself deeper into my throat, almost to the point of pain. He's relentless as he thrusts himself into my mouth, and I fucking love it. I love how he manhandles me and takes what he wants.

His entire body trembles as he pulls me off of him with a wet pop. "Strip," he commands, his own hand replacing my mouth as he stares me down. He's a man barely restrained, and it's now my single goal to make him break—to drive him wild with want and need.

Still on my knees, I tug my top over my head, loving

the way he groans at the sight of my sheer lace bra. His eyes practically glaze over with desire as I pull the cups down, baring my breasts to him.

Reaching around, I pop the clasp and let the lacy fabric fall away. I trail my hands over my chest and nearly hiss as my fingers graze my nipples before sliding down my belly to the waistband of my skirt. But before I can do anything, West is there, his strong body hovering over mine as he pushes me down onto my back.

"What was it you said? *Mmm.*" He licks his lips. "Let me." His voice is a rasp as his hands move to the zipper on the side of my skirt.

In what feels like no time flat and eternity all at once, he has me stripped to nothing, with his lips moving over my feverish skin until he settles himself between my restless thighs.

The first swipe of his talented tongue, and, I swear to God, I see stars as they're being formed. He feasts on me as if I'm his last meal, licking and sucking until I'm a wanton, moaning mess, begging for him to fill me.

"Oh my God," I pant, digging my fingers into his hair as he brings me to the edge of bliss. "I need you."

"Need me to what, baby?" His words are a low growl, a fire to my already flickering flame.

"To fuck me. I need you to fuck me."

With one last long lick, he moves up my body, lining us up just right. "With pleasure," he groans as he pushes into me.

We both moan as he pulls back and rocks into me again. With every thrust, his tempo increases, until he's pounding into me like a man possessed.

My hands claw at his back, his chest, anywhere they can reach as he commands my body with his. Sweat dots his brow, and I fucking love it—I love knowing that it's his pursuit of my pleasure that's exerting him so fully.

"Yes, fuck, yes!" I cry, wrapping my legs around his waist.

"Feels so good," he pants, one hand gripping my chin, keeping my eyes on his as the other reaches between us. "Gonna need you to get there," he tells me as his skillful fingers join the party.

"So close," I moan as he drives into me with enough force to rattle the walls. He pushes my right leg flush with my chest, allowing him to hit a spot I've only ever dreamed about, and before I know it, I am screaming his name as my climax takes me.

Pleasure swims through my veins and over my skin as he continues, relentless in his pursuit of his own release, until finally, his movements falter, and he follows me into oblivion before collapsing on top of me.

"Bet we nailed it on the first try." He speaks the words against my pleasure-soaked skin, and I smile.

"Ah, but this isn't the first time."

West rolls off of me and pulls me into him so I'm cradled against his side with my head on his chest. "I didn't say first *time*, I said first *try*. Pay attention, baby mama."

"Smartass." I tilt my head to look up at him, only to find he's already looking down at me with a soft look. "Think we should try again? You know, just in case?"

"Fuck yes!" He grips me around my middle and moves me to straddle him like I'm a ragdoll. I'm shocked to find he's actually ready to go again, his hardness prodding at my entrance.

With a sexy smirk, I waste no time sinking down onto him for round two.

CHAPTER 29
WEST

The past three weeks with Stacia have been fucking magical. Now that she's only working the one job, our spare time is spent together, usually in between my sheets.

She's even taken to sleeping in my bed most nights, which I love. There's nothing better than waking up to her wrapped around me—well, other than waking up to her lips wrapped around my cock. That's the absolute best.

The two of us have kind of created our own little cocoon. But tonight, our presence has been requested—no, demanded—by Brock and AJ.

He texted me this morning, most likely at the urging of his little spitfire of a wife, and informed me we were getting pizza at seven.

So, here we are, outside of Vinny's at five til seven, waiting on my cousin and Abby Jane to show.

Which they do, at seven on the dot. AJ rushes us and pulls Stacia into a tight hug. I feel a surge of guilt as I watch the two women. I've been selfish with Stacia's time, and that's not fair. Here and now, I resolve to share my girl with the world, even if I'd much rather keep her all to myself.

As they talk in quiet, rapid tones, Brock's keen eye notices me watching her, and he lifts a brow in question. "It's a thing," I say.

"What kind of thing? A *you're into her* thing or a *she's a means to an end* kind of thing?"

Even though it's fair, I bristle at his implication. "It's an *I love her* kind of thing."

Brock rocks back on his heels and whistles. "Didn't see that coming."

His wife spins to us and loops an arm around his middle. "You're the only one then." *Swear to God, she has the hearing of a damn bat.*

"Yeah, whatever," Brock says, pushing the worn, glass-paneled red door open. "Let's eat."

The four of us all groan in anticipation as we step into Vinny's. The scent of fresh dough, simmering sauce, and crushed garlic rushes to meet us.

We grab a table near the window and order promptly when our server comes by—draft root beers all around, with a pepperoni and half black olive and green pepper pie for the married couple, and a meat lovers for Stacia and myself.

"So, strangers," AJ murmurs with an evil glint in her brown eyes. "How long have y'all been official?"

Stacia's cheeks go rosy, and I love it. "About a month."

"Uh-huh, and anything else to share?"

I reach over and take Stacia's hand into mine, silently letting her know I'm here no matter what she chooses to disclose to her best friend.

"We'll catch up soon. I promise."

AJ pins her with a glare, menacingly pointing a breadstick her way. "I'll hold you to that, bitch."

"I'm sure you will, but tonight, let's just have fun!"

Over the course of way too many slices, the four of us catch up. It's insane the amount of shit that can happen in just a few weeks—case in point, Stacia and me. But also, the nonprofit AJ works for received a new grant, and she's over the moon, and Brock is playing in an upcoming PGA Pro Tour qualifier.

Needless to say, big things are happening, and the four of us have a lot to celebrate.

"We should go to Quixote's!" AJ exclaims. "You know, for nostalgia's sake."

Brock gives her a dopey smile. "I'll never say no to having you grind on me, firecracker."

In the past, I'd have fake gagged and told him he was a sap, but now…now I totally see the appeal. "I'm down if you are," I say to Stacia, who is already nodding. "Great, then let's go."

We settle our tabs and head for the nightclub where I first saw my future baby mama.

"Shit, I wish your cousin still worked here," AJ says as we all eyeball the crazy long line.

"Wouldn't that be nice." Stacia pouts. "You know, I haven't heard from him at all since he deployed."

AJ frowns. "That sucks. Where is he?"

My girl shrugs. "Don't know. It's top secret or some shit."

Without an *in*, we head to the back of the line. Luckily, it's fast moving, and it only takes us fifteen minutes to make it to the front. At the door, a big, burly bouncer checks our licenses, only charging Brock and me the cover charge.

Stepping into the club is like entering an alternate reality. Colorful strobes flash overhead as old school R&B booms through the sound system. There are people everywhere, even though it's still early.

The girls immediately drag us out onto the packed dance floor. As Usher croons about having it bad, I pull Stacia into me, her back to my front. With an index finger hooked through belt loops on either side of her ripped-up black jeans, I move her hips to the beat and press my lips to her neck.

"You're wearing the same shoes," I tell her, shifting one hand to rest on her bare belly. When she came downstairs, dressed to kill, in her jeans, black lace crop top, and blue velvet pumps, I almost swallowed my tongue.

"What?" she asks. "I wear these all the time."

I twirl her to face me, palming her ass and sliding my leg between hers. The song changes to a slow jam, and we sway, barely moving but locked together. "The first time I saw you was here; you and AJ had come to dance. Her and Brock got into it. You had on blue lipstick, black leather, and these shoes. You looked like every fucking fantasy I ever had come to life."

I see Stacia gasp rather than hear it with all of the noise. "You remember that?"

I hover my lips over the corner of her mouth. "How could I not? You're unforgettable, Stacia Kellan, completely and utterly unforgettable."

With that, I seal my mouth to hers, showing God and everyone in this club just who she belongs to.

CHAPTER 30
STACIA

We dance through a few more slow songs before "What's Luv" booms out of the speakers. I twirl back around and press my ass into West's groin, rolling my hips as I tease him.

From behind me, he murmurs the iconic Fat Joe line about not being a hater in time with the song. I can't help but smile as I sway my hips seductively, grinding back into him. After all, he loves the way I shake my ass and doesn't want me to stop, right?

Another song passes and by the time it ends, I'm parched. "I need a drink," I tell him, nodding toward the bar.

Not two minutes after we approach the bar, Brock and AJ find us. "Shots!" my best friend shouts. "We need to do shots!" She doesn't wait for a reply as she flags down the overworked bartender and orders a round for the four of us.

The bartender gets to work, pouring a small measure of tequila into each shot glass before pushing them our way. AJ thanks him and slides some cash his way.

We each pinch our glasses between our thumb and index fingers and raise them in a toast before tossing them back. Except the second the scent of the amber liquid hits me, I find myself throwing my glass to the floor and covering my mouth.

Nausea rolls over me, hot and fast. My stomach churns, and my head swims as sweat dots my forehead. "Shit, baby, are you okay?" West asks, bracing me as I sway on my feet.

I pinch my eyes shut and lean into him for support while I wait for the sensation to pass. "Yes. No. Fuck!"

He rubs a soothing hand up and down my back. "Get her a water," he says to someone, and a few seconds later, he's guiding me down onto a barstool and pressing the cool glass between my hands. "Drink this. Small sips."

I do as he says, and the feeling starts to pass. "Not to be a party pooper, but can we go?"

"Absolutely."

"Are you okay?" AJ asks, helping me back to my feet.

"I...I think so. I don't know what happened. I just felt really sick all of the sudden."

"Oh, I heard the stomach flu is going around." AJ giggles. "Or maybe you're pregnant."

West and I both laugh and then exchange a wide-eyed glance. *Could I be pregnant?* Has it even been long enough? Lord knows I don't know much about how pregnancy works. Literally all of my maternal knowledge is from movies, though something tells me they're probably not all that accurate.

"Ha," I offer weakly, "funny."

Outside, we part ways after AJ makes me promise that we'll catch up, just the two of us, sometime this week. In the car, West voices exactly what I'm thinking. "Are you…do you think you could be?"

I shake my head and whisper, "I really don't know."

"Have you missed your period?" he asks.

I rack my brain, trying to recall the last time I had my cycle. My eyes just about bug out of my head when I come up blank. "Maybe?"

"*Maybe?*"

"I was on birth control to help me regulate it; without it, my body kind of just does what it wants."

"Maybe we should buy a test?"

"Yeah, okay." We get about a quarter mile down the road when my nausea returns full force. "Actually, can we just go home?" I ask, trying like hell to keep the contents of my stomach where they belong.

West looks my way. "You okay?"

I shake my head, not trusting my body enough to open my mouth.

"Home it is, then."

For the remainder of the drive, he takes great care to avoid any bumps and takes the curves well below the speed limit to avoid jostling me. His tenderness and care, no lie, have me falling a little harder—oh, who am I kidding? I'm already sunk.

CHAPTER 31

WEST

he very idea that Stacia could be pregnant—that she could have my baby growing inside of her —kept me up all night. Well, that, coupled with my obsessive need to watch over her and make sure she was okay.

She was definitely a little green around the gills last night, but after another glass of water, a back rub, and some tossing and turning, she was able to settle into a fitful sleep.

It's half-past six now, and I'm stirring with this restless energy. I'm equal parts excited and anxious. I want so badly for her to be pregnant—and not just for the trust. Sure, that's where this all started, but it's more than that now.

My feelings for her have morphed and grown into something colossal. Suddenly, she's more than my best friend. She's my future. I want her by my side as not just my baby mama, but my everything.

I watch her sleep for a few more minutes before I slip out of the bed and dress in a pair of athletic shorts and a hoodie. I leave a note on the pillow in case she wakes before I return, but judging from the cute little snores coming from her, she's going to be out for a while.

I almost feel guilty leaving her here, but this is something I want to do for her. Hell, I'd do anything—everything—for her, if she'd let me. But at the same time, I'm glad she won't. Her fire...her tenacity are part of what makes her so damn sexy.

The drive to the lone twenty-four-hour drugstore Cottonwood has is quick at this early hour. I think I only pass one other vehicle the entire way here.

Inside, I quickly locate the aisle I need, taken aback by the staggering amount of options on the shelves before me. Box after box in varying colors lie before me. Some boast early results while others claim superior accuracy. Some are digital and some even estimate how many weeks you are. *Why do I have to choose which thing I want? Why can't they just do it all in one fell swoop?*

"Jesus Christ," I groan before tossing one of each into my basket and heading to the checkout.

The cashier, a sweet-looking older woman, gives me an inquisitive look. I pay and thank her before making a mad dash to my car. As I slide behind the wheel, I can't help but laugh at myself. I'm a twenty-four-year-old man, and I just ran out of that store like a teen who stole a pack of condoms on a dare.

On the way home, I make a quick detour by Stacia's favorite little breakfast spot and pick up two orders of French toast.

At the house, I take great care to arrange our meals on the island. I also make a nice little pyramid with the pregnancy tests. Appraising my work, I decide something's missing. I dart back outside and grab a bloom from one of my azalea bushes and stick it in a shallow bowl in front of my box display.

Satisfied with my work, I head back to the bedroom to wake her.

In my absence, Stacia's wrapped herself in the covers so she looks like a human burrito. Which is just so...*her.* The only way to keep her from hogging the bed is to cuddle her all night. Otherwise, she will spread out and take up every inch—learned that the hard way.

Seeing her now, though, I'm struck with a sense of rightness, like she belongs here, in my home...my bed... my heart.

I lower myself to the edge of the mattress and run my fingers over her messy hair. "Wake up, baby. I have something for you."

She grumbles in her sleep but doesn't wake. "C'mon, gotta get up. Don't you want to see what I have for you?"

Stacia stretches and mumbles, "Already seen your dick, dummy."

I don't even try to fight my grin. "As much as I'd love to be talking about my dick, that's not it."

She peels one lid open. "What?"

"French toast."

She pulls back. "Please tell me you didn't cook."

I bark a laugh. *Little smartass.* "Nope. Swung by Benny's."

Her other eye pops open; I have her attention now. "Benny's?"

"That's right. Come eat while it's hot."

It takes her a second to unravel her blanket cocoon, but she manages to wriggle her way out. She tries to veer toward the bathroom, but I redirect her straight to the kitchen.

It takes her a second to see past the steaming plate of powdered sugar and syrupy goodness, but when she does, she rushes toward the island. "Did you…do this?"

"I did. I wanted you to be able to take a test first thing this morning. Everything I read online said your… fuck, what is it…your something-something-something levels are higher in the morning."

Her eyes go weepy as she stares at me. "You researched this?"

"Of course. I want to be a part of this every step of the way. I want to be there for you, to help you, and to learn with you, so we can give our kid the best of everything."

Stacia throws herself into my arms, almost bowling me over. "I love you," she whispers, surprising us both.

I try to brush it off, not wanting to get my hopes up. "That's just your hormones talking, baby mama."

She reaches up and cups both of my cheeks, pulling my eyes to hers. "No, that's me, speaking from the bottom of my heart. You scare me; this thing between us scares me. But even still, I love you, West Larson, and I'm willing to be brave with you by my side."

Two halves of a whole, we both lean in at the same time. Our kiss is soft and sweet, a preview of what's to come.

It almost pains me to pull away, but I do; nobody likes soggy French toast. "Let's eat and then we—uh, you—can take a test or two. Does that sound good?"

Lightning quick, Stacia pecks my lips one more time before settling herself down onto the stool in front of one of the plates. "Coffee?" she asks around a mouthful.

"On it." I whip up two cups with my Nespresso, placing the creamier of the two before her. We eat in silence, both anxious about the unassuming looking pile of boxes; the result of one of these little sticks is going to change the course of our lives forever, and honestly, I can't fucking wait for the next leg of our journey together. You know…assuming it's positive.

Please be positive.

CHAPTER 32
STACIA

Nerves rattle around in my belly, stealing my appetite as I try and force down the French toast West so thoughtfully brought me. But every time I lift the fork to my mouth, my vision snags on the little tower of pregnancy tests.

Finally, I can't take it any longer, and I swipe the uppermost box and hop down from my stool.

"Now?" he asks, standing as well.

I nod, clutching the package to my chest. "Yeah, now." I turn and walk back to the master bathroom. West moves to follow me inside, but I stop him, a hand to his chest. "Let me uh…you know…and then we can read the results together?"

As I speak, it dawns on him I want privacy to pee, and he looks embarrassed. "Yeah, of course. Just let me know when I can come in." I nod, and he drops a soft kiss to my forehead.

In the bathroom, I open the box and read the directions. Shockingly, for as long as I've been sexually active, this is my first time taking a pregnancy test.

I pee on the little felt pad part and recap the stick, placing it facedown on the counter. "You can come in," I tell West once my pants are up and my hands are washed.

"What's it say?" he asks, sounding both eager and fearful.

"It takes three minutes."

West flips down the toilet lid and sits, pulling me down onto his lap. "No matter what that test says, I love you. You know that, right?"

I lean back into him, loving the protective feel of his strong chest at my back. "Yeah. I love you, too."

Silence settles around us as the remaining minutes tick by.

"Ready?" he asks, checking his watch.

"Ready." I stand and flip the test. Two bright pink lines stare back at me. "Oh my God!"

"That's good, right? It means you're pregnant?"

I nod, tears falling freely. "Yeah. Yes!"

West scoops me up and hugs me tight, pressing kisses all over my face.

Then a horrifying thought crosses my mind. "What if…what if it's wrong?"

Without releasing me from his embrace, West says, "I read online that false positives are pretty rare. Wanna take another?"

"Just to be safe?" I ask, and he nods before dashing out to grab one.

He returns with a glass of water and two more boxes. I eye the water and he shrugs. "Just in case."

I kick him out and repeat the steps of the first test with the two he brought me before calling him back in. This time, I keep them face up and we hover. The first of the two shows two blue lines—one in a rectangular window and the other in a round—before a full minute has even passed. The second is digital and it takes the full three minutes before the word *pregnant* flashes on the small screen.

"Holy shit," I murmur and West echoes the sentiment. "We did it! We really did it!"

West shoots me a cocky look. "Bet it was on the first try, too."

I roll my eyes and grin. As quickly as my euphoria sets in, worry replaces it. West must notice the change in my features because the next thing I know, he's cradling me to him and asking what's wrong.

"Nothing," I assure him. "I'm so happy. I'm just a little overwhelmed, too. There's so much I need to do. I need to make a doctor's appointment. Hell, I need to find a doctor; mine only does the gyno-stuff. I need to tell my mom. Oh, God, how long do you wait to tell people? Oh, and AJ! I need to talk to AJ! I need vitamins…you know those…um—"

"Prenatal," West supplies.

"Yeah, those. And I need to—"

West silences me with a kiss. His skilled lips ease my worries as I melt into him. "Breathe, baby," he croons as he pulls back from me. "I'm here to help, and we're gonna take this one step at a time."

I look up at him with wide, helpless eyes. "What's first?"

"First you call your doctor. His office will be able to make a suggestion on who to see."

"Right. That's smart." I lay my head on his chest. "I'll do that as soon as they open."

"Good. Why don't you take a bath in the meantime? Relax a little?"

"Okay, yeah."

West steps away from me and turns the faucets on the tub. As it fills with warm water, he adds a squirt of his bodywash. "It's not bubble bath, but it will still make bubbles."

"And it'll smell like you," I say as I strip. "Join me?"

He helps me into the tub and steps back. "I actually have a phone call or two to make myself. I'll leave the doors open, just holler if you need me."

I pout.

He grins and walks out of the bathroom only to reenter a moment later with my kindle in hand. "Figured you might want to read."

"You're amazing."

"Damn right, I am. Super sperm and a heart of gold —I'm the total package, baby."

I flick sudsy water at his retreating form before reclining back into the massive soaker tub and diving back into my latest read—coincidentally, it's a surprise pregnancy book from one of my favorite authors—and before I know it, I'm completely lost in the story.

Thirty minutes later, I emerge from the bath pruney and smelling like West. I wrap myself in my robe and head out in search of him.

I find him in the living room, seated on the couch with his laptop perched on his knees. "Whatcha doing?" I ask, settling down onto the cushion next to him with my feet tucked up next to me.

"Research," he says, reaching out to stroke my ankle.

"What kind?"

"Obstetricians in the area. I've found two that are

top-ranked and accepting new patients. But, let's see who your doctor suggests as well."

"Really? That's what you're researching?"

West shrugs sheepishly. "Yeah, and I ordered some pregnancy books from Amazon and downloaded an app to my phone that will update every week with what's happening with our little sprout and…oh, God, I sound crazy."

I lean over and move his laptop off of him, setting it on the cushion next to mine before crawling onto his lap. I sit straddling him, our stares locked. "You don't sound crazy. Not at all. You sound amazing and loving and excited."

"That's because I am. I'm so fucking excited, baby."

My gaze drops to his lips, and I lick my own before moving in. Our mouths clash in perfect synchronicity. I moan as his tongue sweeps into my mouth and his hands move to my hair.

I expect him to rake his fingers through it and tug on it possessively; instead, he uses the leverage to pull me away from him.

"I wish we had time for this, baby, but you need to call your doctor, and you have plans in about an hour."

I cock my head to the side, wondering what he has up his sleeve. "I do?"

"You do. So, get to it."

I slide off of his lap and trek back into the bedroom to get my phone. I dial the number to my gyno's office and sit on the edge of the bed. A quick conversation with the receptionist, and I have the name of their recommended maternal medicine doctor. As luck would have it, it's one of the doctors on West's list.

After looking up the office number, I hit dial, once

again following the answering service prompts. A brief hold later and a perky voice greets me. "Thank you for calling Cottonwood OB-GYN, this is Kaylie. How can I help you today?"

"I was hoping to make an appointment with Dr. Flory."

"Okay, and what would you be coming in for?"

I mentally facepalm; of course she would need to know this. "Oh, um, a positive pregnancy test."

"Do you know the first day of your last period?"

I think back, again trying to remember. "I don't, I'm sorry."

"No worries, our ultrasound technician will get your dates sorted. Are you a current patient of our practice?"

"No, Dr. Presley referred me."

"Alrighty then. Let me get a little info from you." Kaylie proceeds to ask me what feels like a million questions. "It looks like the earliest we can get you in is four weeks from now. Does that work for you?"

A thread of worry loops through me. "Um. Is that… safe? Like, do I need to be seen sooner?"

Kaylie chuckles lightly. "We don't usually see expectant mothers until eight weeks, and most—though not all—usually find out they're pregnant at around four or five weeks. So it should be just fine."

"Oh," I say, breathing out a sigh of relief. "Then yeah, that's fine. Should I get some prenatal vitamins or anything to take?"

"It certainly won't hurt. You can buy them almost anywhere. A few days before your appointment, we'll send our new patient paperwork to the email you provided. If you'll go ahead and fill it out, it will save you time here in the office."

I thank her and end the call, immediately plugging the appointment date into my calendar.

Back in the living room, West is still on the couch. Only now, he's looking at…surely my eyes are deceiving me. "Oh my God, are you looking at car seats?"

He looks back at me. "Don't hate. Kid's gotta have one, right?"

I roll my lips inward to suppress my grin. "Mmhmm. True."

"I feel like you're silently laughing at me."

I tilt my head to the side and lift one shoulder. "Maybe a little."

West places his laptop down and stands to face me fully. "Sure, go ahead and laugh at the man who booked you a spa appointment with your bestie later today."

"Wait, what?"

"That's right. Figured you and AJ could use some girl time since I've been keeping you all to myself."

I stare at him like he's some mythical creature; he's definitely a unicorn among men, that's for sure. "Thank you," I murmur, feeling oddly emotional.

"Like I said, anything for you." He moves closer to me and takes my hand in his. "Did you get an appointment?" As he talks to me, his index finger strokes absently over my left ring finger.

I fill him in on the time and date, and he adds it to his calendar as well. "You better go get ready if you don't want to be late."

I pop up onto my toes and kiss him square on the lips. "I love you; you're the best."

West palms my ass and hauls me closer. "I love you, too, baby mama. And I'm the man you make me want to be. You deserve the best, so that's what I'll strive to be."

His words float over me, wrapping me in their warmth. I don't know how we got to where we are now, not really, but my God, I'm glad we got here.

CHAPTER 33
STACIA

West spared no expense for AJ and me at the spa. He set both of us up with out of this world massages, deluxe facials, and mani-pedis with paraffin wax. Oh, and he even thought ahead to have lunch catered by one of the restaurants within the hotel where the spa is.

From the second she saw me, AJ was chomping at the bit to pump me for information. Luckily, the quiet atmosphere of the massage room kept her questions at bay.

Our facials bought me a little more time—I mean, it's hard to talk with goop and steaming towels on your face.

Now, however, AJ and I are both relaxed and recharged as we sit in side-by-side pedicure chairs. "So, talk to me," she says, her body lightly vibrating from the movements of the built-in back massager.

"God, where do I even start?" I go over my options internally before finally deciding to just throw it all out there. "I'm pregnant."

My teal-haired friend nearly launches herself out of her chair as she yells, "Bitch, say what?"

Every single person in the room turns to glare. But, like the badass AJ is, she glares right back until they all turn away.

"I know you didn't just say you were pregnant."

Sheepishly, I nod. "Yup."

"Since when?"

"I just found out for sure this morning." I laugh, trying to diffuse the tension. Spoiler alert, it doesn't work. "You're actually why I took a test. I honestly would've chalked it up to too much dancing or getting overheated." My bestie stares at me, her brown eyes the size of dinner plates. "Well, I mean, we were trying—so it's not totally out of left field."

"Excuse me," AJ hisses, "what the fuck do you mean you were trying? No, just no. Who are you and what did you do with my bestie?"

I concede, because I'm sure that's exactly how it feels to her. So, while we get our nails filed and buffed and polished, I tell her everything. From my mom having to move home with her parents, to the conditions of West's trust. I tell her about Virtual Kitty and West owning it, and how we angry-fucked each other. I confess about Buck and Lesli's, and how West carried me out of there over his shoulder like some kind of sexy caveman in a suit. Her expression softens as I explain my growing feelings, and how I love him, and he loves me. She looks downright enamored when she learns of all the little things he does for me day in and day out, and when I tell her about the contract he had me sign to protect me, I'm pretty sure she'd say yes on my behalf if he happened to get down on one knee.

Not that I think marriage is in our future—though if I'm being honest, I wouldn't be opposed to it either.

By the time I finish filling her in, my nails are on point and my soul feels fifty times lighter. It's not like us to keep things from each other, and while secrecy wasn't my intention, it still happened.

As we walk out of the spa, AJ stops me. "You know what this means, right?"

"Uh, that I'm going to have a baby?"

She smacks her palm to her forehead, her silver-glitter nails sparkling in the sun. "Obviously that. But more immediately, shopping! We have to go shopping!"

My instinct is to turn her down—but West made it abundantly clear when he slipped me a debit card tied to his account with my name on it that I was to treat myself anytime I wanted. Until now, I've been very judicious with my spending, but today...today feels like a good time to celebrate. "Let's do it!"

Two hours and many, many bags later, AJ and I are utterly shopped out. AJ tempts me with the offer of coffee, but I'm exhausted, and think a nap would serve me far better than caffeine would right now.

We part ways, with a promise to meet up next week as well. I've got to admit, while I think West and I needed that time together, being out with my bestie feels good.

Back at the house, West is nowhere to be found, but he did leave a card on the island along with a small black velvet box with a black grosgrain bow.

With my interest piqued, I slide my thumb beneath

the flap of the envelope and slide the card from it. I crack up when the front of the card comes into full view. On it, in a bold, colorful mismatch of fonts, it reads, "You're as beautiful on the inside as you are from behind."

A laugh rumbles out of me as I open the card to read the inside.

> Stacia,
> You're every good thing in this life I don't deserve, but goddamn if I'm going to let you go. I love you more every day, and I can't wait for the next phase of our journey with you by my side.
> Love always,
> Your baby daddy

Right when I think this man couldn't get any swoonier, he goes and does shit like this.

I place the card back into the envelope before carefully untying the ribbon and opening the lid of the box. Sitting inside of it, on a bed of tissue paper, is a gold necklace.

I remove the necklace with care, running the cool, delicate chain between my fingers before examining the bar pendant hanging from it. The back of the bar has a few small indentations in it and when I flip it over to inspect it, I can't help but laugh. The cocky bastard had it engraved to read *baby mama*. And as ridiculous as it is, it is so fucking *us* and I love it.

Two hours later, I'm vegged out on the couch watching TV when West walks in. "Yo, baby mama!" he hollers as he stomps through the house.

"Shh!" I whisper-shout back, "Clarkson is on!"

He bypasses the living room and heads for the kitchen. "Kelly?"

I scrunch my nose. "What? No. Jeremy. Hush."

I hear the fridge open, followed by him rifling through it. "Isn't that a porn star?"

"Nope. That's Ron Jeremy. Figured you of all people would know that."

West pads into the room wearing just his jeans and plops down next to me. "What? Because I created a porn app, I have to know their names?"

I roll my head to look at him. "One would think."

He reaches out and fingers a lock of my hair. "I'm more fascinated with your porn knowledge."

The sound of an engine revving on the screen gets my attention and I bat his hand away. "Shh! Abbie Eaton is about to take a Lamborghini Huracan Performante around the Eboladrome."

West wraps an arm around my shoulders and yanks me into him. "I don't have a fucking clue what you're trying to say, Stacia."

"Watch, then we'll talk."

He humors me, and we watch as she kicks ass, completing the lap in less than a minute and a half.

"Holy shit!" I squeak out when she finishes and her time flashes on the screen. "That's the second-fastest time on this track!"

West chuckles and I grab the remote and pause the show. "What's so funny?"

He tugs me onto his lap. "Watching you geek out over cars is kind of hot."

I bite my lower lip. "Is it?"

With a firm grip on my hips, he drags my pelvis forward. I moan at the feeling of his hardness beneath me. "Fuck yes, baby. I can just picture you spread out bare-ass-naked on the hood of one of those fast cars you like."

His hands slide down the back of my pants, where he cups my ass, pulling me more firmly against him as he peppers my neck and shoulders with soft kisses.

"Tell me about it," I beg, looping my arms around his neck and swiveling my hips.

He groans. "First, I'd watch you drive. Seeing you command all that power gets me so hot for you. Then, when you came in, I'd yank your hot ass out of the car, lay you down on the hood, and fuck you good and hard, making you shout my name as you came."

His dirty words send a surge of arousal through my system. "I need you," I murmur before standing from his lap.

"Have me," he replies, shucking off his pants and boxers in one go.

I follow suit and strip down so that the only thing adorning my body is my ink, piercings, and the necklace he gave me. I can't help but wonder if he'll notice.

West drags his eyes over my body appreciatively. "You're wearing it," he states, sounding all too pleased.

I move back to him, situating myself back on his lap, poised over him, my back to his front. "Of course I am. I love it."

West wraps my long hair around his fist and pulls

me flush against him. I sink down onto him, letting him control my movements with those hot hands of his until we're both panting and gasping out our releases.

CHAPTER 34
WEST

Freshly showered and redressed after our couch sex, I lead Stacia into the kitchen. "So," I hedge. "That was…"

"Amazing? Unexpected? The perfect ending to an already perfect day?"

I tweak her nose. "All of those things."

"I really love the necklace," she tells me, twisting the bar pendant between her fingers. "How on earth did you manage it?"

Shrugging, I try and play it off. "I may or may not have ordered it the day we inked the contract."

"What? Really?"

"Yeah. Today seemed like the perfect day to give it to you."

"You nailed it. Thank you."

I snag a set of keys from the island. "I have another surprise for you."

"You do?"

"Damn straight," I say, tossing her the keys.

She quirks a sculpted brow at me, but I don't say anything. "C'mon."

Together we walk outside, and I revel in her jaw-dropped expression when she sees the surprise I brought home.

"Holy shit!" She whirls to face me. "This isn't a surprise—it's a freaking second mortgage!"

She approaches with caution, skimming her hand over the matte, olive-green paint job. "Do you like it?"

"I love it." She tugs on the door handle and it opens, revealing to her the fully decked out espresso brown and black leather interior. "Wait! Where's your AMG?"

I walk over to her and nod toward the spacious back seat. "It wasn't family friendly, so I upgraded."

"To a G-Wagon?"

"That's right. Plenty of room for a car seat back there." I wink. "Maybe even two."

She smacks me in the chest. "Don't play." Then she giggles, the sound music to my ears. "Oh my God, you bought a daddy wagon."

She's totally making fun of me, but I don't even care, because deep down, I know how much this means to her. I know it shows her that I'm willing to go the extra mile, that I'm in this for the long haul. And at the end of the day, that's all that really matters.

It's been a month since we found out Stacia was pregnant. And while some days, it still doesn't feel real —for me, at least—Stacia is in the thick of it. Poor thing is constantly exhausted, and her tits are so tender they're officially off limits to the likes of me, which really fucking sucks because *hot damn* have they grown. She also has to pee every five minutes and is experiencing some crazy food aversions. She's pretty much surviving off of french fries, peanut butter toast, and bacon right now; the mere thought of other foods makes her gag.

"You just about ready?" I ask as my beautiful baby mama stomps into the room. One look at her crestfallen face and I know she is *not* ready. "What's wrong?"

She gestures wildly to where her jeans won't button. "How is it possible for me to already be showing? I'm barely two months pregnant!"

My eyes move over her, taking in the barely-there curve of her lower belly. "You look beautiful to me."

She huffs. "Thanks, but that doesn't help my pants button." Oh, did I mention the mood swings? Those are super fun.

I stand and step to her, taking her in my arms. "Buttoned or not, you're a goddess. You are creating life within you. Plus, it's probably just bloat. I read online—"

She steps back from me, her eyes watery. "You think I look bloated?"

Fuck. "No, baby. No, no, no. Not what I said."

Her lower lip trembles. "Yes, it is. You said—"

I swoop in and cover her lips with my own, kissing her until her knees are weak. "I want you to listen and hear me. You. Are. Gorgeous. Your body is changing, and I can imagine that's frustrating. If you want, we can get you some new jeans today, but please don't be sad. Nothing kills me more than seeing you cry."

She inhales a shaky breath. "Okay, yeah. Let me just change."

I send her off with one last press of my lips and

immediately begin googling where to get the best stretchy jeans.

She emerges ten minutes later in a long cotton dress that clings to her chest and floats down to the floor. "Sorry for the crazy," she says, ducking her head.

"You're not crazy," I tell her, hoping like hell she knows I mean it. "Now, are you ready to go see our baby?"

She grins and wiggles on her feet. "Oh my God! So ready!"

We head out to my daddy wagon, as Stacia lovingly calls it, and set off for Dr. Flory's office. Like I've done with pretty much everything since we found out she was pregnant, I've been researching the hell out of what to expect at this first appointment, and I think I'm ready.

Fuck that, I know I'm ready. I'm ready to see the little grainy peanut and hear the heartbeat. I'm ready to know our due date and to meet the woman who will help us usher this new life into the world.

Twenty minutes later, I'm sitting off to the side in a small-ass chair while the nurse sends Stacia into the restroom with a small plastic cup. I wait awkwardly for her to return, feeling very much like a fish out of water.

My phone buzzes in my pocket while I wait; I slide it out to check the screen, only to slip it right back where it came from when I see my dad's name flashing at me. He's been on my ass ever since I blew off our lunch plans. If I didn't know better, I'd think his feelings were hurt. But Roland Larson doesn't have feelings. No, he's just pissed I'm slipping out from under his thumb. He's angry that he's losing his control over me, enraged that I'm no longer toeing the line and playing my role of dutiful son. To a man like him, loss of control—real or perceived—is the end of the world. He's spent so long treating everyone in his life like they're nothing more than pawns on a chessboard. He's in for a rude awakening from me, though, because I'm counting down the minutes until I can tell dear old Dad to get fucked.

After what feels like for-fucking-ever, Stacia emerges, bringing my attention back to the here and now. The nurse directs her to step onto the scale and marks down the three-digit number on the display screen. "Okay, you can go ahead and have a seat, Ms. Kellan."

My heart thumps angrily at the nurse calling her that —which is absurd. Kellan is her last name, but over the past few weeks, my inner-caveman has been whispering to me, begging me to lock her ass down with a ring and a new last name—my last name.

"Do you recall the first day of your last period?" Stacia tells her she isn't sure. "No worries, the ultra-sound tech will get you sorted there. Really quickly, I'm going to check your vitals as well as your iron."

The nurse quickly works her up before moving onto questions about her family history, and mine. Once she's finished, the nurse escorts us back to a small, darkened room. "You can go ahead and get changed. Remove everything and cover yourself with this," she says to Stacia, opening a cabinet and passing her a folded gown, "and then have a seat on the exam table. Your technician will be here in just a few."

Stacia steps into the bathroom, and I take a seat in the chair next to the table. She returns wrapped in a standard hospital gown, looking nervous and unsure as she moves through the room to the table.

She climbs up onto it, and no sooner than she's situated, the ultrasound tech walks in. "Hello, there. I'm Rachel."

Stacia introduces the both of us and then it's go time.

"Great, if you'll just scoot to the end of the table, lean back and place your feet in the stirrups, we'll take a look."

She clicks around on her computer before snapping on a pair of gloves and grabbing a baton-looking thing. She sheaths it in what appears to be a huge condom, squirts some jelly-ish stuff onto it, and rolls her stool over to the end of the exam table.

"Typically, the first ultrasound is transvaginal, simply because it provides a more in-depth view of the uterus, ovaries, tubes, and cervix. You may feel a little discomfort, but I assure you, it cannot hurt the baby."

She drapes an additional sheet over Stacia and directs her to spread her legs and inserts the wand.

Stacia's brow creases, and I reach out and take her hand in mine.

As the tech moves the wand around, white blurs fill the black monitor screen, until finally she finds what she's looking for. "See that?" She points out a little white blob. "That's your baby. And see that flutter right there? That's the heartbeat." She clicks around a little more, and suddenly, a swooshing sound fills the room.

"What's that?" Stacia asks, her voice hoarse.

Rachel smiles. "That…is your baby's heartbeat."

I look from the screen to my girl; she's openly crying. I'm not even going to lie; I have tears in my eyes, too. "I think that's my new favorite sound," I confess.

"Me, too," Stacia agrees. "Oh, God, me, too."

"If you want, you can record the sound with your phone so you can listen to it later."

I whip my phone out of my pocket so quickly, I'd undoubtedly put Wyatt Earp to shame in a fast draw. Rachel plays the sound again, and I record it, knowing full and well we're both going to listen to it obsessively. As I go to put it away, I see I'm up to four missed calls from Dad.

"All right, I'm just going to take a few measurements to determine your due date."

She does her thing while Stacia and I watch along, enraptured even though we don't have a clue what any of the numbers and letters on the screen mean.

"It looks like you're about…eleven weeks along, which puts you due in." She proceeds to rattle off a date, leaving both Stacia and I shell-shocked.

"Are…are you sure?" Stacia asks, worrying the gown between her fingers.

"That's what the measurements say. Why do you ask?"

"Holy shit!" I blurt out. "Told you we got it on the first try!"

Stacia hides her face behind her hands and Rachel laughs. "You can go and get dressed. I'll print y'all some pictures out while you do."

CHAPTER 35
STACIA

n the small bathroom, my tears flow unchecked. Despite the fatigue, the weird food stuff, the sore breasts, and ten million bathroom trips a day, this hasn't felt real.

But now…now I have undeniable and irrefutable proof of the life growing inside of me.

I strip out of the gown and smooth my palms over my minuscule bump. According to the pregnancy book West ordered, our baby is about the size of a lime, which is crazy to me. How in just eleven short weeks, something that started off as a cluster of cells no bigger than a vanilla bean seed is now the size of a small citrus fruit, and that in around six months, it'll be a fully-formed person.

The miracle of life is mind-blowing.

I give my belly one last caress before slipping my panties, bra, dress, and sandals back on. As I step into the room, I'm expecting West to meet me with a tearful yet happy smile. Instead, he's scowling while his fingers fly over his phone screen. "Are you okay?" I ask, grabbing his attention.

He huffs out an annoyed breath. "It's just my dad."

"What about him?"

West slips his phone into his pocket and passes me the pictures from the ultrasound. I quickly flip through them before stashing them in my purse.

"We've been summoned," is all he says.

"Summoned?"

"Lunch today."

"We?"

"Yep."

His tone is full of dread, and I wish more than anything that I could take it away. "Well, then, I guess that solves what we're eating tonight."

"Really?"

I shrug. "Yeah, really. We may as well go ahead and drop this lovely little bomb on them while we're at it."

West is grinning now, his eyes clearer. "Really?" he asks again.

Looking up at him, I bat my sooty lashes. "Sure, why not?"

He kisses the corner of my mouth. "I fucking love you."

"I love you, too," I say just as the tech returns.

"Dr. Flory is actually ready for you." Rachel escorts us down the hall to another exam room. "I know you just got dressed, but go ahead and disrobe again and have a seat on the table. She'll be in soon."

The rest of the visit passes in an uncomfortable blur, though I don't know who felt more awkward during the vaginal exam, West or me.

"Stacia, I'll want to see you back in about four weeks."

"Sure, that's fine." I bite my lip, debating on whether or not I should ask the question lingering on the tip of my tongue.

I decide to bite the bullet and ask, but West beats me to it. "When can we find out gender? I've seen a lot of different answers online."

Dr. Flory smiles heartily at his eagerness. "We offer a sneak peek ultrasound package at sixteen weeks. If you want, you can schedule that appointment when you leave today as well."

"Thank you so much."

She pats my hand. "Of course. See you in four weeks."

***

"Are you sure about this?" West asks for the millionth time as we turn onto the private drive his parents live on.

"Positive."

"Okay. Just…if they're rude—"

I lay my hand on his arm. "West, breathe. Your parents being rude to me won't break me. Let's go in there with our heads held high, see what they need, announce my pregnancy, and then leave."

"Okay. But just so you know, I wanted to take you shopping after your appointment. Not bring you to purgatory."

I snort out a laugh. "It can't be that bad."

Twenty minutes later, I am more than willing to admit it's that bad. Roland and Prissy Larson are hands down the most superficial, petty, skin-deep people I've ever met.

The entire time we've been here, all they've done is complain, gossip, and pointedly ignore me. Seriously, when we stepped out onto the patio, his parents acted like I wasn't even there. But I'm trying to keep the peace—for West's sake.

"Tell me, son," his dad starts, and I know he's about to spew some bullshit designed to piss his son off. "What's kept you so busy you couldn't make time to see your parents, let alone answer your phone?"

West rolls his shoulders and takes my hand in his, laying them on the tabletop. "She has."

Prissy titters. Roland glares. All of the sudden, I'm no longer invisible. "Oh, that's so nice you're helping Stacy while her dad is—"

Thankfully West shuts his mom up before I can. "Her name is Stacia. And I'm not helping her with anything, Mother. Actually, we have some news."

His father blanches, as if he knows what's coming. "Stacia and I are expecting."

"Expecting what?" his mom asks. *God bless, this woman is slow on the uptake, isn't she?*

West grits his teeth and replies, "A baby. Congrats, you'll be grandparents by year's end."

"Son, can I talk to you? In private?" Roland jerks his head toward the french doors leading back into the house.

I worry for a split second that West might actually leave me out here with his mother, but he makes no move to stand. "Anything you want to say to me, you can say in front of Stacia. There's no secrets between us."

Roland's eyes spark with evil intent. "Really? No

secrets? Then I'm sure she's aware she's nothing more than a paid whore paving the way for you to gain your inheritance?"

Now West is up from the table, up and in his dad's face. "Stacia is not a whore, and, so help me God, you will either speak to her with respect or not at all."

I stand and move to where the two men are at one another's throats. "It's not worth it, West."

He turns to look at me, his eyes flashing with barely restrained anger. "You're wrong. You're more than worth it."

Roland sneers my way. "So you're okay with being a means to an end?"

I square my shoulders and place my hands on my hips. "I'm not a means to an end, sir. I'm the end game. West and I are more than a business transaction. I love your son, and he loves me. It's too bad you and your wife have your heads shoved so far up your own asses that y'all can't see it."

He laughs, and it's a dark sound. "Love," he spits the word out as if it's coated in venom. "He doesn't love you. He'll leave before that kid's first birthday, and you'll be alone *and* a fool."

West moves in front of me. "Thanks, Dad." Mr. Larson's eyes spark with intrigue, like he thinks his son is suddenly and miraculously coming around to his point of view. "Thank you for showing me exactly what *not* to do. Thanks to your shining example, I know all the right ways to be the best husband and father possible. I'm ten times the man you are without even trying."

He grabs one of the ultrasound pics he stashed in his pocket when we arrived and lets it flutter to the table. "There's your grandkid. She's eleven weeks along, by the way. We'll know the gender in a month. If either of you want to be a part of this baby's life—you know what? Fuck it. You're both far too selfish to change. Have a nice life."

And with that, he wraps an arm around my waist and escorts me out the way we came.

WEST

"Good news, baby mama," I say as I walk into the house.

"In the bedroom," Stacia calls back, her voice an octave higher than usual.

I march back to our room—yeah, that's right, *our* room; I moved her ass downstairs with me the day after her OB appointment, while she was at work, and that was that—and stop in my tracks when I see her sitting in the middle of the bed with her red hair piled on top of her head, dressed in one of my shirts and a pair of tall socks, surrounded by scraps of paper, markers, and glitter. *So much glitter.*

"Stacia, baby, wanna tell me why it looks like a craft store puked all over our sheets?"

She huffs in frustration, and damn if she doesn't look cute as hell. Not that I'd ever tell her that—she'd probably stab me with those scissors lying on the nightstand.

"Well, it's simple really," she bites out, shooting lasers at whatever is on the bed. "I wanted to make a card to give my family to announce our pregnancy. But, apparently, I craft as well as I cook."

I nod slowly. "So, not at all?"

Her frustration melts away into a smile. "Exactly. Not at all."

I lean back against the doorjamb. "It can't be that bad, can it?"

Her eyes flit from me, down to the bed, and back again. "Uhh…"

"Let's see it."

She nibbles on the side of her lower lip. "You have to promise not to laugh."

"Okay, promise." I'm totally lying right now, even got my fingers crossed behind my back.

"Ugh, fine." She holds up what appears to be a piece of cardstock with the words "You better sit down" written sloppily—and by that I mean the words are liter-ally dripping down the page—with glitter across the front.

"That's…it's…um." I try and find something positive to say. "The colors are nice."

"You jackass. You promised!"

I hold up my hands and contort my face into the very picture of innocence. "Hey! I kept my promise; I didn't laugh."

She rolls her pretty brown eyes. "I didn't laugh at your cookie cake decoration."

"And I'm not laughing now, I'm just suggesting that we maybe go with something…store-bought."

Stacia laughs. "Fair enough. So, you said something about good news?"

"That I did." I walk over to the bed and extend a

hand down toward her. "Let's go talk somewhere less…sparkly."

"Can we talk over some ice cream? I *reeeeally* want some ice cream."

Ice cream—specifically mint moose tracks—is her new favorite thing. She'd eat it three meals a day if she could. "Can do."

In the kitchen, I spoon two heaping scoops into a bowl and pass it to her. "So, I was talking to Colton today."

"And…c'mon!" She waves her spoon in the air impatiently.

"And he was able to work some kind of voodoo. If we can secure proof of your pregnancy, the trustee is willing to allow early access to the accounts listed in the trust."

Stacia freezes, her spoon midair and all. She doesn't even blink for at least a minute. "Wait, wait, wait." She spins to face me completely. "You're saying if we offer proof that I'm pregnant, they will grant you access to the money in the trust?"

"That's right."

"Which means we could post my dad's bond?" The pure hope in her voice is a vise around my heart.

I nod.

"What kind of proof do they need? What do I need to do?"

"Hang on, Colton sent it to me in a text so I wouldn't forget." I grab my phone and unlock the screen. "Okay, we would need a notarized letter from Dr. Flory."

"Easy!"

"Time and date stamped ultrasound images."

"Done!"

"And…something called an amniocentesis test to prove that I'm the father."

"What…what's that?"

"Honestly? No clue. Let's ask Dr. Google."

Stacia abandons her ice cream and comes to stand beside me. I type the word into my search bar and watch as thousands of results load. I tap on the second link, and together, we read.

"That sounds…not so fun," I say once we reach the end of the article.

"Clearly needles don't scare me," Stacia says, gesturing to her colorful and pierced skin.

"My little badass." I kiss her cheek. "So, is this something you're willing to do?"

She stares at me. "Dude. I was willing to do porn. I worked at a topless steakhouse. I can handle this easily. The question is, are you?"

I smooth some flyaways back from her face. "Absolutely."

"Are you sure?"

"Does a cow have spots?"

"Um, not all cows—"

"Well, this cow does, baby mama. So, when we go to your appointment next week, we can set this up. Okay?"

She cozies up next to me and my heart beats a little faster in my chest. "Okay."

"Great, now that that's settled, why don't we strip the sheets off the bed, hop in the shower, and have a little fun?"

Her brown eyes twinkle. "Fun, you say? What kind of fun?"

"The wet, soapy, naked kind."

Stacia takes off for the bedroom. "Race you!"

"Cheater!" I call back, giving chase to her sexy ass.

Today's Stacia's fifteen-week appointment, which means we get to talk to Dr. Flory about setting up the amniocentesis test.

Stacia tried convincing me to skip this appointment since things at VK are absolutely insane right now.

After everything that happened at Buck and Lesli's, I decided not to work with Hellerman. If you ask Colton, he'll say it's because of the way Dirk stared at Stacia's tits, and yeah, that's definitely part of it. But, mostly, the way he operated left me feeling slimy.

It ended up being for the best, too, because shortly after, another company—Fun for All—reached out with a proposal. They're pretty much my vision for Virtual Kitty's expansion come to life.

Together, we're working on a line of novelty toys, merch, and eventually, we plan to move into a more diverse range of videos.

However, balls-to-the-wall busy or not, there's no way in hell I'm missing a single appointment. No way, no how.

The sound of my ringtone for Stacia sounds from my pocket. I fish it out and answer. "Hey, baby mama, you on your way?"

"Yup."

"Me, too."

"You know you don't—"

"Stacia Iris Kellan, don't finish that sentence. I told you from the start, I'd be at every single appointment. That wasn't an empty promise; I meant every word."

Plus, I have something to give her. Finding new ways to surprise and spoil her has quickly become my favorite thing. And this time, I went all out.

"Okay, see you soon. Love you."

"Love you, too," I reply and end the call.

Thanks to midday traffic, I roll up five minutes after her scheduled appointment time. I rush through the parking lot and into the building, relieved to see she's still in the waiting room.

"So sorry," I murmur, slipping into the chair beside her.

"No worries, they haven't called me back."

No sooner than she says the words does a nurse pop her head out and do just that.

We head back together, and I'm once again relegated to the small-ass chair while she and the nurse do their thing. A urine sample, weight check, and blood pressure later, we're waiting in the exam room for Dr. Flory.

She doesn't keep us waiting long. "Hello, Stacia and West. How's everything?"

"Good. Really good," Stacia says before frowning. "Though, I've been having a little pelvic pain."

"You are?" I ask, worry thrumming through me. "Why didn't you say anything?"

Stacia and Dr. Flory both hide smiles behind their hands. "Because I knew you'd go all he-man alpha on me."

I huff. "Act like you don't like it."

Stacia cuts her eyes at me, and I settle down.

"Can you describe the feeling?" Dr. Flory asks.

"It's kind of like a mild cramping feeling."

"Any bleeding at all?"

"No."

"It's most likely discomfort from your uterus growing. But we're going to have a listen to the baby's heartbeat anyway, for peace of mind."

Stacia leans back and lifts her shirt. The good doc squirts some jelly onto her stomach before smoothing a little handheld Doppler over it. A whooshing sound fills the air, and I finally breathe easy.

"Everything sounds great. One hundred-and-forty-five beats per minute." Stacia and I lock eyes over the doctor's head; she looks as relieved as I feel.

"All right, any other questions?"

"One more," Stacia says, looking to me for help.

"Due to familial and legal reasons, we need to have an amniocentesis test set up for paternity. We both know I'm the father, but we need it in writing from you, along with ultrasound pictures, and the amnio test results."

Dr. Flory regards me, her face neutral, before turning to Stacia. "Is this something you want to do?"

My girl nods. "It is. Very much so."

"Okay, then, we'll set it up, but first, I need to go over the risks of the procedure with you to make sure you're making an informed decision."

Dr. Flory goes on to explain the risks, benefits, and possible side effects. Stacia and I unanimously decide it's worth it, and through a stroke of luck, we're able to schedule it at the same time as our ultrasound next week.

As we walk outside, I ask, "Do you have time for a late lunch?"

"I'll never turn down food. Hey, where's the daddy wagon?"

It's go time. "I drove something else," I say, playing it cool.

"What? What does that mean?"

I feel for the keys in my pocket and hit the start engine button as we approach where I'm parked. The growl of the turbocharged engine catches her attention, as I knew it would, and she eyes the vehicle appreciatively.

"You like that?" I ask.

Her eyes rove over the grayish-white Jaguar SUV. "Uh, yeah, it's a beautiful, beautiful beast. Like a mom car on crack."

Fist pumps. "Glad you think so, because it's yours."

"What?" she shrieks, loud enough for at least a one mile radius to hear.

I toss her the keys. "Yup. Had it built for you."

"You what?"

"Go ahead, take a look."

She opens the driver's side door and peers inside. Her sharp inhale tells me she very much likes the murdered-out interior—all black leather everything.

"This...this is too much." Her eyes are watery and her voice trembles. *Gotta love those pregnancy hormones.*

"So you like it then?"

"West! You can't keep doing things like this."

"Like what?" I ask.

She stomps her Vans clad foot. "Don't be obtuse. These insane, over the top gifts. It's too much."

I step into her space, backing her into the open door before picking her up and plopping her behind the wheel. "Nothing, and I mean *nothing,* is too much when it comes to you and our baby. Y'all deserve better than the best, and that's damn sure what I intend on delivering any and every chance I get."

She parts her pretty lips to reply, but I don't give her the chance.

"You've been driving the same car for what, six years now? Safety standards have changed. Not to mention, while yeah, you had a back seat, it was still a two-door. Talk about inconvenient with a car seat. And trunk space…don't even get me started on trunk space."

With an exaggerated roll of her eyes, Stacia barks out a laugh. "Okay, fine. You got me."

"Uh-huh. Anything else you wanna say?"

Another eye roll. "Thank you."

I wag my brows. "You can thank me tonight."

She shoves at my chest. "You dog!"

"Woof!" I give her my best bark and growl. "Now let's eat. I'm starving."

CHAPTER 37
STACIA

Today's the freaking day we get to find out if we're having a boy or a girl! I'm so excited I hardly slept a wink last night.

It's also the day they're going to stick a needle into my belly, and while that sounds like far less fun, it's for a good cause, because it puts me one step closer to putting my family back together.

The downside? It's not even eight o'clock, West is still asleep, and my appointment isn't until eleven. Which leaves me wide awake and all alone.

It's while I'm lying here, playing on my phone in bed, next to West, that genius strikes. He's always going above and beyond for me, and it's high time I do something sweet for him.

As quietly as I can, I slip out of the bed and pad out into the kitchen. After some fruitless rummaging, I find what I need—a pen and paper.

I pop a Nespresso capsule into the machine to make myself a cup of coffee and get to work.

Thirty minutes later, I have small little folded notes

placed all around the house for West to find. Each one contains a reason why I love him and how thankful I am for him and our journey together. I'm pretty damn proud of myself; I know it's not extravagant like a freaking brand new Jaguar F-Pace, but hopefully the sentiment behind it is enough.

A quick check of the clock tells me it's now pushing eight forty-five. West usually wakes me with coffee, but this morning, it's my turn to return the favor. I quickly make him a cup—and myself another—and head back into the bedroom. Balancing both mugs, my phone, and one of my notes is a feat, but…I make it.

I place both mugs and my phone onto his bedside table and sit on the edge of the bed next to him. I almost feel bad waking him; he's been burning the midnight oil, so to speak, and working long hours, but I think I might actually combust if I wait any longer.

"Good morning," I singsong into his ear, my voice soft and husky. "It's time to get up."

West groans this deep masculine sound that makes my thighs clench. I feather kisses along his chest, neck, and jaw. I'm just about to go for his lips when two strong arms band around me, and, in the blink of an eye, our positions are flipped and he's running his lips all over me.

The burn of his scruff is a delicious kind of torture as he turns the tables. "Good morning, indeed," he rumbles as he sucks my nipple into his mouth through the thin material of my tank.

He begins kissing his way down my body, shoving my shirt up and my shorts down as he goes, and before I know it, he's wedged his wide shoulders between my thighs and is eating me like I'm a five-course, Michelin-star meal.

In record time, I'm shaking and moaning and clawing at the tops of his shoulders, his name a prayer on my lips as my climax takes me, overwhelming all of my senses. To say this isn't how I saw our morning going would be an understatement—to say I'm disappointed would be an outright lie. The things this man can do with his tongue is the stuff of fairy tales—*highly sexual* fairy tales.

"Now that's the way to wake up," he murmurs, and I peel open my eyes just in time to see him swipe the back of his hand over his lips.

I sigh contentedly.

"You won't hear me complaining." I reach for the prominent bulge in his boxers, but the sexy jackass knocks my hand away and moves out of my reach. *How is it that even when I'm trying to do something nice for him, I'm the one reaping the benefits?*

"Consider that my *happy gender reveal day* gift to you."

I pin him with a steely look. "It had better be the only gift you have planned today."

He shrugs in that devil-may-care way of his, and I roll my eyes.

"I made you coffee. You got me off so fast, it may even still be hot!"

West laughs and moves me over to my side of the bed before plopping down next to me. He passes me my mug before taking a long sip from his. "Warm enough."

He drains it in another long pull, and when he goes to set it back down, he notices the folded sheet of paper I'd brought with me. "What's this?"

I bat my lashes. "I don't know…why don't you open it?"

His large fingers unfold the paper with care before he reads the words aloud. "Because your selflessness and generosity know no bounds." *Talk about an accurate note to kick things off with.*

West looks to me with a cheesy grin. "What's this?"

"One of the reasons I love you."

"Well, shit, baby mama. I love you, too."

West found two more of my love notes—*because you make me the best version of me* and *because your sense of humor matches mine*—before we left for my doctor's appointment.

He's been rocking a perma-grin ever since; even now as we sit in the dimly lit ultrasound room waiting on Rachel to come do her thing, he's smiling.

"Good afternoon," she greets when she walks into the room. "Are y'all ready to find out the gender?"

"Yes!" I say, nodding fervently.

"Great, let's do this."

I lift my top, as per her instructions, and she tucks a disposable towel into the waistband of my pants—stretchy as hell jeans West surprised me with—and squirts a bit of warm jelly onto my stomach.

She plays the sound of our baby's heartbeat, which brings tears to my eyes, before rolling the Doppler all over my belly in search of the money shot. "Your little one is shy," she murmurs, laughing lightly.

She keeps at it for about fifteen more minutes before

calling it quits. "Well, guys, I'm sorry. Y'all's baby is determined not to give us a show."

My heart sinks a little, but I smile anyway; it's not her fault the kid is stubborn—I mean, look at its parents. "That's okay. We can try again another time, right?"

Rachel nods. "Absolutely." She begins clicking around on her screen. "I'm going to take some measurements now, and then Dr. Flory will be in to perform the amnio."

Both of our eyes stay riveted to the screen in case the baby decides to put on a show, which is silly, because Lord knows neither West nor I know how to read an ultrasound. Unless Rachel specifically points something out, it all kind of looks the same. I mean, obviously, a head is a head and the spine is the spine, but otherwise...yeah, no.

"All right, hang tight. Dr. Flory will be here in a minute."

Ten minutes later, it's go time. My shirt is gone, I've been draped with a cloth, prepped with an antibacterial iodine solution, the baby's position is on the screen, and the needle is poised and ready for insertion.

West reaches out to hold my hand, and Dr. Flory inserts the needle. She withdraws the required fluid and then removes the needle. Aside from a small pinch and a little cramping, it's a fairly easy procedure.

"Okay, we'll get this off to the lab. Dad, you've already provided your DNA sample, correct?"

West nods. "Yes."

"Great, we should have the results within a week or so. Stacia, you may experience cramping, fluid leakage, and irritation around the puncture site. If any of these complications happen, it is not immediate cause for alarm, unless they persist or worsen. If you have any questions, don't hesitate to call."

CHAPTER 38
STACIA

The results from the amnio test came after a week. As expected, the probability of paternity is 99.998 percent.

What a total shocker.

With the test results, combined with the ultrasound images and notarized letter, Colton was able to work his magic and have the accounts moved into West's possession; as promised, West had my name added the second he could. The whole process, start to finish, took two weeks, which is kind of mind-blowing to me.

However, Colton had one caveat in all of this. He wanted to meet my father before moving forward with full representation, and I get that, I do.

Which brings us to the here and now.

"You okay?" West asks from the driver's seat of the daddy wagon.

"Just nervous," I mumble back, sitting on my hands to keep them from shaking.

"Don't be, baby. I know your dad hasn't wanted you to come see him, but this is a good thing."

"But what if he turns us away?"

West and Colton exchange a knowing glance in the front seat. "He won't," the latter assures me.

"But—"

"Baby mama," West soothes, "it's gonna be okay. I promise you."

West turns off of the highway onto a long, winding, scenic road. A drab gray box of a building looms in the distance, an angry mark on the otherwise pastoral scenery. It sends chills down my spine to think of my kind and lively father being locked away in here.

We turn into the facility and follow the signs to a secured parking lot, where an armed guard searches our vehicle before granting us entry. The entire time, my knees are knocking with nerves. Not because I think he'll find anything, but because I haven't seen my dad in so, so long that silly, superfluous thoughts are crowding my brain, like—*what if he doesn't love me anymore* or *what if he looks different now*. I know I'm being ridiculous, but I can't seem to shut my brain off.

I'm surprised we have to be searched again upon entering the building, but at the same time, I guess it makes sense. The three of us pass through a metal detector on our way into the sad-looking lobby. It's gray cinderblock as far as the eye can see. Colton guides us to a check-in desk of sorts, where we all fill out paperwork.

The whole time, I keep expecting a prison official to turn us away, to tell us my dad is refusing our visit, but it never happens.

After an agonizing twenty-minute wait, a stocky guard with an epic mustache calls for us. "Before we head back, I'm going to need to verify your IDs to your paperwork."

He checks each thoroughly before finally hitting a button on the wall to buzz the door open. We're led down a long hallway and then into a midsize room full of tables; it's almost set up like a cafeteria—if a cafeteria served doom and gloom.

My eyes ping all over the room until finally they land on him. He's a mere two tables away. I draw up short, scrutinizing him from a distance. His usually clean-shaven face is scruffy, and his hair is overgrown. It may be my imagination, but his cheeks seem a little hollow as well.

It only takes a few steps for the guys to notice I'm no longer with them. West gestures for me to follow, but I can't. My feet are rooted to the spot.

As if he can sense me, Dad looks up, locking eyes with me. A single bead of sweat rolls down my back, and my hands shake. My fight or flight instinct is going hog wild as I stare at my hero, dressed in a generic gray sweatsuit with a name badge clipped to the front.

I can't help but wonder which of us will break first.

"Stacia." It's him. He does. "My sweet wildflower." The hitch in his voice tells me everything he's left unsaid. He loves me, he's missed me, he's happy to see me—he's still my dad, and I'm still his little girl.

I want so badly to run to him, to throw myself into his arms—the very same ones that protected me from the boogeyman as a child—but I don't. It's against the rules.

Bitterness sweeps through me, cold and slithery, but I fight through it. He'll be out of here soon enough.

"Daddy!" I take the seat to his left, tears wetting my cheeks. "I've missed you so much."

West claims the seat by me, leaving Colton to take the

one on my dad's right. The two men wait quietly while my father and I catch up in hushed tones.

"Mr. Kellan," Colton says when there's a lull in our conversation. "I'm Colton Banks; it's nice to meet you."

Dad appraises him in his crisp navy suit, pressed white shirt, and coral tie. "I figured as much. It's nice to meet you."

"Since we talked last, I've been doing some research. Digging, if you will. I have a few things I'd like to talk to you about more in depth, but we'll discuss those matters once you're out."

"Out?" my dad asks with a shaky voice, but all I can think of is *when in the hell did he and Colton talk?*

"That's right, sir," West speaks up, covering for me. "We were able to raise your bail; it's being posted first thing tomorrow. We just wanted to talk face-to-face first."

My dad's brown eyes, so much like my own, shine with a heartbreaking mixture of shame and gratitude. "Thank you."

I finally find my voice. "It took longer than I wanted, but I'd never leave you here, Dad. Mom needs you. I need you." I almost blurt out that his future grandbaby needs him, but now is definitely not the time to announce that. This baby is one of the best things to ever happen to me, and I refuse to give this awful place even an ounce of that happiness.

"Where did the money come from?" he asks, most likely afraid to know the answer.

"West helped," is all I say, and thank the stars, he takes it at face value.

Dad and I fall quiet again and after a minute he asks, "How'd you get to be so good, wildflower?"

I offer a soft smile. "I learned it from you."

CHAPTER 39
WEST

"Wake up, baby mama, we gotta go!" I say, jostling her lightly.

"Five more minutes," she mumbles, rolling away from me.

"No can do. We have plans!"

She flops halfway over onto her back and blinks up at me. "What time is it?"

"Eight."

"West," she whines, "my appointment isn't until ten-thirty!"

Technically, she's not wrong. But I have something up my sleeve, and she needs to get her hot ass up and ready. "They called and had to move it." I'm lying through my teeth; hopefully she's too sleepy to question it.

"Why would they call you?" she asks.

Shit. "Beats me, but we have to be there at nine now."

She stretches her arms over her head and the covers slip down, revealing her bare breasts to me. *Why do I find it so sexy that she went to bed naked after I fucked her into the damn mattress last night?* "That's in an hour!" she squeals, shooting out of the bed.

My eyes trail hungrily over her body. Stacia was already a goddess in her own right, but pregnancy has been good to my girl. Her breasts are larger, her hips are a little wider, and don't even get me started on the roundness of her belly. It's—no lie—the hottest thing I've ever seen, and I find myself making up reasons to touch it. There's just something about knowing that our child, a life we created together, is growing inside of her that really blows my mind.

"No! Stop that!" she barks, snapping me out of my inner ramblings.

"Stop what?"

"Stop looking at me with those sex-eyes. We don't have time!"

"Five minutes," I challenge. "I could get you off in five minutes."

Heat and indecision flare in her eyes. She's torn between getting a shower and getting an orgasm. I bet I can flip the tides completely with a little persuasion.

I crook a finger her way. "C'mere, baby."

She shakes her head, but she's biting her lip and smiling.

"I'll wake you up better than any shower."

Stacia takes a hesitant step toward me, trying to play like she's still on the fence. But I can tell from the way she's rubbing her thighs together; she's already made up her mind.

She takes another small step, and I reach out and grab her hips to pull her to me. I kiss and suck my way from one breast to the other, paying special attention to her pebbled nipples before growling, "Hands and knees, Stacia."

I rise up from the bed and take a second to appreciate all she has on display for me before freeing myself from my jeans. I tease her opening with the blunt head of my cock before pushing inside of her.

As promised, I have us both climaxing five minutes later, leaving her with just enough time for a quick shower before we have to rush out the door.

It may sound lame as hell, but I'm fucking giddy with excitement as we wait to be called back at the OB's office. Maybe because I know the real reason we're here an hour and a half early.

By the time the nurse calls us back, I'm practically bursting out of my skin.

"What's your glitch?" Stacia asks, elbowing my side as we walk to meet her.

"Just in a good mood, baby mama."

"Uh-huh." She clearly isn't buying what I'm selling.

The nurse leads us back to the ultrasound room. Stacia's twenty weeks pregnant, which means we're doing the anatomy scan, which is perfect, because it keeps my girl from being suspicious.

"Good morning, you two," Rachel says when we step into the room. "Are y'all ready?"

Stacia bounces on her toes. "So ready. Hopefully this little sprout cooperates this time around."

I help her up onto the table, where she lifts her top and lies back.

"I'm gonna take a few measurements and then we'll

listen to the heartbeat." She clicks and measures, clicks and measures, clicks and measures before finally that amazing swoosh fills the room. "One-hundred-and-fifty beats per minute…perfect."

Stacia looks my way with a soft smile on her face, one that I return easily before grabbing her hand.

"All right, let's see if we can find out if you're having a boy or a girl."

She switches to a different Doppler, and the image on the screen changes from black and white to more of a sepia.

Stacia's gaze swings to Rachel. "Why is it different?"

"Because we're doing a four-D ultrasound now." She presses the paddle, moving it until an image forms on the screen.

"Oh my God," Stacia breathes out, awe lacing her every word. "That…that's our baby."

I choke up a little, too, at the sight of those chubby cheeks and little button nose.

Rachel moves and clicks again, and this time, our little one has a hand pressed up to their face.

"Okay, let's see if baby is going to show us what we want to see."

It feels like ages before another image forms. "Oh, there we go. Congrats, Mom and Dad, you're having a boy!"

Stacia and I are both openly crying—and I don't give one single fuck if that makes me less masculine. I just found out I'm having a son; I'm allowed to be emotional.

"Holy shit, baby," I say as I stand, pressing a kiss to my girl's temple. "Can you believe it?"

She scoffs through her tears. "Believe that your super

sperm managed to produce a boy? Yeah, I can believe it."

Rachel laughs softly. "Do y'all have any names picked out?"

"We have a running list," Stacia admits, "but we haven't settled on anything just yet."

"I have a little game I play with my patients. Though, sometimes it doesn't end well." Rachel sort of laughs. "Want to give it a try?"

Stacia and I exchange a glance before agreeing —hesitantly.

"Great. I'm going to count, and on three, you'll both say the name you like the most."

I toss my head back and laugh; yeah, I can see this game causing some arguments, but I think Stacia and I have got this.

"One…two…three!"

"Asher!" we both shout, grinning like fools.

"Really?" Stacia asks with a gorgeous grin tipping her pink lips up.

"Really. Asher…Asher Kenneth Larson."

She nods, teary eyed again. "Yes. It's perfect."

"Hey, Asher, it's your daddy."

The sound of West murmuring to my belly as his big hands cradle it wakes me from my nap. I'd be pissed if I could, but hearing him talk to our son turns me into a big pile of mush.

Wanting to eavesdrop a little longer, I keep my eyes closed and breaths deep and even.

"How are you today, bud? Are you giving your mama a hard time? You must be keeping her up at night; she passed out after lunch today."

He pauses, as if the baby is going to reply. *Gah! The cuteness!*

"We're excited to meet you. I know your mama can't wait to hold you. Your aunt AJ, too."

It takes serious self-control to keep from smiling, but with herculean effort, I manage.

"I bet you're gonna be handsome as hell, little man. Gonna be making all the little girl babies swoon in their diapers. Hell, their mamas, too."

I can't take it a second longer. A lighthearted, love-drenched giggle breaks free.

West peers up at me with a tender smile before bringing his attention right back to my belly. "Your mama's up now; I wonder if you can tell when she's awake from your little place in there?"

I groan and stretch before sitting up, resting my back against the headboard. "Sorry I fell asleep."

West moves to sit next to me, and I drop my head onto his shoulder. "No worries, baby mama; I hear growing a human is hard work."

I nod. "It is, very."

"You ready for tonight?" he asks, looping a strand of my hair around his index finger.

"I think so, yeah. I mean, I'm nervous for sure, but ready."

"It's gonna be great. Everyone will be excited."

"You really think so?" I ask, my stomach hollowing as anxiousness jitters through me.

"I do, baby."

<hr>

The second we walk into my grandparents' house, a sense of deep contentment fills me.

Football plays on the television, the volume turned up a hair too loud as my dad and Grandpa yell at every call the ref makes.

The smell of homemade apple crumb pie and from-scratch chicken and dumplings fills every square inch of the small house.

It's loud and chaotic and warm—*really freaking warm*

—but it's perfect, and I wouldn't change a single thing. Even better is that West wastes no time in jumping right into the fray.

"Dinner's ready!" Gramma yells, and even though the game isn't anywhere near over, everyone scrambles into the kitchen to make their plate. Football may be sacred in the South, but my grandmother's food is a straight-up religious experience.

"Smells good, Mrs.—Gramma," West groans, inhaling deeply as he piles his plate sky high.

My grandma cheeses big time as he adds enough food for his Styrofoam plate to bend under the weight.

"You can always get seconds," I say, laughing under my breath.

"You hush up. He's a growing boy."

I sputter out a laugh while West looks fifty shades of smug. "Yeah, I'm a growing boy."

I shoulder past him to make my own plate. "Only thing growing on you is your ego."

West laughs and takes my plate from me, somehow managing to carry both of our plates to the table without a catastrophe.

Mom brushes by on her way into the kitchen. She was napping when we got here. "West, Stacia, so happy y'all are here with us."

She's improved drastically since Dad was released, but it seems as though her anxiety is here to stay, and some days are easier for her than others. I think, deep down, she's scared his name won't be cleared and that she'll lose him for good.

Once we're all gathered around the table, my grandma bows her head and blesses the food. "Lord, thank you for your many blessings. From this food, to the company we're sharing it with, we're grateful. In your name, amen." She looks up and asks, "Who's gonna start us off?"

"I'll go," Mom says. "I'm thankful for us being here together." Her eyes stay locked onto her husband as she speaks. A sense of rightness engulfs me, knowing that I helped bring her joy back to her.

My dad goes next. "I'm thankful beyond measure to eat food that is actually palatable."

Gramma tsks. "Kenneth Kellan, my food is more than *palatable*."

He bows his head. "You're right; it's the best I've ever had."

You'd think Mom would scoff, but my lack of culinary prowess came from somewhere. Grandma blames Grandpa's side of the family.

"I'm glad the refs are only half blind this game," Grandpa says, making us all laugh.

"I'm grateful there won't be any leftovers for me to store."

"None? Really?" I whimper. I was already planning on chowing down on some dumplings for a midnight snack.

West reaches out and runs his thumb over my wrist in a soothing gesture. He knows good and well that I've been waking up most nights and raiding the kitchen.

"I set some aside already," Gramma says. "Calm your britches. What are you grateful for, West?"

"That I'm here with all of you." I'd say he's laying on the charm, but I know he means every word; his family —save for Brock—sucks.

I heave out a deep breath. It's my turn. *You're good, Stacia, do it just like you planned.* "Tonight, what I'm most thankful for is…" My words trail off as nerves steal my voice. *Get it together!* I clear my throat and start again. "What I'm most thankful for is that in about twenty weeks, West and I will become parents to a sweet baby boy."

Other than my mother's sharp inhale, the room is dead silent.

Finally, after an uncomfortably long amount of time, my mom speaks. "You're pregnant?" Her eyes shine with emotion, but I can't get a read on exactly how she's feeling.

West takes my hand in his and squeezes. "Yes," I whisper, "we are. Hooray!"

All of the sudden, everyone starts talking all at once, and judging from their tones, they're happy for us.

Mom pushes back from the table and comes to me, wrapping me in the kind of hug only a mother can give. "My sweet girl. I'm so happy for you."

Dad's next. "Wildflower…never thought you'd make me a grandpa before sixty."

I smirk. "And yet here we are."

He grins. "Smartass."

Grandpa offers his congratulations from his seat with a raise of his glass and a tilt of his chin. "Happy for y'all."

The only person who has yet to say anything is my grandmother. Nope. She's been watching the revelry with a guarded expression. My heart aches at the thought of her being let down or disappointed.

Finally, she speaks, though instead of offering her

congratulations, she pins West with a hard look and asks, "Now that you've knocked up my granddaughter, tell me, do you plan on making an honest woman out of her?"

I groan, wishing like hell the floor would open up and swallow me whole. "Gramma! It's the twenty-first century; a man doesn't have to marry a woman simply because she's having his child."

"Now hold on," West says. I whip around to look at him. "I certainly wouldn't be opposed to all three of us sharing the same last name; Stacia's the only holdout at this point."

"What?" I ask, in complete disbelief.

"You heard me, baby, I'd put a ring on your finger in the blink of an eye."

"You would?" I can't believe we're having this conversation in front of my family, but right now, I'm too interested in his reply to care.

"All day long. The second you're ready, I'll be down on one knee."

Tears cloud my vision and my heart feels too big for my chest. "I love you," I tell him. "I love this family we're creating and this little life we're making."

West scoops me into his lap, sidesaddle. "I love you, too, and there's no one else I'd rather have by my side. You and Asher are my whole world."

"Good enough for me," Gramma says, and we all burst out laughing.

Conversation picks up around us, but all I can think about is how damn lucky I am. This certainly isn't the path I envisioned myself walking, but I am so glad it's where I ended up.

There's a saying I heard once, "It doesn't matter

where you're going, it's who you have beside you for the journey," and I have to say, the sentiment has never rung more true, because no matter where we end up, with West and Asher by my side, I know we're exactly where we're meant to be.

EPILOGUE
WEST – ONE YEAR LATER

ife as a family of three is better than I could have ever imagined. Sure, toward the end of Stacia's pregnancy there was some worry over bringing Asher into the world.

Admittedly, Stacia's worries were far more complex than mine. She fretted over breastfeeding versus bottle. How her body would look postpartum—*spoiler alert, totally fucking bangable.* She worried about returning to work and childcare. She obsessed over establishing a routine for Asher, and so on and so forth. You know, all of the typical first-time mom worries.

Meanwhile, my biggest concern was when I'd have time to show my girl just how much I appreciated all of the new curves her pregnancy produced. That probably makes me sound like a douche, but the thing is, I knew the other things would fall into place.

And they did. Stacia took to motherhood like a duck to water. Sure, there were hiccups—like Asher looking like an extra from the set of the Coneheads thanks to the use of forceps during her delivery; and I think she cried every time she nursed him for weeks. Seeing her in pain literally killed me, so I Googled the shit out of it one Monday and came home with a pack of nipple shields. In that moment, Stacia looked at me as if I were a God among men. Not even going to lie either, I loved it.

But that's just me—I love taking care of her; I live to make her smile. Asher, too, now; he's eight months old now and his gummy, drooly, toothless grins are one of my favorite things ever. I'm ninety-percent positive he said "Da-da" the other day, but Stacia's not buying it. But I know what I heard.

However, as great as everything has been, some-thing's missing. It took me a while to put my finger on it, which is crazy in hindsight. The answer was so glaringly obvious, I don't know how I didn't figure it out sooner.

Now, though, I'm a man with a plan. And I mean that quite literally. After months and months of careful planning, today's the day I'm—*hopefully*—going to fill the gap.

And by that, I mean put a ring on her finger. Lord knows, I've been fantasizing about asking her for a hell of a long time. Brock and AJ have been giving me shit for waiting so long, but I know my girl.

With her dad being freshly released and everything with his trial, her family needed time to bond and catch up; they needed time to prepare for his trial and to cele-brate the subsequent clearing of his name. That's right, Ken was innocent. His shady-ass partner, on the other hand, was crooked as fuck and set him up to take the fall.

I contemplated proposing when Asher was born, but ultimately decided it wasn't the right time. After all, our little dude needed to be the center of attention for a while.

We also started renovating Mimi Jean's house around the time our guy was born, too. Stacia thinks the house won't be finished for a few more weeks, but it's actually ready today and I can't fucking wait to see her face when she walks through the front door.

"You ready, mini-man?" I ask the cooing baby in my back seat.

Clearly, he doesn't reply, but I know he's ready.

AJ—who is totally in on and in favor of my plan—has been keeping her busy all morning. But, now, it's fucking go time.

ME

Thirty minutes.

AJ

See you soon.

I swing by the local flower shop to pick up my order before heading home to set everything up.

Stacia had full rein decorating our house and now, our sparkling new kitchen full of top of the line appliances neither of us know how to use is the perfect place for a proposal.

I park around back and carry Asher and the bouquet inside, setting the vase on the island and the car seat on the floor so I can grab Asher's new highchair. To the back of it, I tie the gold, silver, and white balloons I picked up this morning.

Asher watches me as I drag the highchair out into the entry hall, making it the first thing Stacia will see when she enters. Once it's situated just right, I start arranging all of the other goodies I ordered for her, because go big or go home is kind of our gift-giving style and even though I've splurged like crazy on all of this, her agreeing to marry me will be the most epic gift of all.

On the floor to the left of the highchair is a massive bouquet of wildflowers. And to the right is a glossy white gift box with a gold bow tied around it.

My phone buzzes in my pocket and I slide it out. Holy shit! They're ten minutes away! Without bothering to respond, I shove the device back into my pocket and grab Asher, car seat and all.

"We gotta get a move on, little man. Your mama's gonna be here soon and everything needs to be perfect." Asher coos and reaches his pudgy little hands up toward me.

In his nursery, I make quick work of changing him into the onesie I had made for the occasion before hoofing it back downstairs. Once my little guy is secured into his highchair, I fly back to our bedroom to grab the ring box.

Right as I make it back to Ash, I hear the sound of tires on gravel, letting me know they're here. "It's go time, mini-man," I say to my son as I place the ring box down onto the tray of his highchair.

STACIA

AJ's been acting cagey all day. When she wasn't whispering to her husband, she had her nose in her phone. She picked me up at eight this morning for a girls' day, which Brock promptly crashed at lunchtime. And we've been running around ever since.

Now, it's almost five and my makeup is flawless, my hair is on point, and my nails are fresh. I look like a thousand bucks—which is fitting because it's probably what West spent on my primping. Pretty much, I'm dressed up for a night on the town and all I want to do is go home and snuggle up on the sofa with my two guys.

"Hey, what are you doing?" I ask when Brock passes the turn-off for my house.

"I was thinking before we took you home, we could check out the progress on the new house," AJ says, answering for him.

I manage to hold in my frustration—shockingly. More than anything, I want to go home, take off my bra, and just…be. *She doesn't have kids yet,* I remind myself and some of my discontent slips away.

"I guess, but don't expect much. West says they won't be finished until the end of the week, so I imagine it's probably a mess."

AJ wiggles in the passenger seat and claps her hands together. "I know, I know. It's still exciting though!"

When we roll up, I'm expecting there to still be construction materials in the driveway, but there's nothing there. "They left the outside lights on," I murmur as Brock pulls into the driveway.

"All the better to see inside with," my bestie singsongs and I laugh.

"C'mon, let's get this over with." We all climb down from Brock's massive truck. "Let's peep in the windows and hit the road."

"Or…" AJ hedges, "we could try the front door!"

Scoffing, I say, "Girl, it will be locked."

"Let's just try," Brock adds, backing her up like the

good little husband he is. *Kiss ass, he's a total freaking kiss ass.*

"Shit better be locked," I grumble under my breath as AJ drags me up the front porch steps.

"It's open," Brock says when the door handle gives way under his touch.

"Are you fucking kidding me?" I try and pull my arm out of AJ's grasp. "Let me call West, he needs to know—"

Brock pushes the door open and my best friend yanks me forward and over the threshold. The sight before me both boggles my mind and fills my eyes with tears.

The house isn't under construction, not at all. It's more than finished; it's furnished and looks like my *Future Home* Pinterest board come to life and in the middle of the foyer are my two guys looking as handsome as ever.

West drops down to one knee. "What…what is this?" I gasp, struggling to come to terms with everything before me.

"Shh, baby mama, I'm trying to make you my wife."

"What?" I ask again, because clearly my brain is not functioning at its usual capacity.

West remains kneeling and nods his head toward our son. He coos under my attention and it's then I notice he's gnawing on a ring box and not a toy of some kind. "Whatcha have there, mini-man?"

He reaches for me with one hand and I pick him up. "Can Mama see that?" I ask, trying to pry the drool-covered velveteen box from him. As I finagle it away, I read the words printed on the front of his onesie aloud. "Will you marry my daddy?"

I nod and West swoops in, pressing a kiss to my cheek before taking Asher and passing him off to AJ. He turns back to me, takes the ring box, and flips it open, revealing to me the single most stunning ring I've ever seen.

Nestled in the box is an emerald cut black diamond framed by two white diamonds in a gold setting. "It's…"

"What, baby? Tell me," West urges as he slips it onto my ring finger.

"It's breathtaking. The most beautiful thing I've ever seen."

West nods, pleased. "Good, because I bought the one that made me think of you and you're absolutely breathtaking; the most beautiful thing I've ever seen."

I hold my hand up, admiring the way the ring looks on my finger. "I love you, West Larson. I love you and our son and this amazing little life we're creating together."

He presses a kiss to my neck. "So that's a yes, then?"

"It's a hell yes!"

His lips meet mine and he dips me low as he deepens our kiss. "Now, why don't you open your other gifts?"

My eyes fly up to meet his. "Other gifts?"

"That's right, baby."

He bends over and passes me a huge bouquet of wildflowers, which I promptly sniff before placing them on Asher's highchair tray. "They're amazing. Thank you."

"That's not all, baby," he says as he hands me a glossy white gift box topped with a golden bow.

I carefully tug on the end of the ribbon and it falls away. Slowly, I lift the lid only to be met with gold dotted tissue paper. I pull it from the box, sheet by sheet, until its contents are revealed.

The first item I retrieve is a pair of black lace pumps with the iconic red sole. "These are…wow."

West ducks his head. "They weren't actually meant to be a part of the gift, but I saw them and immediately imagined you walking down the aisle in them." He leans in and whispers in my ear, "I also imagined you wearing only them with your legs wrapped around my neck."

I suppress a moan—barely—as I set them aside and move on to the next item: a pale pink leather cat collar with a diamond encrusted heart-shaped tag with the letters D and Q engraved into it. "What? What is this?" I ask.

"Keep going, baby."

I do as he says and pull out food and water dishes that look like teacups along with a myriad of cat toys. "You know we don't have a cat, right? And while role-play can be great…this is not my kink."

West snorts out a laugh. "A little more."

I roll my eyes and retrieve a card from the bottom of the box. I open the envelope, smiling as I read the outside of the card. "I can't wait to spend the rest of my life trying to decide what's for dinner with you." I flip it open and a picture falls out and onto my lap.

Lifting it, I see it's a picture of the fluffiest Himalayan kitten there ever was. "She's so cute!" I coo, rubbing my finger over the image.

"Good because we pick her up tomorrow. Surprise, baby!"

"You got a cat?"

West smirks. "I mean, I figured it was pretty obvious, what with the collar, food bowls, and toys."

"You got a cat and named it after Dairy Queen?"

Now he outright laughs. "No, baby, I got a cat and named it DQ after you, my defiant queen."

My lower lip trembles. "Like my username?"

"Just like it. You applying for Virtual Kitty was the catalyst for all of this in a way. I don't know." He shrugs sheepishly. "It just seemed fitting."

"I love it. I love you. All of it. You're so good to me and Asher."

West hauls me into his arms and gestures for AJ to hand our son to him. He holds both of us close, murmuring all the while about how much he loves us. "You're it for me, Stacia. You and Asher are my whole world. You two are my entire reason for existing, my purpose. You're my sunrise, sunset, and everything in between. I want to love you and your rebel soul for the rest of our days until we're old and gray, though knowing you, you'll probably be old and purple. But that's just another reason I love you. You're so unapologetically you."

The tender moment is ruined when Asher lets out a wail worthy of a battle cry. "You hungry?" I ask as West snuggles him closer.

"I'll feed him a bottle before we head out," AJ offers.

"Head out? Like, with Asher?" I ask, perplexed.

West grins and passes our son to my friend. "I figured we could use the night alone to, you know, celebrate."

I swipe my tongue over my lower lip, already antici-pating the many ways this night could end—lucky me, every single scenario includes multiple O's for me.

"You've just thought of everything, haven't you?" I ask.

West steps into me. "I like when a good plan comes together."

I tilt my head back to smile up at him. "I like it when we come together."

Brock groans and AJ laughs. "Well, that's our cue to head out. Have fun, lovebirds. Don't make anymore babies."

"Don't tell me what to do," I call back as West claims my lips.

His kiss is chaste so we can both love on Asher before he leaves. This is his first night away and it's kind of a big deal, but at the same time, I trust my bestie and I'm thrilled West and I will get to christen our new home sans any interruptions, because God love him, Asher seemingly has an internal alarm that blares whenever we're about to fuck. *Pint-sized little cockblock.*

After the trio leaves, West walks me back to the master bedroom. "Oh my God," I murmur, my hand flying to my chest. "It's…"

"You like it, right?" he asks, sounding unsure.

"I love it," I tell him, and I do. It's everything I wanted and more. From the pale gray walls to the funky tone-on-tone wallpapered accent wall behind our bed, it's perfection. He even scored the white-washed bedding set and one of those coma-inducer comforters I've been seeing ads for.

I spin to face him. "I love you." I pull off my shirt and shimmy out of my jeans, leaving me in only my panties and bra. "I fucking love you."

West growls, eyeing me appreciatively before he hauls my soft body against his hard one. He moves us toward the bed until the back of my legs hit the mattress and I tumble down onto it, pulling him with me.

He settles between my thighs, claiming my lips possessively with his before moving his way down my body. "I love you," he groans as he kisses his way down my belly. "Now and forever, baby, I love you."

He slides my panties down my legs and peppers my thighs and the aching space between them with hot open-mouthed kisses, teasing me and working me into a frenzy of want and need.

"God, yes," I moan when he sets to work in earnest, flicking his tongue against me until I shatter into a million pleasure-soaked pieces.

"Fuck, Stacia. This is us, baby, forever." He speaks the words against my fevered, damp flesh and I can't help but grin. Most girls dream of riding off into the sunset with their prince charming, but here I am living the dream, deep in orgasmic bliss thanks to the tongue of my dark knight and I couldn't think of a more fitting way to start our forever.

Because like West said—this is us and I wouldn't change a fucking thing.

THE END.

BEFORE YOU GO

LK'S OTHER TITLES

All of LK's titles can be read as standalones & are available with Kindle Unlimited. An * beside a title denotes it is also available in audio.

Sweet Little Nothing * (an enemies-to-lovers/bully romance)

Dirty Little Secret * (an older brother's best friend/second chance romance)

Pretty Little Thing * (a single mom/forced proximity/mistaken identity romance)

Best Laid Plans * (an older brother's best friend/secret baby romance)

Best of Intentions * (a friends-to-lovers/little sister's best friend romance)

Best of Me * (a second chance at love/forbidden twin romance)

Rebel Heart (an enemies-to-lovers jock/tutor rom-com)

<u>Rebel Soul</u> (an arranged baby/friends-to-lovers rom-com)

<u>Rebel Desire</u> (an unrequited soulmates/surprise single dad rom-com)

<u>Coming Up Roses</u> * (a small-town/single mom romance)

<u>An Uphill Battle</u> * (a frenemies-to-lovers romance)

<u>Weather the Storm</u> (a second chance at love romantic suspense)

<u>Come What May</u> (an age gap/single dad romance)